The Advocate's Conviction

Teresa Burrell

Silent Thunder Publishing

This book is a work of fiction. References to real people, events, establishments, organizations, or locales are intended only to provide a sense of authenticity and are used fictitiously. All other characters, and all incidents and dialogue are drawn from the author's imagination and are not to be construed as real.

THE ADVOCATE'S CONVICTION. Copyright 2012 by

Teresa Burrell.

Edited by Marilee Wood

Book Cover Design by Karen Phillips

ISBN: 978-1-938680-05-2

Silent Thunder Publishing

San Diego

Dedication

To all mothers everywhere and in particular to both of mine, Clara and Virginia, who each in their own way provided me with guidance, clarity, and love. Clara, for her spiritual guidance, protection, and her selfless devotion to her nine children until she left this earth far too early. And to my stepmother, Virginia, who came into my life at a time when I needed her most, teaching me the importance of independence, developing my self esteem, and affording me unconditional love and encouragement. May they both rest in peace.

Acknowledgments

A special thanks to my friends and family for their help with research and for making this book possible; Bob Pullman, Jerry Leahy, Richard Arroyo, Eric Orloff, Chris Broesel, JP Nelson, Charles and Shellie Settle, Ron and Kim Vincent, and especially Marilee Wood.

Also by Teresa Burrell

THE ADVOCATE SERIES

THE ADVOCATE (Book 1)
THE ADVOCATE'S BETRAYAL (Book 2)
THE ADVOCATE'S CONVICTION (Book 3)
THE ADVOCATE'S DILEMMA (Book 4)
THE ADVOCATE'S EX PARTE (Book5)
THE ADVOCATE'S FELONY (Book 6)
THE ADVOCATE'S GEOCACHE (Book 7)
THE ADVOCATE'S HOMICIDES (Book 8)
THE ADVOCATE'S ILLUSION (Book 9)
THE ADVOCATE'S JUSTICE (Book 10)
THE ADVOCATE'S KILLER (Book 11)
THE ADVOCATE'S LABYRINTH (Book 12)
THE ADVOCATE'S MEMORY (Book 13)
THE ADVOCATE'S NIGHTMARE (Book 14)

THE TUPER MYSTERY SERIES

THE ADVOCATE'S FELONY
(Book 6 of The Advocate Series)

MASON'S MISSING (Book 1)
FINDING FRANKIE (Book 2)
RECOVERING RITA (Book 3)
LIBERATING LANA (Book 4)

CO-AUTHORED STANDALONE

NO CONSENT
(Co-authored with L.J. Sellers)

Prologue

The fourteen-year-old girl struggled to break free from the bindings on her hands and feet. One woman on each arm held her as she fought. Her feet were in stirrups, and the unbearable pain shot through her abdomen. Her blonde hair was wet with sweat. She yanked her right arm away but the heavy-set woman holding her arm threw her body across the teenager, pinning her down on the hospital bed.

"No," the teen screamed. "No! Don't take my baby."

"Push," the body-blocker said. "Just push." The tall, thin woman holding the teen's left arm spoke calmly. "You need to stop fighting and breathe. Your baby is coming. You need to push."

The girl looked around the small, dirty room for help, but all she saw was a man wearing a surgical mask sitting at the end of the bed between her legs, waiting for her to give birth. He would be no help. After all, she had agreed to this. The candles flickered around her, casting soft shadows around the room. The oak tree painted on the wall and the circle around her bed would protect her, or so she was told. But she hurt so badly and no one seemed to care.

The heavy-set woman was face to face with her. The girl could feel her breathing and smell her garlicky lunch. "Just push," she said again. The girl screamed.

"This is your child's fate. Your baby must be sacrificed. Are you a believer?"

The girl wanted to say no. She didn't know what to believe, but fear won out. "Yes," she said.

"Yes, what?"

"Yes, I believe. I believe in the power of the oak. I believe in the power of the oak."

She was chanting now and the two women joined her. "I believe in the power of the oak. I believe in the power of the oak."

The young girl screamed again as another contraction shot through her. She pushed as hard as she could, then stopped.

"Again!" the man at her feet yelled. "Push!"

She pushed and screamed in agony until she felt the mass exit her womb. Her body lay limp on the bed as she heard the baby cry. The heavy-set woman continued to hold her in place while the tall woman took the baby to the back of the room and out of sight. The baby's cries still filled the room.

Then, silence.

A few minutes later the woman returned without the child.

The girl turned her head away and closed her eyes. What have I done?

Chapter 1

Attorney Sabre Orin Brown hurried through the crowd at San Diego Juvenile Court toward the clerk's office. She thought about the newspaper article that reported child abuse was down. Where were they getting their statistics? The halls were so crowded she had to squeeze through. The construction in the lobby didn't help, either. The powers that be had decided it would be a good time to move the information desk from the middle of the room up against the wall. It wouldn't provide any more space and it didn't really look any better, but it might make it a little easier for the clerks to go from the work room to the desk. She was on calendar for detentions this morning and she was running late. It was the first morning she could remember that she hadn't arrived at court an hour early.

"You okay, Sobs?" Bob, Sabre's best friend, asked. Sobs had become her juvenile court nickname. S.O.B. were Sabre Orin Brown's initials and her colleagues were quick to tease her about the nickname. At first it was only Bob that called her Sobs, but the name had caught on and some of the other attorneys used it as well. Bob had nicknames for a lot of his co-workers, most not as lovingly applied as hers. "I can't believe I beat you to court."

"I just had a little trouble getting rolling this morning, but I'm fine now." Sabre gave a half smile. "How many detentions are on calendar?"

"We have three. And there's just you and me on detentions. There's an out-of-control teenager, a drug baby, and . . ." Bob stood there in his gray suit and Marshalls- bought Florsheims, shuffling through the blue petitions. A quirky smile came over his face.

"What is it?"

"Heh, heh," Bob made a strange sound with his throat. "I'm not sure, but it looks like one of those ritual cases."

"Another one? There was one last week and I'm pretty sure Wagner had one last month. Why are they filing this stuff? Most of it is just ludicrous. I wonder how many more there are that we don't know about."

"It's about time we got something interesting. I'm bored with broken arms, tox babies, and creepy guys who molest little children." Bob picked up the social worker's report and started to read through it.

Sabre shook her head. She knew Bob cared as much about the children as she did. She watched his expression turn from grin to grimace as he read through the report. Although he was in his early thirties, his full head of hair had already started to gray. She figured hers would too if she continued in this line of work. "So what is it?"

Bob leaned in closer to her and in a deep, creepy voice said, "Goat blood and chicken feet."

"No." Sabre said in disbelief, grabbing the report out of his hand. "Give me that."

Bob laughed as he picked up another copy from the box on the desk.

"Ewww. It does say goat blood and chicken feet were found in the home."

"You take the kids." Bob said "I want the mom on this one. I can win this. It'll be another win for the king." He threw his fist in the air.

"You're sick, but you are the king of juvenile court. You have more jurisdictional wins than anyone." Sabre separated the other petitions, glancing at the potential appointments. "Do you want the tox baby or the teenager?"

Bob tilted his head down and looked over his glasses. "You can have the teenager. I hate working with teenagers. For that matter, you can have the tox baby, too, if you want."

"No, that's fine. I'll take mom. If they all go to trial, you'll have too much prep to do. Not that there's that much to do on the drug baby cases, but still . . ."

"Fine. You have the kids on Johnson and Lecy and I have the baby on Hernandez. There are no appointments for the fathers, right?"

"Nobody in the picture on any of these cases right now." Sabre picked up her files, her petitions, and the reports. "Let's go find our clients."

They walked out of the closet the county called an attorney's lounge. It was originally a storage room, but space was so tight now they needed every nook and cranny to use as a courtroom. A lounge for the attorneys was the least concern to the county. Bob watched a large-breasted woman with a low-cut blouse walk across the hallway.

Sabre flicked his arm. "Hey, you're a married man."

"I'm married, not dead." He grinned at her. "Nice tie, by the way," Bob said as he sauntered away.

Sabre received her first Jerry Garcia tie as a present from her brother, Ron, when she entered law school. He teased her about holding her own in a male-dominated profession, but if she was going to do it, she should have the Grateful Dead by her side. Sabre wasn't sure if he ever meant her to wear the tie, but as a tribute to her brother it became the first of a large collection.

Sabre walked across the floor where the information desk used to be, catching her three-inch heel in a rough spot on the floor and almost turning her ankle. Another wardrobe staple, the heels stretched her to a full 5'7". She reported the spot on the floor to the desk and they quickly placed a caution sign on it to avoid further incident.

Sabre stopped in the restroom. The stalls were full and she turned toward the mirror while she waited, taking a rare moment to just breathe. She looked slim, well-dressed, not unattractive. It seemed she needed to reassure herself these days. She smoothed the jacket on her suit, took her sunglasses off, and ran a brush through her shoulder-length, brown hair. She pushed her sunglasses back on her head, using them as a barrette to hold her hair off her face.

Moments later, Sabre was back in the crowd. The room was filled with people, some trying to get their lives in order, others just fighting the system. She saw a couple leaning against the wall entwined in each others arms. The woman was dressed like a hooker and was obviously high. The man wasn't in much better shape. His hair looked like it hadn't been combed in weeks and he was in serious need of a haircut and shave. Sabre smiled to herself. *There seems to be someone for everyone if they look in the right places.* For a brief moment she wondered if she'd find someone again. Her thirtieth birthday was fast approaching and she was still happily single . . . most of the time. She didn't want to be married, and as much as she loved them, she didn't plan on having children. She was satisfied with her work and passionate about the people she worked to help. But occasionally she wanted a relationship. Then she'd think of the last time she was involved and change her mind.

Sabre walked through the lobby until she found her client, Maria Hernandez, on the drug baby case. She was young. It was her first baby and her drug activity seemed to be fairly new. Maria agreed to enroll in all the programs and Maria's mother was willing to help out with the baby. The social worker recommended detention with the grandmother as soon as the baby was released from the hospital and was willing to let Maria stay there as long as she was active in her court-ordered programs. Sabre saw Bob talking with grandma and knew he'd be okay with the recommendations if he was comfortable that grandma could protect the baby. When everyone worked toward what was best for the child, the cases were easy. Sabre believed this was one of those cases.

The two of them left the courtroom just in time to witness an arrest at the metal detector. A twenty-nine-year old woman emptied her pockets into the tray and walked through the machine. The sheriff picked up the contents of the tray, opened a vial containing cocaine, and placed the handcuffs on Karen Lecy.

"Uh oh," Bob chuckled and shook his head. "Stupid woman."

"What is it?" Sabre followed Bob toward the arresting officer.

"That's the mom on the detention. The one with the out-of-control teenager."

"Gee, that might explain some of the kid's problems."

"Excuse me, Jerry," Bob said to the sheriff. "That's my client. Can I talk to her?"

"I'll put her in an interview room after we book her."

Bob turned to Karen Lecy. "Don't say anything until we talk."

Sabre stared at the woman being taken away. "She's the mom?" Sabre asked, not really expecting an answer. "She looks like a teenager herself. She's so young."

The crowd in the room had stopped buzzing as they stood around and watched the arrest. Some were probably feeling bad for her; others appeared glad to have the attention off themselves, even for a moment, but everyone was gawking as the woman was taken back to the holding tank.

"You ready on the Johnson detention?" Sabre asked.

"Yeah, mom's denying everything. She swears she doesn't know anything about any rituals, satanic or otherwise."

"And how does she explain the goat blood and chicken feet?"

"She can't explain the goat blood, but she has a very plausible explanation for the chicken feet."

"I can't wait to hear this."

"It's simple really. They eat them," Bob said with a straight face.

"Ewww ... what's to eat on a chicken foot? There's no meat on them—just dirty, scaly-looking skin that's been walking around in chicken feces."

"Really, Sabre." His voice serious. "I think she may be telling the truth. She's having a tough time making ends meet and she can get chicken feet free. She said her mother used to make them when they were kids."

"And you're buying this?" Sabre looked at Bob, her face quenched in disbelief.

"Leanne Johnson is either a really good liar or she's just trying to feed her kids. The part that got to me was that even though she's devastated about losing her children, she knows they'll have food." Bob shrugged. "I don't know. See what the kids say."

"I will. I'll go to Polinsky this afternoon and see them. I have to see the Lecy girl, too. Now that her mother has been arrested, we have another issue to deal with on that case."

Chapter 2

Sabre walked up the brick walkway leading to the Polinsky Children's Center, reading some of the names on the bricks as she went. She had dedicated a brick herself in honor of some friends who had lost a child a few years ago. She still hadn't seen the brick with his name on it but she knew it was there somewhere. One day she would take the time to find it. But not now. Now she had to determine what was going on with the Lecys and the Johnsons.

The clerk recognized Sabre when she entered. She exchanged some pleasantries and then placed her ID on the counter and requested to see the Johnson children.

"All of them at once?" the clerk asked, her eyebrows rising quizzically.

Sabre looked at her petitions. "Bring me Cole first. In about ten minutes bring Hayden, and then I'll see Alexandria, Blake, and Wyatt all together."

Sabre waited in the lobby, reading through her reports until a counselor showed up with a tall, lanky, eight-year-old boy with brown hair that fell below his ears. Sabre watched his body language as he approached. He carried himself like he was in charge, yet he appeared guarded. The counselor called Sabre aside while Cole waited.

"I just thought you'd want to know. Cole has been hoarding food. He puts apples, bananas, chips, or whatever he can into his pockets and takes them back to his room."

"What's he doing with the food there?"

"At first he was saving it for his siblings, but even after he knew they were receiving plenty of food, he still wanted to keep it with him. This morning one of the counselors saw him offer a bag of chips and half of a sandwich to his mom."

Sabre took a deep breath and walked back to her client. She introduced herself and took him into an interview room for privacy. They sat on a small sofa with about a foot between them. She explained who she was and assured him that anything he said was confidential.

"Do you know why you're here, Cole?"

"The social worker said we needed to be here to be safe, but we were safe at home."

"What was it like at home?"

"I dunno." He shrugged. "Good, I guess."

"Does anyone else live with you besides your mom and brothers and sister?"

"Nope."

"Do you have any other family around?"

"Sometimes my Aunt Ella comes and stays the night."

"Does your Aunt Ella live nearby?"

"No, she lives in Riverside."

"That's about an hour and a half away. Do you see her very often?"

"Nope."

Sabre watched as Cole sat very still answering her questions. It bothered her that so many of the children she interviewed seemed so grown up. "Cole, do you like school?"

"Yup."

"How do you get to school?"

"We take the bus, and then I drop Hayden and Allie off at their classes and I go to mine."

"Allie? Is that Alexandria?"

"Yup. We call her Allie, but sometimes we call her Sissy because she's the only girl."

"What grade is Allie in?"

"She started kindergarten this year. Mom has to pick her up because she gets out too early, but Hayden rides the bus home with me."

"It says in the report that you've all been missing a lot of school lately. Is that true?"

Cole looked directly at Sabre as if he were trying to figure out the correct answer. "We've missed some. Mom's been sick and I've had to help her with the babies."

"Has anything unusual been happening at your home?"

Cole shook his head. "Nope."

"What's it like here at Polinsky?" Sabre asked.

"Good. The food is good."

Just then the door burst open, and a sinewy little six-year-old boy with his hair standing straight up in the back burst into the room.

"I'm sorry," the counselor standing in the doorway said. "Hayden didn't give me a chance to knock."

"It's okay. Come on in."

Hayden ran up to Cole and pounced on him, pulling him off the sofa onto the floor. "Hayden, stop!" Cole tried to push him off, but Hayden held on and soon they were rolling around, Cole a willing participant.

Sabre spoke to the counselor. "Why don't you bring me the other siblings. I'd like to see them all together."

"You sure?"

"Yes, please." Sabre smiled

Sabre watched the two boys play for a bit. She tried introducing herself to Hayden, but he ignored her.

"Is he always like this?" Sabre chose her words carefully. "So active?"

"He's a pain in the tush," Cole said adamantly, as he held his arm straight out against Hayden's head to keep him from attacking again. Hayden just smirked, ducked, and grabbed Cole around the legs.

Sabre had them just about calmed down when the door opened and Allie and Blake stepped in, followed by the counselor carrying Wyatt. As soon as Hayden saw Blake walk in, he turned and wrestled him to the floor. He was too forceful, though, and before long, Blake was crying. Cole stepped in and separated them. Then Allie quickly gave Blake a kiss and led him over to some toys in the corner of the room.

Sabre took Wyatt from the counselor and carried him around, introducing herself to each of the children as best she could. She wondered if she should be concerned about Wyatt's safety, although he seemed to have survived the first year and a half of his life amongst these "active" children well enough. He was the only one of the five that had any extra weight on his body.

The dynamics of this little family were interesting to watch. After a while, Sabre called for the counselors to come take the children back. A sigh of relief overtook her when they all left. She had learned a lot from her encounter with the Johnson sibs, not the least of which was to see them individually next time. Perhaps then she could ask about the chicken feet.

Chapter 3

Tired and irritable, it probably wasn't the best time to meet a teenager, but Sabre read through the report while she waited for the counselor to bring Bailey Rose Lecy to the interview room. There wasn't anything too surprising in the report. Bailey had run away several times, her grades had started to drop last semester, and by spring she hadn't attended school at all. From her behavior, the social worker suspected drugs, but no real evidence supported the theory.

Sabre closed her file and laid it down on the table when Bailey walked in. Her dyed-black hair made her aqua-blue eyes more evident, almost frightening. Bright red lipstick on her full lips added the only color to her pale skin. In spite of the cover-up, Sabre could see a natural beauty under her gothic disguise. Her features were perfect—a   small nose, straight teeth, clear skin, and a tiny dimple in her left cheek. She wore a green sweat shirt and khaki pants that Sabre assumed were Polinsky issue, since the report indicated she only wore black.

Bailey stepped inside and stopped a few feet from the door with her arms folded.

Sabre took a step towards her. "Please come have a seat." Sabre motioned to the sofa.

Bailey stood still. "Do you have a cigarette?" She asked.

"No. I don't smoke. And even if I did, you can't smoke in here."

"We could go out and you could buy me some."

"No. I'm sorry, Bailey. I couldn't do that." Sabre walked over closer to Bailey. When Bailey took a step backwards, Sabre stopped. Although it was a small room, she felt uncomfortable trying to converse with the eight feet or so between them, but putting her client at ease was more important than her own comfort. "By the way, I'm your attorney, Sabre ..."

"I don't need an attorney," she growled. "I haven't done anything."

Sabre spoke softly. "There's been a petition filed on your mother and that's why you've been temporarily removed from her care. When that happens the court appoints an advocate for the child. That would be me." Sabre paused. "Bailey, do you know what confidentiality means?"

"I'm not stupid."

"Of course you're not. Sorry. Just so you know, anything you tell me is confidential. So you can feel free to talk to me about anything and I can't divulge that to anyone else unless you give me permission."

"So if I tell you I'm going to kill someone, you can't tell?" Bailey said with teenage sarcasm in her voice.

"Actually, in that case I would have to tell because it is a future crime. But anything you have already done or anything that has happened to you stays between us. Understand?"

"Right." Bailey said as she shuffled her feet but kept her distance.

Sabre took a couple of steps closer to Bailey and when she didn't back up, Sabre angled a little closer to her, still keeping about some distance between them. "In this case, the petition on your mother is based partially on your behavior." Bailey didn't say anything, still standing with her arms crossed. "It says here you refuse to go to school. Is that correct?"

"School sucks."

"Why's that?"

"It just does." Bailey looked around the room.

"It looks like you were doing really well in the beginning of the school year. What happened to make things different?"

"Nothing."

"Something must've happened. You went from perfect attendance and straight A's to F's and now complete refusal to attend." Bailey didn't respond. "I'm here to help you, but I need to know your side of this story. There's always more than one side to a story."

"Don't act like you care. I know you don't care. Nobody cares."

"I know you don't know me and obviously don't trust me, but I do care and I want to help you. I know it all seems hopeless right now and like no one is listening to you, but I am listening. You just need to talk to me or there's nothing to listen to."

"Can I go back now?"

Sabre took a business card out of her briefcase and handed it to Bailey. "If you decide you want to talk, just tell one of the counselors and they'll call me."

"Sure" Bailey's face was expressionless as she took the card, turned toward the door, and pointedly flicked the card into the trash can.

Chapter 4

Sabre, early as usual for court, rifled through the junk in her mailbox in the lounge. She was alone except for her friend and colleague, Regina Collicott, who was reading the petitions. Regina was a tall, attractive woman with a page-boy hairdo and blunt-cut bangs. Sabre couldn't help like her since she was one of the few attorneys who shared her obsession for shoes. She was from California, but something about her always made Sabre think "southern belle with a smoking habit."

"Are you on detentions this morning?" Sabre asked.

"Yes, there's only one. It's some kind of ritual case."

Sabre stuffed the papers back in the mailbox and stepped towards Regina. "Another one? Let me see that." She reached her hand out and Regina handed her the report.

"There've been others recently?"

"Yeah, we got one yesterday and Wagner had one last month."

"That's a lot," Regina said. "In the six years I've been working juvenile court I've never had any kind of ritual case. I remember once there was some kind of satanic thing, but it turned out to be just some social worker's overactive imagination. I wonder what's going on."

"Who do you have on the case?"

"I have the kids. Why?"

"Do you remember JP, my investigator?"

Regina smiled. "Tall, good-looking cowboy, easy on the eyes?"

Sabre nodded.

"He's hard to forget."

Sabre chuckled. All the women, young and old, found him charming and indeed he was. "I'm going to have JP look into the case. Maybe you'll want to hire him, too. There shouldn't be a conflict. And if there is a movement out there, it would help to have some continuity."

"I'll call him this afternoon," Regina said as she walked out the door.

Sabre grabbed the papers back out of her mailbox, shoved them in her briefcase, and walked out to an already crowded hallway. Bob spotted her and yelled, "Sobs!"

"Hi, honey," Sabre said when Bob approached. "Guess what? There's another ritual case on calendar this morning."

"Really? Do you think Satan is running rampant in San Diego? Or maybe aliens are taking over our planet." He chuckled.

"You laugh, but it's a little frightening."

"Speaking of which, did you meet the children on my case? The Johnson tribe?"

A half smile crossed Sabre's face. "Oh yeah. Your client has her hands full. Delightful bunch of kids, but a little wild. And you're right. They have been going hungry. The oldest one, Cole, has been hoarding food at Polinsky."

"I know. The mom said he tried to give her food when they had their visit. She really wanted to take it because she was hungry, but she refused because she didn't want him to not eat because he was saving his food for her."

"You're convinced this mom is telling the truth, aren't you?" Sabre asked.

"I tend to believe her. I think she needs some help because she obviously can't feed all those kids."

"Wasn't she receiving aid?"

"She recently started getting it, but she was too far behind to catch up with the bills. The father left about a year ago, although I'm not sure how much help he was. Mom was working at Subway part time, but she lost her job and it barely covered daycare anyway. Although she resisted going on welfare for a long time, she's been on it for a few months now."

"So she should have enough for food for the kids."

"Yeah, that's where it gets a little foggy."

"If the money isn't going for food, where's it going? I realize it's not a lot, but these kids haven't been eating well. It shouldn't be as bad as it is." She tilted her head as if pondering. "Do you think it could be drugs or gambling, maybe?"

"She doesn't strike me as a druggie or a gambler and there's no evidence of either," Bob said.

"It's probably not cheap finding someone to perform rituals. And what about the expense of draining the blood from a goat? And don't forget about the cost of the chicken butcher." They laughed, but Sabre wasn't entirely convinced that it wasn't true.

Sabre finished her morning calendar, had lunch with Bob, and then went to her office to meet with JP. She was feeling a little nervous about seeing him, although she knew it was silly. She hadn't worked with him for several months, not since her breakup with her last boyfriend. JP had been such a support for her through that mess, but she didn't want to lean on him and she didn't want to give him the wrong impression.

JP sauntered into her office. "Howdy," he said, tipping his black Stetson hat and speaking in his ever so slight Texas accent. It was most evident when he used one of his grandfather's colloquialisms. "It seems like I haven't seen you since Moses was a pup."

Sabre laughed and was suddenly at ease again. "I've missed you, too. Are you ready to go to work on another case for me?"

"I don't know. Is it safe?"

"Probably not. But hopefully you won't get shot at or beat up or anything this time."

"All in a days work. Whatcha got?"

"There are two cases I'd like you to look into. We have the minors on both. The first is the Johnson case. Five hungry kids with truancy issues. Mom claims she's just down on her luck. The social worker thinks there's some ritualistic thing happening."

"What do you think?"

"I don't know, but something's going on. There was a case with similar overtones filed a couple of weeks ago, and another one came in today. I'll talk to the minors' attorney on the first one and get back to you. Regina Collicott is on today's case and she may be hiring you as well, if you want the case, of course. Do you know Collicott?"

"We've howdied but we ain't shook yet."

"So you haven't been formally introduced?"

"That's what I just said."

Sabre smiled. "I thought dealing with a similar case might help narrow things down if there is, in fact, a rise in this activity in San Diego."

"You never give me anything boring. I have to say that for you."

"The second case may be. If not boring, at least frustrating. You get to talk to a bunch of teenagers."

"That's not so bad. I was once one myself." JP flipped through the paperwork. "What's this one about?"

"The Lecy case is similar in that truancy is a big part of it. It appears to be an out-of-control teenager. She's been running away, her grades have dropped, and she quit school. She was doing really well until sometime this last year. Her mom was busted with cocaine at court yesterday so that might be the major problem. I want you to talk to her friends. Actually, she has only listed one. Her name is Shellie Ingraham, but I suspect she will lead to others. There's no mention of a boyfriend, but talk to the neighbors and mom's friends. See what you can find out."

Chapter 5

Coffee cup in hand, Sabre stepped out on her front porch to enjoy the early morning sun and listen to the birds chirp. She liked taking these few moments in the morning before she joined the circus they called juvenile court. She enjoyed her work and after six years she knew the Welfare and Institutions Code and Rules of Evidence better than just about anyone she worked with. Her colleagues often sought her out for advice or clarification on legal issues. She usually had the answers and always acted confident, but she still felt like she had fooled everyone into thinking she was smarter than she was. It was a feeling she had since she was in grade school, and she'd never conquered it. She remembered when she graduated from college and then from law school how strong the feeling was that she had tricked everyone. But she would go to work every day with her head held high wearing her "I'm competent" face and continue to fool the world.

Just as she started to open the sliding glass door, her phone rang out with a Leonard Cohen song. She didn't need to look to see who it was, as the ringtone was set especially for Bob.

"What's up?" she asked.

"Turn your TV on to local news."

"What am I looking for?" Sabre set her coffee cup down on her fireplace ledge, picked up her remote and searched for channel ten. She watched in astonishment as the cameras spanned the inside of an old, abandoned house on Sixty-Fourth. She saw the huge pentagram on the floor drawn in a red-brown color around a hospital bed, burned candles, and blood splattered everywhere. "Never mind, I found it."

They both listened in silence as the reporter spoke. "The footage was provided by a concerned citizen." The cameras switched to live coverage of the house surrounded by police. "Evidence of satanic rituals and sacrifices filled the rooms. The video was shot sometime between last Sunday morning and today . . ." the camera zoomed in on Sunday's newspaper showing the front page's date, ". . . as you can see by the newspaper on the table." The screen split showing the citizen's recording of the inside of the house and the television station's version outside with the police. The video continued through the small house, the camera stopped and lingered on a wall with the numbers 66 painted in red, and the reporter added her own comments. "The numbers 666 were found in several places in the house. It appears this one was interrupted somehow...the last 6 was left off."

A yellow police ribbon did little to keep the curious onlookers back from the house. Police cars continued to arrive with some officers going inside, guns drawn, while others worked on crowd control.

Sabre hung up the phone and immediately called JP. "Are you watching the news?"

"The devil's house?'"

"Yeah. There may be a connection to our case. I mean, how many of these cults can there be in one city at a time?"

"I'm on my way. I'll call you when I have something to report."

Sabre finished drinking her coffee, watching ritual signs and splattered blood instead of listening to chirping birds. Not exactly the way she planned to start her morning.

JP approached the house on Sixty-Fourth looking for someone in the police department he recognized. He had worked there a long time and had accumulated many friends before he had been shot and put on permanent disability. He hated leaving the department. Police work was his life. Private investigating wasn't the same but it gave him a little taste of his life passion. He walked along the police ribbon, still looking for a familiar face. They were becoming fewer and fewer as his friends reached retirement or changed to desk jobs.

"Hey, Mark," JP said to a slightly overweight detective standing near a police car.

"JP, how've you been?"

"Good, thanks. What's going on here?"

"We received a report that there were human sacrifices going on in this house."

"Whoa. Have they found any bodies?"

"No, none in the house anyway. There's evidence of fresh digging in the backyard, but we haven't started on that yet. Who knows what we'll find. But there were a couple of small hearts found in the refrigerator."

"Human?"

"We don't know yet."

Chapter 6

Although she wasn't on the detention calendar, Sabre checked the petitions to see if there were any more satanic ritual cases filed. She picked up the one new petition and read the allegations. Someone had shaken a three-month-old baby so hard it had caused brain damage. She read through the report, not finding anything outside the norm.

Sabre walked out of the lounge into the hallway and saw the social worker on the Johnson and Lecy cases. "Good morning, Gillian."

The woman with mousy-brown, not-so-fluffy hair, turned when she heard Sabre. "Oh, hi." Gillian smiled.

"I'm representing the minors on Johnson and Lecy. You have both of those cases, right?"

"Yes, have you met the children?"

"I have. The Johnsons are quite a handful. I saw them all together. I thought I might go back to Polinsky and see them individually today."

"You may want to call first in case they've been placed in foster homes." Gillian pulled her knit, slightly-tight blouse down over the top of her black slacks. Sabre noticed she had put on a few pounds since their last case together. She appeared to be trying to fit her somewhat overweight body into last year's clothes.

"Did you find a placement for all of them together?"

"I've been trying, but it's not easy putting that many children in one home, and I'm not about to leave them in Polinsky if I can find homes for them," Gillian said defensively.

"I'm sure you're doing your best."

"I'm trying. By the way, I found a foster home for Bailey. She'll be moved this morning." She took out a pad of paper, wrote on it, and handed it to Sabre. "Here's the name of the foster mother, address, and phone number."

"Thanks, I'd like to go talk with her again."

Sabre watched as Gillian gathered up her files. She looked tired. She had the kind of job that drained the life out of you if you weren't careful. Gillian had a reputation for working hard, but she wasn't that easy to work with and she was exceptionally good at covering her actions. Even when her position didn't necessarily seem like it was best for the children.

Bob walked up to Sabre and Gillian. "Hi Sobs," he said, looking at Sabre. Then he turned toward the social worker and said in a business voice, "Good morning, Gillian. My client on the Johnson case just called me and said she arrived at Polinsky for a scheduled visit, but they wouldn't let her see the children because they were all being moved to foster homes. She also said they were being split up."

Sabre spoke up. "I thought you didn't have homes for them yet?"

"I didn't say that. I told you to call because they may be gone. That's because I found homes. I didn't know they were being moved this morning."

"How many homes?" Bob asked.

"Four."

"Four? Four is the best you could do?" He stepped a little closer to her. "You know, I bet if you tried a little harder you could have placed them in five homes."

Gillian raised her voice. "Don't get huffy with me. We're lucky to have placements for them. Those kids are a handful."

Sabre spoke up. "So, where are they? I need to go see them."

"I don't have the addresses on me. I'll have to call you."

Bob gave Sabre a "what's wrong with this picture?" look.

"Gillian, is there a problem here?" Sabre asked.

"No problem. I'll give you the names and addresses of the foster parents as soon as I am back in the office."

Bob piped in. "Are they in Vista? I hope you at least did that much so they're closer to their mother. You know it's been difficult for her to get to Polinsky, so this could be a good thing."

The social worker snorted. "I placed them where I could find homes. The mother will just have to work it out."

Sabre saw Bob's face redden. She placed her hand on his arm. "So, where are they?" she said calmly.

"Cole and Hayden are in homes in Chula Vista, Allie is in Jamul, and Blake and Wyatt are together in Alpine."

Sabre swung around and took a step closer to Gillian. "You can't be serious. How are those kids going to maintain contact with their mother, let alone with each other? That is ludicrous. Have you thought about what this is going to do to those kids? Cole is going to be devastated." This time it was Bob putting his hand on Sabre's shoulder as her voice grew louder.

The social worker said, "I think it's best if Cole is separated from the others. He is way too parentified. He needs to be a little boy, not the father of that family."

"So you're willing to trade that for abandonment issues? Those kids are really close. They need each other and they need to spend time with their mother."

"I'm not willing to risk her applying some crazy rituals on them. My job is to protect those children and that's what I'm going to do."

"Do you think they're going to perform rituals on each other?" Sabre's voice escalated.

"I think it's best for the children. Who knows what Cole has been trained to do?"

"Do you have some reason to believe he has been trained to do something?"

"He's been drawing pictures of unicorns."

Sabre threw her hand in the air. "Oh, well, that explains it!" The color in Sabre's face deepened. Bob took her by the arm and led her away.

"Come on, Sobs," he said. "We'll deal with this another way."

"I'm setting a special and asking for a court order for sibling visitation. This will devastate those kids," Sabre said, stomping her foot. "Unicorns? Is she nuts?"

"You're wound up this morning. Did you have a bad night's sleep?" Bob asked.

"I was fine until I ran into Gillian. I just hate when they split the children up like that. It's just not right. They go through enough losing their parents; they don't need to lose each other, too."

"And then be spread all over the county. She couldn't have placed them any further from their mother if she tried."

Bob put his arm around Sabre's shoulder and escorted her to her hearing in Department Two. She felt so blessed to have Bob in her life. He was her best friend and like a brother to her. His actions and his sense of humor often reminded her of her real brother, Ron. She hadn't seen Ron for nearly a year and then it was only for a few hours. Although Bob couldn't replace Ron, it sure helped having him around.

Sabre finished the last case on her calendar. When she left the courtroom she saw Gillian coming out of Department One. Sabre stepped back inside to give her time to pass. She was too angry to deal with her again. Sabre came out of the courtroom just in time to see Attorney Wagner exit Department One cussing as he walked toward her.

"What's the matter, Wags?" Sabre asked.

"Judge Shirkoff. He's so damn stupid. He doesn't know the first thing about juvenile law. And he's so damned arrogant on top of it all. How the hell did he get to be presiding judge?" Wagner didn't wait for Sabre to respond. He just stomped off.

Sabre drove to her office to draft a motion for a special hearing on the Johnson case regarding sibling visitation. After she wrote the motion and made copies, she began driving back to the courthouse to file it. A few blocks down the road, she hesitated. She was so angry that the children had been detained in four different homes she really hadn't thought it through. She should give the social worker a chance to arrange visits, or not arrange them, before she set a hearing. Then she thought about her own brother and how much she would have missed if she hadn't been able to grow up with him. She wasn't going to wait. She'd obtain an order for the social worker to make every effort to have the children detained together and an order for sibling visitation. Those children did not need to be apart. They needed each other.

On her way to court, Sabre called Bailey's foster mother and set up an appointment to meet her later that afternoon. It would be a quick visit, just long enough for Bailey to know she was looking out for her. Perhaps she'd get some information from her that would help with JP's investigation on this case.

Court had already commenced when she arrived. Sabre entered the courtroom quietly and handed the papers to the bailiff. He in turn took them to the court clerk. Sabre sat down in the back of the courtroom and waited for the ongoing case to finish. The case had been trailed from the morning calendar and the parents had been waiting all morning for justice to be dispensed. The mother was wiry. She twitched and squirmed in her seat, a behavior Sabre recognized as a result of drug use. An older gentleman sat next to her, and although he wasn't her husband, he was claiming to be the father of at least two of her children. Sabre would have easily mistaken him for the children's grandfather or even great-grandfather. When the court ordered the children detained at Polinsky instead of with the alleged father, Sabre saw tears well up in his eyes. The mother's response was, "Hmpf."

Between hearings, the judge signed the order for a special hearing to be set on the Johnson case. Sabre made copies, put one in each of the attorneys' mailboxes, and drove to the County Counsel office to drop off their copy. They would, in turn, notify their client, the social worker.

Sabre then proceeded to the address the social worker had given her for Bailey's foster home. Sabre had had children in this foster home before, and the foster parents were very caring people. Mr. and Mrs. Venable were both teachers, although Mrs. Venable hadn't taught school since her own children were born. When their two children entered high school, they started taking in foster children and so she continued to stay home and raise the girls. The children they took in were ones who had trouble in school. Their determination to keep these children in school and their patience shone through with their many hours of tutoring.

Bailey had only been in the home a few hours when Sabre arrived, and she didn't appear too pleased to see her attorney. Mrs. Venable had apparently already made an impression on Bailey because she was able to coax her into at least talking with Sabre.

They walked out onto the back porch. Sabre motioned for her to sit down on the bench, but Bailey perched herself on the porch railing a few feet away.

After a few not so pleasantries, Bailey said, "You're my attorney. Get me emancipated."

"Why do you want to be emancipated?"

"So I can live where I want and do what I want."

"Where did you hear about emancipation?"

"At Polinsky. All the girls are talking about doing it. Amy said her cousin's friend got emancipated and now no one can tell her what to do."

"It's not that simple, Bailey. You need to be able to support yourself."

"I can take care of myself."

"You have to show that you have a place to live and an income to support yourself, and you're only fourteen."

"I'll be fifteen in a few months."

"Six months."

"Well, I can take care of myself. You're my lawyer. You need to file the papers or do whatever you need to do."

"There's nothing to file until you have a means of income and a place to live."

"I'll steal the money if that's what it takes. Or I can sell drugs like my mom's skuzzy boyfriend."

"It has to be legal income."

"Then I'll get a job at McDonald's or something."

"It's hard to get a job until you're sixteen, Bailey." Sabre reached out her hand and placed it on Bailey's shoulder. Bailey pulled away. "And what's this about your mom's boyfriend? What's his name?"

"Scott Jamison. He's a loser."

"What makes you think he's a drug dealer?"

"You're kidding, right?" Bailey snarled. Sabre waited. "He only has drugs on him all the time. People come by all hours of the night to get things from him and give him money. What do you think? He's selling comic books?"

"Why haven't you told this to someone before?"

"Like anyone cares. Mom doesn't care. She gets all the drugs she wants."

"I'm so sorry you have had to live like that. You know, I was a teenager not that long ago. I didn't always get along with my mother, but I can't even imagine what it must have been like for you."

Bailey lowered her voice a little. "At least when she's high she's not on my case, but you don't know the half of it."

"What do you mean by that?" Bailey didn't respond. "Bailey, is there something else going on in that home?"

"Naw." Bailey hopped down from the railing and started to walk toward the door. "I don't want to talk anymore. Can I go in now?"

Sabre left the foster home and as soon as she was in the car she called her mother.

"Hi, Mom. Are you busy Saturday evening? I'd like to come see you."

Chapter 7

"Are you smoking?" Sabre yelled as she walked up to Bob, who was waiting for her just outside the courthouse. She smacked Bob on the forearm. "You bozo. Why would you do that?"

Bob pulled back, missing the full force of her swing. "Calm down, Sobs. I only have a couple a day."

"Yeah, for now. And soon you'll be back to a couple of packs a day."

"What can I say? I'm a weak man, controlled by a cancer-producing agent wrapped in white paper disguised as my friend while it overwhelms me and takes over my need to feel euphoric if only for a few seconds in time."

"Oh, please."

"It could be worse. I could be drinking vodka."

"You do drink vodka."

"Yeah, but not in the morning." Bob held the cigarette in his right hand. He put his left arm around Sabre, turning away from her to blow the remaining smoke out of his mouth. "Come on, Sobs, allow me to have my one . . . uh . . . or two vices."

Sabre's voice was calmer. "I just worry about your health." She looked up at Bob. "Does Marilee know you're smoking again?"

"My wife is as upset as you are."

"Good. Let her stay on your case. I think I'll call her and see if she needs any help tormenting you about it." Sabre took a couple of steps away from the courtroom wall.

"Anyway, it's partly your fault," Bob said.

Sabre stopped and looked up. "My fault? How is it my fault?"

"You practically got me killed last month."

"Oh, don't be so dramatic."

"So dramatic? I was shot! In the head!"

Sabre reached up and touched the side of Bob's head. "Look, your hair has almost all grown in. You won't even be able to see the scar."

Bob walked over to the stone ash tray that stood next to the courtroom door and stuck his cigarette butt in the sand. "Let's go eat."

"JP is joining us."

They took Bob's car to Pho's, their favorite lunching place. JP got out of his car just as they pulled into a parking spot directly in front of the restaurant. His black Stetson rose above the car three spots down.

"Do you two ever eat anywhere else?" JP asked, as he walked up to them.

Sabre shook her head. "Bob has a very limited palate, but I'm working on him."

"I just know what I like. And I like this food."

"You've only eaten one dish. It's always the same dish," Sabre said.

"See, I know what I like."

The three of them walked into the restaurant, past the big gold Buddha and the bright gold fish swimming in the tank. A waiter led them into the next room and seated them at a table with the same pink polyester tablecloths that had adorned the tables for as long as they had been eating there, which was well over five years. Bob snickered when Sabre and JP ordered the #124 just as he had.

Before the waiter began to walk away, Sabre had already started shop talk. "JP, I need you to check on the mother's boyfriend in the Lecy case. His name is Scott Jamison." She turned to Bob. "Is there anything you can tell us about him?"

"According to mom, he's a model citizen," Bob responded.

"Right," Sabre said.

"I've been trying to catch up with Shellie Ingraham, the friend of Bailey's that is listed in the report, but I keep missing her," JP said. "I think she may be avoiding me."

"I'm sure you'll get to her," Sabre said, as she reached into her briefcase and took out a paper and handed it to JP. "Here's the memo I wrote after speaking with Bailey yesterday. See what you can find out about the mother's boyfriend." Before he could say anything, Sabre added, "And on the Johnson case, follow up on the mom's story about where she's been getting her chicken feet and goat blood."

Bob spoke up. "It was just a little bit of blood. It's not like she had quarts of it sitting around. She says they were hungry and she bought the cheapest meat she could find to feed the kids. I tend to believe her."

"Just because chickens have wings don't mean they can fly," JP said. "I'll check it out." Sabre and Bob both smiled at JP's Texas slang. They called them "JP-isms." He seemed to have one for everything.

Sabre asked, "Have you discovered any other friends of Bailey?"

"Not yet. Most of the kids at school are tighter than bark on a tree with their information, but I've got a couple of leads that I'm following up today."

The waiter walked up with the food. Silence ensued as they began to eat, but it wasn't long before they were in full conversation again about the cases they were all involved in. Bob finally changed the subject. "I'm laying some brick this weekend for the walkway to the new patio in the backyard. What are you two doing?"

JP said, "I'm investigating these new cases."

"I am too. I'll be driving all over San Diego County visiting the minors on the Johnson case."

Bob looked at JP, then at Sabre, and back again. "You two need to get a life."

Chapter 8

A good night's sleep had become foreign to Sabre and last night proved to be no exception. Although it was Saturday, by five o'clock in the morning she was lying wide awake in her bed. The strange cases that were coming into juvenile court were weighing heavily on her mind. Another one had been filed yesterday. It wasn't her case, but she had been watching the detentions as they came in to see if there was some connection to her own case. They all varied in location and each had only a hint of ritual in them, just like hers with the chicken feet and goat blood. If it hadn't been for the house with the pentagram and the splattered blood that was shown on the news, Sabre would've thought it all nonsense. Fortunately, the small hearts that were found in the refrigerator were from pigs rather than humans, according to the eleven o'clock news last night.

Sabre's day was fully scheduled with home visits. She had mapped it to spend as little driving time as possible, but with the Johnson children spread all over the county, it would be a full day. Her first visit was scheduled for eight o'clock in Alpine with Blake and Wyatt. From there she would drive to Jamul to see Allie, and then to Chula Vista to see Cole and Hayden in their respective homes. She enjoyed seeing the children, but was already dreading the long drive.

Sabre took her little red notebook out of the nightstand next to her bed. This was a gift from her brother, Ron, and it was where she kept her secret goals. She had been writing in it since she was six years old when she decided her first goal was to marry the little boy who lived next door, Victor Spanoli. It was the only goal she had written that she hadn't achieved. That and her last one, which was to run a marathon, but she was still training for that. She'd been thinking a lot lately about traveling. She loved to travel and she hadn't been anywhere in a long time. She had such a hard time getting away from work, but she knew if she scheduled it, she'd make it happen. She picked up a pen and wrote, Travel to Cancun. Her Spanish was good, though not what she'd call fluent, but it would be great practice. She had studied for a while in Guadalajara, but it had been so long ago and her language skills were rusty.

Sabre felt good. She had a new goal and not only would it be fun, it would be educational. Now she just had to come up with a time frame and maybe a traveling companion. After gingerly closing the notebook, she placed it back in the drawer, stood up, and dressed for a morning run.

The cool air in her face and the adrenalin pumping through her helped her forget about work for the next hour. This was her favorite time of year. The summer heat was gone and the weather was perfect. Morning was her favorite time to run, but she usually had to wait until afternoon to fit it into her schedule. Weekends were different. She could go out first thing and then start her work. She didn't seem to play any more. It was all about completing the next task. Her social life had tanked with her last relationship and she wasn't sure when she'd be ready to try another. But running was good. Running cleared her head and gave her a new perspective on things. She still had about eight months to train for the next San Diego marathon. But if she picked up her game, she could possibly be ready for the Carlsbad run.

Sabre checked her watch, picked up her speed, and headed home to get ready.

About an hour later, Sabre was driving east on Highway 8 toward Alpine. She turned on the radio and sang along with Taylor Swift, feeling more and more frustrated as she drove toward the home of the two youngest Johnson children. Forty-five minutes later she arrived at the foster home of Blake and Wyatt. The foster mother invited her inside. Sabre heard Wyatt cry as she entered the spotless living area and saw Blake trying to console him.

"Is he okay?" Sabre asked.

The foster mother picked Wyatt up and he started to calm down, still whimpering as she coddled him in her arms. "He cries a lot. Sometimes Blake can soothe him, but most of the time I just have to hold him until he falls asleep."

"Has he been checked by the doctor?"

"Yes, he's fine physically." The foster mother gently stroked Wyatt's hair. "He's especially bad at night. I think he just misses his mother. She called last night and he calmed right down when he heard her voice on the phone."

"Has she seen him since he's been here?"

"She's scheduled to come tomorrow, but with all the transfers, it'll take her about four hours to get here by bus, so I've agreed to meet her in El Cajon. That will cut a couple of hours off and she'll be able to see Allie at the same time. Allie's foster mother has agreed to bring her because she needed to go that way anyway. I don't think she'll make a habit of it because she wasn't too pleased with the idea."

Sabre looked at the room where Blake and Wyatt slept. Then she visited with the boys for a while before she started on the road to see Allie. She arrived at the scheduled time but no one answered the door when she knocked. Sabre walked around the big yard, trying to calm the black-and-white, mixed-breed dog that kept barking at her. Sabre went to her car and looked up the phone number to call the foster mother. Just then, a large, white van drove up the driveway.

When the van stopped, five children emptied out of it. Allie ran up to Sabre. "Where's my brothers?" she asked.

Sabre knelt down on one knee and looked her in the eye. "I just saw your two little brothers and they're doing great. You'll be able to see them yourself real soon."

"I miss my brothers. And my mom, too."

"Well, I'm going to see your older brothers this afternoon. Is there anything you want me to tell them?"

"Tell them to come see me." Allie started to follow the foster mother into the house. "And tell them I have a dog named Jingles."

"I'll do that." Sabre went into the house. She was amazed at the contrast between the two foster homes. This one had loose toys lying around, jackets and shoes in odd places, and dirty dishes on an already cluttered counter in the kitchen. This foster mother growled at the kids to pick their things up and take them to their rooms. The last one had such a gentleness in her voice. Sabre wasn't judging. One didn't necessarily seem any better than the other; they were just different. And the children seemed to be adjusting about as well as could be expected.

After her visit, Sabre said her goodbyes and drove to see Cole in Chula Vista. The drive customarily took about forty minutes, but her GPS sent her the wrong direction and added another ten minutes to the already maddening drive. Sabre had to park halfway down the block due to all the cars in front of the house. One of them was a police car. Sabre's heart began to race as she walked up to the house.

A policeman met her at the door. "I'm Sabre Brown, Cole Johnson's attorney. Is he all right?"

Gillian, the social worker, came out of Cole's bedroom. "Cole is missing," she said.

"What do you mean, missing?"

"He apparently ran away."

"How long has he been gone?" Sabre asked, looking over at the foster mother who was sitting on the sofa crying as the policeman took her statement.

"We think he left in the night," Gillian said.

"What do you mean, 'you think he left in the night?'" Sabre's voice came out a little louder than she intended. "Don't they know how long he's been gone?"

"We're not sure. The foster mother saw him last night just before he went to bed. The other little boy in his room said Cole was gone when he woke up this morning, but he just thought he was somewhere else in the house or outside or something."

"What time was that?"

"About nine o'clock. Since it was Saturday, the children were allowed to sleep in."

"Why wasn't I called?" Sabre asked.

But before Gillian could answer, a detective walked up to Sabre, introduced herself, and said, "We've got a full force out there looking for him. Do you have any idea where he might be?"

Sabre shook her head. "I've only met him once so I don't know him that well. I do know he's very close to his siblings and his mother, so if he was trying to find someone, I expect he'd be headed home. But I doubt if he knows his way around here since he grew up in Vista."

The detective wrote something down on her notepad. "We have someone at his mom's house right now. He's not there and it appears he hasn't been there." She shrugged her shoulders. "Unless she's lying to us."

Gillian walked toward where the foster mother was sitting.

The detective spoke again. "The social worker says this is a satanic ritual case. Do you know if it ties into the house with the pentagram that was just on the news?"

"The evidence of satanic ritual abuse consists of a finding of chicken feet and goat blood in the Johnson house. That's all we have. I have a private investigator on it as well, and we haven't come up with anything else yet. So, I really don't know anything more than that. It worries me, though, that there may be a connection." Sabre took a deep breath. "Do you think someone may have kidnapped him?"

"We haven't ruled it out, but he did take his backpack with him and some food was missing out of the refrigerator. That's the main reason we think he's a runaway, but someone could've set it up so it just looked that way."

Chapter 9

Anxious to finally get to the gym, JP pulled into the parking lot, tossed his Stetson in the trunk, and walked towards the entrance. His phone rang. Sabre was frantic. She explained to him what she knew about Cole's disappearance. Before JP even hung up from the call, he had started to walk back toward his car. His workout would have to wait.

JP met Sabre at the foster home so he could obtain first-hand information from the foster family and the investigating officer.

"Does he have any money?" JP asked.

The foster mother shook her head. "Not that I know of. I checked my purse and I still have cash, but I don't know how much I had. If he did take any, it wasn't much."

JP put his arm around Sabre. "Hey, kid, I know you're worried."

"What if this satanic ritual thing is real? What if someone has taken him?"

"I know it's scary and I'm going to do whatever I can. The cops will be looking for foul play, so I'm first going to hit the ground looking in places he may be hiding. And I'll try to follow up on this ritual thing ... whatever it is, but we really have very little to go on there."

JP started his hunt. He canvassed the neighborhood questioning everyone he could, adults and children, but he couldn't find anyone who knew Cole. He hadn't been in the home long enough to become acquainted, and no one had seen anything suspicious in the night or early morning.

JP stomped through all the local parks and looked inside the boys' bathrooms, covered the local school grounds and ball fields, and questioned everyone he saw, but found nothing that led him to Cole. He seemed to have vanished.

Satisfied he wasn't going to find Cole on his local search, JP called Bob. "I'd like to speak to your client, Cole's mother, at her home. Would you like to go with me?"

"Sure. I think Mrs. Johnson would appreciate it. We're all on the same side, at least for the moment."

"I'm in Chula Vista. I'll swing by and pick you up."

"How about if I meet you in Fashion Valley? It'll save you a little time. In front of Bloomingdales?"

"That would be great. Who knows how much time we have."

JP drove to Fashion Valley, picked Bob up, and they started the thirty-minute trek to Vista.

"How is the Mom taking this?" JP asked.

"Like any concerned mother. She's devastated. She has no car or means to search by herself. Besides, the cops told her to stay home in case he found his way there."

"You don't think he has contacted her?"

"I don't think he could. She has no phone. She used the cop's phone to call me. The neighbors aren't real close and besides, she didn't think Cole had any of the neighbors' numbers."

The GPS said to exit on Deer Springs Road and go west. JP followed the road around some curves and then turned right onto another street.

An odor of sulfur filled the air just before they reached a hand-painted sign that said, "Eggs for sale." In smaller writing scrawled underneath it read, "Chickens too." About a half mile later they pulled up to a small dilapidated house.

"This is the address," JP said. "She's really out in the sticks, isn't she?"

"Yeah, it's no wonder she has such a hard time using the bus service to go see her kids."

Leanne Johnson came out of the house before they reached the door. "Did you find Cole?"

Bob answered, "No, I'm sorry, Leanne. We don't have any leads yet. That's why we're here." He nodded his head toward JP. "This is JP, a private investigator. He's working for Cole's attorney and trying to find your son. He'd like to ask you some questions if you don't mind."

"Sure." Tears were welling up in Leanne's already red and swollen eyes. She opened the front door. "Please come in and sit down."

JP and Bob walked into a small living room with a sofa, chair, and a television smaller than any JP had seen in a really long time. It made him feel a little guilty about his forty-two-inch plasma. The kitchen sat off to the left, which was small and meager but clean. JP stuck his head into the kitchen.

"He's not here. God, I wish he was. You can look around if you'd like. The cops already did that, but feel free."

JP responded, "No, that won't be necessary." He paused. "Unless you think he could've gotten in here without you knowing it."

"The place isn't that big."

"Mrs. Johnson, has Cole ever run away before?"

"No, never. He's a really good boy. Oh, he fights with Hayden a lot, but Hayden usually antagonizes him. And mostly, they just wrestle."

"What about Cole's father? Any chance he may have taken Cole from the foster home?"

"That creep. I wish. At least it would be better than Cole being out there all by himself. Although, just barely, when I think about it."

"How do you know he's not with him?"

"His dad's not around. I'm sure he doesn't even know where the kids are. He left us about a year ago."

"What else can you tell us about his father?" JP made a few notes in his notebook. "Do you have an address?"

"No, this was his last address. He's probably living on the streets. He kept crawling deeper into the bottle, and he had started getting more abusive. I finally couldn't take it anymore. One night he yanked me around by my arm and pushed me into the stove. I sprained my wrist and burnt my arm." She pulled her sleeve back to expose the scar from the burn. "The kids were setting him off a lot easier and I was afraid he was going to start hurting them. So the next morning when he was sober, I asked him to leave. I haven't seen or heard from him since."

"What about friends of Cole? Is there anyone close around here that he played with?"

"There's not really anyone his age close enough to hang out with. He played mostly with his brother, Hayden. And he was a big help around the house. He did a lot of chores for a little guy."

"What about school friends?"

"There was one kid he talked about a lot. His name is Jacob. But that's about all I know. He never came to visit Cole, and Cole never went to his house. They just hung out at school."

"Do you have any relatives that he might contact?"

"There's no one local. Their dad's family is from Arkansas and I don't have much family at all. I have an aunt who lives in Riverside, Aunt Ella."

"Do you think he might try to call her?"

"He might. He may even remember her number."

"Would you like to call her to see if she has heard from him?" JP handed her his cell phone.

"Thank you." Leanne punched in the numbers. "I hope I don't upset her. She's seventy-two-years old and not in the best of health; otherwise, she would've taken the children herself."

JP and Bob listened as Leanne spoke to her aunt. They could tell by her side of the conversation that it wasn't good news. Leanne hung up, shook her head, and said, "Nope."

Chapter 10

JP checked with the neighbors to see if anyone had seen Cole and also if they knew a boy named Jacob, hoping he rode Cole's bus. With the information he gathered from the other students who rode the bus, he was able to track the route to the school. He finally found someone who knew someone who knew Jacob.

It was nearly eight o'clock and dark by the time he approached Jacob's house, which was directly across the street from the elementary school. A gangly, freckle-faced boy with red hair answered the door.

"Are you Jacob?" JP asked.

"Yes."

"Are your parents home?"

"Dad," Jacob yelled. "Someone wants you."

A short, slightly overweight man in his forties walked out onto the porch. In his right hand were a pair of metal tongs with grease dripping from them. JP introduced himself and explained he was there looking for a lost child, Cole Johnson. "Do you mind if I ask Jacob a few questions?"

"No, not at all," Albert said. He then turned to Jacob and said, "Have you heard from Cole?"

Jacob shrugged his shoulders and said, "No."

Holding Jacob's gaze, Albert pointed the tongs at him and said, "You better not be lying to me, kid. This boy's life could be in danger."

"I'm not lying. I don't know where he is."

Jacob's eyes opened wider and his mouth turned down. He took a step back from his father. His father reached out with his left hand and grabbed him by the arm, yanking him forward until he was within a few inches of his face. "Do you know where Cole is?"

Tears started to well up in Jacob's eyes. "Honest, Dad. I don't know. He left school a couple days ago. I haven't seen him since."

JP stepped forward turning toward the father. "Do you mind if I speak to him alone for a minute?" He lowered his voice to almost a whisper. "Sometimes kids will tell me things they may not want to tell their parents."

Albert nodded his head. "Yeah, you're right. Go ahead." He turned to walk off and then he looked at Jacob and shook the tongs at him. "You tell him the truth now." He was still looking back at Jacob as he entered the house.

JP sat down on the wooden railing and coaxed Jacob into taking a seat near him. "Look, Jacob, I'm not here to hurt you. You're not going to get in trouble if you tell me where Cole is. There are people looking all over the city for him and we just want him returned safely."

Jacob shrugged. "I don't know. I haven't seen him."

"Have you talked to him since he left school?"

"No."

"Has Cole ever been to your house?"

Jacob put his head down, avoiding eye contact with JP, and shook his head from side to side. JP reached under his chin and gently pulled his head up with one finger. "Jacob, please tell me when he was here. I won't tell your father."

Jacob looked toward the door and back and said, "Sometimes, at lunch, we sneak off the playground and go to my house to play video games. But we almost got caught last week, so we haven't done it since. And then a couple of days ago, Cole left school. I didn't even know he was leaving."

"I know. There have been a few family problems that Cole's mom has to take care of."

"Is he coming back?"

"I don't know. I'm sorry. I wish I could tell you more." JP stood up and took a business card out of his pocket. He handed it to Jacob. "Please call me, or have your father call me, if you hear from Cole, okay? It's really important. His mom is really worried about him."

Jacob took the card, holding it with both hands. He bent it back and forth. "I'll call," he said.

JP leaned in toward Jacob. "Will you be all right when you go inside with your father?"

"Oh yeah. He yells a lot since mom divorced him, but he's okay."

JP waited until Jacob went in the house and then he lingered for a few minutes to see if he heard any yelling. It was quiet. JP walked to his car thinking he was pretty certain Jacob was telling the truth. Before he started his car, his phone rang.

"Hi, Sabre. I'm sorry, I'm just hitting dead . . ."

"JP," Sabre said interrupting him, "Bailey's missing."

Chapter 11

Sabre drove up to the home where Bailey lived with her mother. JP hadn't arrived yet, but she knew he was close behind. Sabre walked across the dead lawn and up to the door. The house was in serious need of paint, and broken glass formed a sharp, jagged point in the front window. The dilapidated door opened slightly as Sabre knocked on it.

"Who is it?" a man yelled over the loud eighties music that emanated from the house.

"I'm Bailey Lecy's attorney," Sabre yelled back. "Is she here?"

No one responded. About thirty seconds passed before an emaciated looking, unshaven man came to the door. His shirtless body bared a large, poorly drawn scorpion tattoo across his chest, and his pants hung below his waist showing the top of his green boxer shorts. His disheveled hair almost reached his shoulders. The front hung down partly blocking the glazed look in his eyes. When he opened his mouth to speak, black gaps on each side of his mouth appeared where teeth once were.

The man slowly moved his eyes from Sabre's face all the way to her feet and then back up to her face. "Well, hello," he said.

Sabre suddenly wished she had waited for JP. The way he looked at her made her feel dirty. "Do you know Bailey Lecy?"

"Come on in. We'll talk about it." He moved his left hand toward the door motioning her to enter.

"I'm good." She backed up slightly. "Are you Scott?"

"Yes," he said, looking directly at Sabre's breasts.

Sabre ignored his stare. "Have you seen Bailey today?"

"That fat little wench." Scott reached up and took hold of Sabre's arm. When she tried to pull away he held on tighter. "Come on in. I'll tell you all about her."

Sabre took a quick step backwards. Scott lost his balance and stumbled but reached with his left hand for Sabre's other arm. She flung it backwards and his hand landed on her rib cage. He pulled her toward him. "You're as feisty as your little Bailey," he said.

Sabre swung her right hand around as quickly as she could, smacking Scott on the side of the head with as much force as she could muster. Her angle was bad and he had pulled her too close to him, but it was enough to make him lose his grip on her side as he tried to stop the blow. Scott's drugged condition gave Sabre a little extra time to react. She pulled back her hand and with the base of her palm jammed it against his nose. Scott let go of her arm and Sabre fell backwards onto the ground. Before she could stand up, he slammed a bare foot into her stomach.

Suddenly the weight lifted from her abdomen and Scott sailed through the air as JP grabbed him by the arm and flung him to the ground, pinning him down with his knee.

"Are you okay?" JP asked Sabre.

"I'm fine," Sabre said as she rolled over, stood up, and dusted the dirt off her pants.

"Didn't I tell you to wait for me?" JP sounded exasperated.

"I guess you were right this time," Sabre said.

JP shook his head. "This man is so low he'd steal the nickels off a dead man's eyes."

"I expected to meet up with a teenage girl." Sabre looked at Scott lying face down in the dry grass. "Not some psycho, drugged-out baboon." The adrenalin still flowing through Sabre's body, along with the fear and disgust of his hands on her, made her want to kick him, but she held back. Instead she leaned over him and said, "You didn't answer my question. Have you seen Bailey today?"

"I can't remember," Scott said. JP pushed his knee deeper into the Route 66 tattoo on Scott's back. "Okay. Stop with the police brutality." JP pushed a little harder and then let up some as he started to talk. "They came by here about an hour ago."

"Who was with her?" Sabre asked.

"That little punk she calls a boyfriend."

"Does he have a name?" JP asked.

"Apollo."

"His last name?"

"I don't know." JP applied more pressure. "I never heard his last name, and I never cared enough to ask."

"What did they come here for?" Sabre asked.

"She just picked up some of her things. Then the punk threatened to kill me."

"Why?"

"Because he's been working out and he thinks he's a super tough guy now."

"No, what did he threaten you about?" Sabre spoke slowly and clearly.

"About Bailey . . . like I'd want that little whore."

JP pushed harder with his knee on Scott's back and asked, "Did you do something to Bailey?"

"I never did anything she didn't ask for." Scott snickered.

JP leaned over him, trying to block Sabre's view, and popped him in the side of the head with his elbow.

"Damn," Scott bellowed.

"I saw that," Sabre said.

"No, you didn't," JP responded. He turned toward Scott. "She's only fourteen years old. You pig."

"Where did they go?" Sabre asked.

"They didn't say and I didn't ask."

JP let Scott up but not before he threatened to return and do some serious damage if he ever touched Bailey again.

JP walked Sabre to her car. "You need to see a doctor."

"No. I'm fine."

"I still think you should be checked out." JP examined her face for damage.

"I'm really okay. I didn't hit my head or anything. I was going to go see my mother tonight, but I'll cancel. I'm just going to go home, take a hot bath, and get some rest."

JP looked at her and frowned.

"Really. Just promise to call immediately if you turn up any information on Cole or Bailey."

Sabre called her mother on her way home. She canceled the visit and assured her she would try to make it next weekend.

JP drove off to find Apollo and Bailey. This was the first he or Sabre had heard of Apollo, or any boyfriend for that matter. In fact, Bailey had denied having a boyfriend, but she was a teenager and not exactly forthcoming with any information.

JP drove to see Shellie Ingraham, Bailey's best friend according to the social worker's report. As he walked up to the door he heard a beautiful, melodic young voice radiate from inside. He waited until she finished the song before knocking, enjoying every note. A dishwater blonde teenager opened the door. Her soft round features added to her innocent look. Though they matched the voice in their purity, she appeared much younger than her voice.

"Hello," she said.

"Are you Shellie Ingraham?"

"Yes."

Just then a man walked up to the door. He was holding a guitar and was apparently providing the back-up music for

Shellie's singing. "Hello, I'm Jim Boller, Shellie's stepfather. Can I help you?"

"My name is JP Torn. I'm an investigator for Bailey Lecy's attorney. We're trying to help her through a rough time. I'd like to ask Shellie some questions, if you don't mind."

"Come on in."

Jim spoke briefly with JP, offered him something to drink, and then left them sitting at the table. He positioned himself across the room. JP was impressed with his protectiveness toward his daughter.

JP turned to Shellie. "When did you last see Bailey?"

"About a week ago, a few days before they took her to Polinsky."

"I understand you two are best friends. Is that correct?"

"We're not as close as we used to be."

"Did you have a fight?"

"Not really." Shellie said.

"So what happened?"

"I dunno." Shellie shrugged her shoulders.

"Did it have something to do with Apollo?"

Shellie looked up, wide-eyed. "You know about him?"

"Yes, we do, and we're worried about Bailey. She's missing and we think she's with Apollo." JP waited to see Shellie's reaction, but her expression didn't change. "What can you tell me about him?"

"Not much. I don't know him that well. He was from a different school and I only saw him a couple of times."

"What does Apollo look like?"

"I dunno." She wrinkled her nose. "He's kinda cute, I guess. He's short, has dark hair. He had a Mohawk the first time I saw him, but the last time he was wearing a baseball cap so I don't know if he still had it." She closed her eyes for a second as if to picture him in her mind. "Oh, and he wears round glasses, like Harry Potter."

"Anything else?" JP asked.

"He's built pretty good, like he works out a lot." She snapped her head toward JP. "Oh, and he has a tattoo of a star on his wrist."

"A star? How many points does the star have?"

"Just four, I think. Well, I think it was a star. It was about this long." She held her fingers about three inches apart. "But two of the points were only a couple of inches long. Maybe it wasn't a star, maybe it was a cross, but it had points like a star. Oh, and it had something written inside it. Numbers, I think. I couldn't tell for sure."

"So you only saw him twice?"

"Yeah, that was it."

"When did you last see him?"

"It's been a few months. Bailey and I didn't hang out much after she met him."

"Why is that?"

"She was different. She spent all her time with him. She started dressing differently, wearing black all the time like Apollo, and then she stopped going to school. I didn't see her at all for four or five months until after ..." She looked toward her stepfather. He was facing them as he quietly picked on his guitar.

"Until after what?" JP asked.

"Nothing," Shellie said.

"It's really important that we find her."

Shellie looked concerned. "How long has she been missing?"

"Not long, but she ran away and we're afraid she may be in danger."

"I don't know anything about that."

JP believed her but was certain she knew more than she was telling. He continued to try to get more information about Apollo and Bailey, but Shellie seemingly didn't know anything else. "Did you ever go to Bailey's house?"

"I used to when we were little, but I'm not allowed to go anymore."

"Why's that?"

"Ever since Bailey's mom started hanging out with Scott, my dad hasn't let me go there."

"But you've gone anyway?" JP had a hunch.

Shellie glanced toward her father and lowered her voice. "Just once." She wrinkled her face in disgust.

"What happened?"

"Scott's a creep."

"What did he do, Shellie?"

"He kept touching my hair and acting all lovey-dovey." Shellie clenched her teeth, turned her lip down, and shook her head and shoulders. "Aachh," she said, sticking her tongue out. "I left and never went back."

JP saw Jim look toward them. "And you didn't tell your parents?" JP asked.

"No, I'd be in big trouble and Jim would probably kill him."

JP nodded, thinking he'd like to do the same. When JP stood up, Jim walked back to the table. JP handed them each a business card and then, looking first at Shellie and then at Jim, said, "If you hear from her or think of anything else that may be helpful, please call me."

Chapter 12

Sabre woke up as the sun rose after a restless night of very little sleep. She rolled over, fluffed her pillow, shut her eyes, and tried to go back to sleep. She turned over again, trying the other side. Her eyes popped open. It was no use. She had two children out on the streets—two children she was assigned to protect. She knew it wasn't her fault they had run away, but somehow she blamed herself for not being able to find them. Bailey was one thing; she was older and more streetwise. Although Sabre knew little about Bailey's boyfriend, Apollo, she somehow felt better that they were together. She knew they could get in plenty of trouble, but with two of them together, and one of them male, the chances were slightly less likely that they'd be preyed upon.

But Cole, little Cole, was only eight years old and he had been missing for nearly twenty-four hours. Where could he be? Did some pervert have him in his clutches? She made herself stop the thought. It was unbearable. She sat up and flung her legs over the side of the bed, paused for a second and then stood up and ran her hands across the pink sheets, removing the wrinkles. She laid her pillow on the side of the bed that hadn't been slept in, straightened the blanket, and then pulled the soft, pink handmade quilt across the blanket and sheets. Five pillows with matching quilted covers were stacked on the right side of the bed. She put them in place. The pillows covered half the bed, but the bed was still easy to fix since she slept alone and used only half of it. There were some advantages to living alone.

Sabre brushed her teeth and put on a pair of jeans and a t-shirt. She grabbed her sweatshirt and phone and dashed out the door to her car, calling JP as she walked to the garage knowing full well he had probably been up for a couple of hours already.

"Did you wake the roosters up this morning?" JP asked.

"I couldn't sleep. I was too worried about Bailey and Cole."

"Me, too. I'm on my way now to retrace the ground near his foster home."

"Can I go with you?"

JP hesitated for a second, then said, "Sure, why not?"

Sabre drove to meet JP, fighting the demons that were reminding her of all the awful things that may have happened to those children. She tried to think positively, but she knew the longer it took to find Cole, the less likely it would be to find him alive. She spotted a coffee kiosk and ordered a medium decaf coffee.

Sabre met JP at a park near the foster home. He stood near a palm tree about ten feet from his car. He was gazing out at the park, looking from side to side, then up the street toward the foster home as she walked up.

"What are you thinking?"

Without turning around, JP said, "Just assume for a minute that Cole ran away on his own. That no one else was involved. Why would he do that?"

"To get home?"

"Yes, but remember he's the 'man' of the house ..."

"... So, he would want to protect the other children and get them home, too," Sabre finished his sentence.

"And the only sibling he knows the whereabouts of is Hayden."

"But they questioned Hayden yesterday and everyone was convinced he didn't know anything."

"That was yesterday; he could try to see him today or tomorrow."

"And in the meantime he would stay close by." She looked at JP. "Do you think he's here in the park?"

"I don't know, but it's worth the time to ask a few questions."

"But there's no one here but the homeless and a few runners."

"And they were likely here yesterday morning as well, and many of them were here last night."

"Let's roll. I'll start at the other end of the park," Sabre said as she headed off.

"No, stay with me," JP snapped, then paused. "Some of these people will respond better to you."

Sabre smirked. She knew JP didn't want her off by herself in the park for her own safety. She felt better, too, so she acquiesced.

They started their questioning with the joggers they saw along the trail. It was an area that had been carved out primarily for runners and bikers. No one had seen any sign of Cole, but some recognized his picture from the news and the Amber Alert. As they walked, JP checked behind each bush or structure.

"You think he may already be dead, don't you?" Sabre asked, as JP trampled through some bushes.

JP looked at Sabre. The lines on his forehead seemed deeper and his eyes gave away his concern. He took a breath and his face lightened a little. He reached out and took her hand. "I think he may still be alive. I think he could be hiding. I think he could be hurt, tired, hungry, scared. And yes, I think there are other possibilities, but I choose to think he's still alive." He let go of her hand. She sighed and they continued to talk with everyone they met.

They woke a man asleep on a bench, covered with a dirty overcoat, and showed him Cole's picture. "Nope. Never seen him."

The next man they met asked for some money. He wore a mangled hat that looked like it was once a light brown but now was dark from dirt and grease. His shoeless toes on both feet protruded out of soiled socks. He reeked of alcohol and urine. JP took a dollar bill out of his wallet. He started to hand it to the man, but held on to it as he showed him the picture of Cole. The man shook his head. "Sorry, man," he slurred. JP let go of the bill.

They continued for several hours through the park, covering ground and killing time until it was late enough to contact Hayden's foster parents and interview Hayden again. Before they reached the opposite end of the park, they encountered a woman fumbling through a trash can. She was methodically sorting, removing the bottles and cans as well as discarded bags of half-eaten food. She picked up a bag that read McDonalds across the side, opened it up, and then tossed it back. She pulled out two soda cans and placed them in her shopping cart, along with an empty beer bottle and two plastic water bottles. She leaned into the trash can again and pulled out a bag from In-N-Out. She opened it, removed a half-eaten tray of French fries, and set them in a cardboard box in the basket portion of her cart. Sabre and JP stood there watching her as she continued to stash bottles and cans into her cart, but placed a piece of donut, left-over Chinese food in its paper carton, and a Styrofoam container of Mexican food into her cardboard box.

They approached her cautiously so as not to startle her. Sabre spoke. "Good morning, ma'am."

"Hmpf," the woman responded.

"Excuse me. We're looking for a missing child." Sabre showed the picture of Cole to the woman. "Have you seen this boy?"

"Lots of boys everywhere. Boys play. Boys help. Boys drink and eat." She reached in her basket and picked up a donut. "Hungry?"

"No, thank you. You keep it." Sabre felt a tug at her heart for the generosity of this poor woman. "Have you seen this boy?" Sabre extended the photo.

"Nice boy."

"Do you know him?"

"Good boy."

"Have you seen him here in the park?" Sabre tried again.

"In the park. Yes, in the park."

"You've seen him here in the park?"

"No." The woman returned to the trash and started digging again.

"Thank you," Sabre said and started to walk away.

The woman pulled out another fast food bag with a partially eaten hamburger and placed it in her box. Sabre thought she heard her say, "Food for the boy."

Sabre turned to JP. "Did you hear what she said?"

"It sounded like she said, 'Food for the boy.'"

"Do you think she has seen him?"

"It's hard to say. She's not making a lot of sense."

Sabre walked back to the woman and showed her the picture again. "Do you know this boy's name?"

"Boy," the woman responded as she reached her hand toward the photo and moved her finger across it, as if she were caressing his face.

"What do you call him?" Sabre asked.

"Boy." This time she didn't look up.

"His name is Cole. Do you know where he is?" The woman continued to dig through the trash, not looking or responding to Sabre's question. Sabre asked again, "Do you know Cole?"

"Boy," the woman said. She pushed the trash can back up in place, picked up some papers that had fallen to the ground, and pushing her cart, walked away from Sabre.

Sabre walked back to JP. "What do you think?"

"I think she feels compassion for the lost boy, but there's no way to know if she has seen him. Even if she did, I don't think she could tell us anything."

Sabre took a deep breath. "You're probably right. I just want to find someone who has seen him, and the way she touched the photo it seemed like she might have connected with him somehow."

"I can follow her and see if it leads us anywhere. We don't have anything else at this point."

"Why don't you do that. I'll go see Hayden and see if he has heard from him."

Sabre left JP to keep an eye on the old woman. She called the foster parent as she walked to her car and made arrangements for a visit. Hayden was living only about three blocks from the park so Sabre arrived within a few minutes. The foster mother greeted her at the door and invited her in.

"He's in his room. I'll get him," the foster mother said. She motioned to a chair. "Have a seat." She paused. "He keeps asking to see his siblings, especially Cole. Is there any word on him?"

"No. We have nothing."

"Hayden doesn't know he's missing. Are you going to tell him?"

"No. I don't think he needs to know at this point, but I want to make sure Hayden lets us know if he hears from him. I believe that if Cole has a way to get to his siblings he will, and Hayden is the closest."

"We will certainly watch for any signs."

"Thanks, I appreciate that."

The foster mother walked upstairs, returned with Hayden, and then left the room. "Hi, Hayden," Sabre said as she stood up. "Do you remember me?"

"Yeah, you're the 'tourney.'"

"Very good memory. How are you doing here?"

"I miss my mom. Can I see her?"

"We're working on that." Sabre turned to keep Hayden from seeing the sadness in her face.

"Can Cole and Allie come play with me?"

"When did you last see Cole?" Sabre asked, since she had an opening.

"At my new school."

"Did he tell you when he would see you again?"

"I'll see him at school." Hayden dashed around the corner to the kitchen to his foster mother and said, "When is school again?"

"Tomorrow," she said.

He ran back in the room. "I'll see him tomorrow at school."

Sabre was sorry that she had brought it up. Hayden was obviously looking forward to his next contact with his brother and she knew Cole wouldn't be at school for him to see. "Hayden, next time you see Cole, whether it is at school or wherever, will you please tell your foster parents so they can let me know. And also ask him to call me." She handed Hayden her card. "Do you have one of these?"

"Nope."

"This is my business card. It has my phone numbers on it. You hold onto this and if you ever need me for anything you call me, okay?"

"I don't have a phone."

"I'm sure your foster parents will let you use the phone to call me."

Hayden darted around the corner again. "Can I use the phone to call my 'tourney?'"

The foster mother came back in the room with her arm around Hayden's shoulder. She said, "Of course. You can use the phone anytime to call your attorney."

The dog in the backyard barked and Hayden ran out the back door. Sabre said, "He seems to be bonding with you."

"He's a wonderful child. He's so playful and lovable. He likes to be cuddled, and he really misses his mother and his siblings."

"I'm going to make an extra effort to have them detained together. His mother is clear out in Vista and she doesn't have a car, so it's difficult, and the other sibs are in Jamul and El Cajon."

"If we need to find a central meeting place, I'll do what I can. Hayden is just so precious, a little bit wild, but so sweet. He looks so sad sometimes when he talks about his family. You can tell how lonely he is. At night he cries for them and he keeps crying until he finally falls asleep."

Chapter 13

Juvenile court detention hearings had another strange case on the calendar. Bob spotted it as he rifled through the detention hearings.

"Are you on detentions this morning?" Sabre asked.

"No. I was just curious to see if there were any more bizarre cases." He handed the blue petition to Sabre. "And voilà."

"What kind of case is it?"

"It has several allegations."

Sabre looked at the petition and then glanced at the detention report accompanying it. "It has neglect and abuse. Drug use by both parents. It says here that they were passed out in the living room while twin toddlers roamed the house." Sabre scrunched her face. "Dang, the twins took a dive out a window from the second story. They both survived. One fell on a chaise lounge and the other on top of the first. Just one broken arm and some bruises. Boy, were they lucky."

Bob read over her shoulder. "And 66 is written on the walls in lipstick."

"Stupid people." Sabre shook her head in disgust.

"Yeah, don't they know they're supposed to use blo-o-o-od to write with?" He stretched out the word blood.

"You goofball." Sabre tapped Bob shoulder with her open hand. "Seriously, what do you think is going on here in San Diego?"

"Beats me. JP said he heard about a few reportings by the police about some strange happenings in criminal cases—besides the house that was on the news, I mean."

"Do they have any suspects for that house?"

"They don't even have any serious crimes to attach to it. They did find some human blood but very little and it was real old, probably belonged to the last tenant. Mostly they found animal blood, and there was no real indication of animal abuse or ritualistic behavior. The pentagram on the floor was drawn with blood, but it was beef and pork blood and could've been obtained at a supermarket. The only other thing they really have is trespassing. It was an abandoned building. The fingerprints haven't led them anywhere, at least according to JP's inside sources."

"So, what the heck is going on?"

"I don't know." Bob changed the subject. "Did you know my client, Karen Lecy, got out of jail this morning?"

"Bailey's mom?"

"Yup. Any word on Bailey, yet?"

"No. JP is still looking. Maybe she'll try to see her mom."

"I'll be talking with Karen today. I'll tell her to report it if she sees Bailey, and I will carefully explain the legal ramifications if she doesn't. I'm sure she'll be happy to cooperate."

"Yeah, right."

"Anything more on Cole?" The concern was evident in his voice.

"No. The police were following up on the 'sighting,' if you can call it that, by the homeless woman, but no news yet. JP went to Cole's school this morning and gave photos of him to all the teachers in case he went there to see Hayden. I'm so worried about that little boy."

Bob put his arm around Sabre's shoulder. "I know. Me, too. I'd be going out of my mind if that were Corey." Sabre knew he understood. Bob's son, Corey, was about the same age.

Bob and Sabre worked through their morning calendar, went to Pho's for lunch, and then back to court for an afternoon trial. After several hours of negotiations on a tox baby case, the trial was settled. Bob's client, the mother, had already completed an in-house drug program and continued to attend Narcotic Anonymous meetings on a daily basis. The baby was placed with the mother in the grandmother's home. The father was allowed supervised visitation until he successfully completed his programs and then supervision could be lifted by the social worker if Sabre, the minor's attorney, concurred.

Bob spoke as they walked out of the courtroom. "That took forever. We could've done the trial more quickly."

"Yeah, but we may not have had the same result."

"I would've won that one."

"Only because we were on the same side. That baby needed to be with her mother. I've never seen anyone work so hard to obtain sobriety. I just hope she stays that way."

"She's pretty determined and she has great support from her family. I think she'll make it."

As they walked out the door toward their cars, Sabre received a text. She read it and said, "I'm going to go meet JP. He has a lead on Cole."

"Did someone find him?" Bob's eyes opened wide.

"No, but it seems someone saw him. That's about all I know. He told me not to go there, but I'm going anyway." Sabre opened up her car door and stepped inside. "I'll keep you posted."

As Sabre drove to meet JP at the park where they had spoken to the old woman, she was excited they had a lead, but nervous about what they might find out. JP was waiting for her when she arrived. "I thought I told you not to come here."

"So, why are you here waiting for me?"

"Because I knew you'd show up and I didn't want you wandering around here by yourself."

Sabre smiled. "Thanks."

JP mumbled something Sabre couldn't understand and then said, "I stayed with the old woman yesterday for a couple of hours but she didn't lead me anywhere. When she lay down under a tree and fell asleep, I left. But then I came back today and spoke to a homeless man who said 'the woman' would know. When I asked him 'what woman' he pointed to the same woman we talked to yesterday. He said she goes to the bridge every day about this time. So, I'm going there to see what it's all about. You wait here."

Sabre tipped her head to the left and rolled her eyes upward. "I'm going with you." Sabre popped her trunk open, stepped out of the car, and walked to the back. She slipped off her heels and replaced her shoes. "See, I even have my walking shoes on. Let's go."

JP shook his head. "You're a pain some times, you know?"

Sabre smiled sheepishly.

"Well, stay close to me. Don't wander off. We're going to be about as welcome as a skunk at a wedding."

Sabre laughed.

They walked through the park and across a field toward a bridge that no longer appeared to serve any purpose. It once crossed over a street, but now it ended in mid-air and was blocked off at the end. Brush scraped against Sabre's pant leg, sometimes sticking through the fabric. Sabre hadn't quite expected all the debris and she was glad she had at least changed her shoes. The closer they got to the bridge, the more garbage they encountered. She stepped on a piece of glass that wrapped around her shoe and stuck to it without cutting her foot. She stopped and removed the broken bottle.

"Ah," Sabre said shaking her bleeding finger.

"Are you okay?" JP asked.

"I just cut my finger. It's nothing, just a little puncture."

JP mumbled something again. She chose not to ask him to repeat it.

As they approached the bridge, the smell of garbage grew stronger. Sabre took a deep breath, expecting it to be the last good air she was going to breathe for a while. She was right. The stench became so strong she wanted to vomit as they passed a pile of trash near the opening. "I think the skunk has already been here," Sabre said.

JP didn't respond. Sabre knew he was a little bit upset at her for insisting that she go along, but she knew he'd get over it as long as she didn't do something really stupid.

Up until that point they hadn't seen anyone, but just as they went under the edge of the bridge, they saw a group of people at the other end approximately thirty feet away. There appeared to be about ten men and women sitting around on boxes and rocks and a few others lying down. They could hear the chatter as they approached. Several shopping carts were parked haphazardly in the bushes. Another lay on its side, bent almost in half. Old clothes were strewn about, food cartons spattered the area, and a small red-and-white shopping bag that appeared almost new was leaned against the wall near where the old woman was sitting on a stack of boards. The stench of garbage was not as strong as it was at the opening, but the smell of alcohol was more powerful.

By the time they reached the group, the conversation had stopped. Some of them stared. Others hid under their blankets or coats. The group seemed to be going up to the old woman one at a time as she doled out food. She stopped and looked up.

Sabre said, "Hello again. We met in the park yesterday."

The old woman said nothing. She nodded at the next person in line. He stepped forward and she gave him a container with what looked like half of a burrito.

Sabre removed the photo of Cole from her bag. She held it up, moving it from side to side, for all to see. "Has anyone seen this missing child?"

A murmur passed over, but no one volunteered anything. Several of them looked toward the old woman. Sabre turned to her again. "What's your name?" she asked.

"The boy," she said.

"No, what's your name?" Sabre asked again, pointing at the woman.

She didn't say anything. A younger woman spoke up from where she sat in the dirt, eating some French fries very deliberately and slowly. Sabre wondered if she was trying to make them last longer. "We call her 'Mother Teresa' or sometimes just 'Mama T.'"

"Okay, 'Mama T' it is. Have you seen this boy?"

"The boy," she said, shaking her head from side to side, "the boy."

JP stood close to Sabre, observing the crowd. He noticed the younger woman nodding her head as Mama T repeated "the boy." The younger woman's eyes darted back and forth. JP stepped closer to her. "Will you come over here please," he asked softly. "I want you to get a better look at the picture."

She stood up and walked toward them. Sabre showed her the picture.

"You've seen him, haven't you?" JP asked.

She nodded her head.

"When?"

"He was here for two days, but he ate too much. Mama T gave him the best food." She looked at Mama T, but the woman seemed to ignore her and started handing out more food.

"So what happened?"

She lowered her voice to a whisper. "Some of the guys got mad and told him he had to go away. So he left. Mama T was very angry. She liked the boy."

"Do you know where he went?"

"That way." She pointed to the right of the park.

"When did he leave?"

"This morning."

Chapter 14

Bob dipped his cigarette butt into the sand at the top of the tall, stone ashtray that stood in front of the San Diego Superior Court Juvenile Division. The perfect brittsommar day, as his Swedish grandmother would have called it, made him want to be anywhere but here. He walked through the metal detectors and upstairs where he had agreed to meet his client, Karen Lecy. Noon seemed like a good time since he knew his client wasn't an early riser. He would rather have done this in his office, but it was easier for Karen to go to the courthouse.

Bob walked over to the wall that stood about four feet high and looked over. From there he could see the entire lobby as well as the front door. Karen was late. Bob expected nothing else. He'd be surprised if she even made it at all. It wasn't unusual for his juvenile court clients to make appointments and not keep them, especially the court-appointed cases. The clients who paid out of their own pocket were much more considerate of his time.

Bob opened his manila file folder and glanced quickly through the detention report. There was nothing in there he didn't already know. He returned it to the file where it lay loosely inside. Bob never attached anything to the folder and seldom had more than the latest report. He kept the facts in his head, and when he needed something else he generally borrowed it from Sabre if she was on the case. He checked his watch. His client was nearly ten minutes late. He gazed over the wall at the remaining attorneys with their clients, who were waiting their turn to learn what would be the next step in their pathetic lives. It was relatively quiet down below—he could see ten or twelve defendants, about a half dozen attorneys, two marshals, and a Chinese interpreter he recognized from the Vu case. Most of the courtrooms had recessed for lunch. Bob looked at his watch. It read 12:14. He'd give her a few more minutes.

A while later, Karen Lecy passed through the metal detector, apparently smart enough to not enter with drugs this time. She looked around and then started for the stairway. Bob met her part way. She smiled when she greeted him but made no mention of being late. He didn't know the client very well, so he didn't know if she was just rude or if it was drug-induced self-centeredness. Karen's red eyes surrounded by the dark circles coupled with her disheveled appearance indicated that she hadn't wasted any time getting a fix upon her release from custody.

Bob led her to a couple of chairs and a small table that sat in one corner of the large hallway next to the four-foot wall. "What is the status of your criminal case?" he asked.

"I entered a plea for possession. I shouldn't have, though. They wasn't my drugs."

"How did they get in your bag?"

"Someone must have put them there."

"Who do you think would do that?" Bob was toying with her now.

"I don't know, maybe someone behind me who didn't want to get caught with their stash. Maybe they just dropped them in my purse."

"Did they check them for fingerprints?"

"They said they had mine on them, but I dig in my purse for stuff all the time. Maybe I touched them without knowing."

"But then they would've had to be in there a while before you put your bag on the conveyer belt to go through the metal detector."

Karen wiggled in her chair. "It must've been someone outside before I came in then. I seen this one guy who was acting all crazy. It was probably him."

Bob didn't really care about her drug use except how it affected this case. If she was stupid enough to use, then it was her problem. "You're probably right," he said. "When do you go back to court?"

"In two weeks. I have to go back for sentencing. The DA agreed to probation. My attorney said it shouldn't be a problem."

"Who's your attorney?" Bob picked up his pen to write down the information.

"Uh . . . Betts. Mr. Betts."

"Do you have his card?"

Karen reached in her purse and pulled out a pack of cigarettes. She looked around. "Can I smoke in here?"

Bob shook his head. "No, I'm afraid not."

She laid the cigarettes down on the table, reached back in her purse, and took out her wallet. She fumbled through it and removed a card. "Barry. Barry Betts," she said.

Bob reached for the card, copied the information, and handed it back to her. The card didn't have the government logo on it, which meant he was in private practice.

"Was this attorney court appointed?" Bob asked.

"He's not a public defender or nothing like that," Karen replied.

"So did you hire him?"

"No." Karen picked up the pack of cigarettes.

"So, how did you get him as your attorney?"

"He was just there."

"What do you mean 'he was just there'?"

"He came to see me at the jail. He said he likes to do some 'bono' work or something and he was taking my case." She flipped the cigarette pack back and forth in her right hand.

"Pro-bono. That means he takes the case for free."

"He offered to do this case here, too, but I told him I already had an attorney."

"You know you're free to make that choice."

"No. I like you. You seem to know what you're doing."

"Thanks," Bob said. He sarcastically thought how flattering it was to have one more druggie's approval. "So let's talk about this case. Have you had any contact with Bailey?"

"No. I heard she ran away from the foster home. They take her away from me, and they can't take care of her any better than I can. Now we don't know where she is. At least I knew where she was when she was with me." Karen's voice got louder. "They need to just end this case. She'll come home. Can you do that for me?"

"It's not quite that easy. And the court won't do anything until Bailey is found, so we need to start there. If she does contact you, you must report it."

"So how do I get my kid back from the government?"

"You need to start by getting clean."

"I am . . ."

Bob raised his hand, palm facing her. "And stay clean. You need to attend the programs they have suggested. And Scott, your boyfriend, is a known drug dealer, albeit small time. He has to go."

"What's he got to do with this? He hasn't done nothing. And how am I going to pay my rent?" Karen opened the cigarette pack and removed a cigarette. She laid the pack on the table and rolled the cigarette around with her index finger and thumb, occasionally reaching it up to her mouth without putting it in. "They already took my check. How do they expect me to live?"

Bob was frustrated with her stupidity, but she had lost control over her pathetic existence and for that he was sorry. However, she was an adult and at some point she had to grow up and start making appropriate choices. He couldn't do that for her and although he would do everything he could for her case, he knew he couldn't do much until she started to help herself. He didn't know what sparked his clients to take that control back. For some, losing their children was enough. Others had to completely hit bottom and end up on the streets with no where to go but up. And others never did get it. Bob knew what his choice would be. Losing his child would be about the worst thing he could think of, and it was difficult to understand how people could believe otherwise.

"Karen, there are programs in which you can live and work through all this. That's what the social worker is recommending, and it would be very helpful for your criminal case if you were already enrolled prior to your sentencing."

She put the cigarette in her mouth, holding it between her index and middle fingers, simulating her habit. She pulled it out and held it as if it were lit. "Yeah." She nodded her head in agreement. "I'll do that. And I'll dump Scott, too. Whatever it takes."

Bob thought her voice held little sincerity. She was patronizing him now, just as she would do with the Department of Social Services. He stood up. He was done. "I know you will," he said.

They walked down the steps together while he explained what she needed to do to enroll in a program. He also encouraged her to call if she heard from Bailey but knew full well she wouldn't do either. They walked outside and Bob took out his cigarettes and lighter. He lit her cigarette for her, then his own, and watched her leave.

Bob was about halfway through his cigarette when Sabre pulled up to the courthouse and drove past him. While talking on the phone, she pulled into an empty parking spot and then backed out, driving toward him again. He stepped into the street. She stopped when she saw him. "Hey, you're in Department Four this afternoon, right?" Sabre asked.

"Yeah, do you need me to do something?"

"Could you cover this case for me?" She handed him a file. "We're submitting on the recommendations. If there's a problem, they'll just have to wait for me. I'll be back. JP just called and I need to meet him at the school. A teacher thinks she saw Cole."

"No problem. Keep me posted," Bob said as she drove off.

Chapter 15

The school secretary directed Sabre into the vice-principal's office where JP sat with an attractive, thin, brunette woman. She didn't look more than twenty years old. JP stood up when Sabre walked in. "This is Miss Adrienne DeLozier. She's the teacher who saw Cole."

Sabre reached her hand out to shake hers. "Hi, Ms. DeLozier. I'm Sabre Brown, Cole's attorney."

"Adrienne, please," she said, her voice sounding even younger than she looked.

"Adrienne. Are you sure it was Cole?"

"I'm quite certain. I was so concerned when I heard he was missing that I studied his photo carefully. I do that whenever I see a picture of a missing child. I try to plant it in my mind, just in case I see one in a grocery store or something."

JP said, "Tell us what you saw exactly."

"I was on yard duty for recess. While walking around the playground, I saw Hayden talking with an older boy. I teach kindergarten and we did an art project with the other kindergarten classes last Friday. Hayden was new to another class and he needed some art supplies. I remembered him because he was so charming when he asked." She paused. "Anyway, I was kind of keeping an eye on Hayden since we were told Cole might try to see him. Although seeing an older boy on the playground was suspicious anyway because there should only be kindergarten students on the playground at that time."

"Did you approach them?" JP asked.

"I did. They were walking toward the side of the building. Cole was holding Hayden by the hand, but I could see that Hayden was going willingly. He wasn't fighting him or anything. I hurried because I didn't want to lose sight of them."

"Did you talk to him?" Sabre asked.

"No. Cole saw me come around the corner. He leaned down to Hayden and said something in his ear and then took off running."

Sabre shook her head. "That poor kid. If he just knew how much we want to help him." She looked at JP and then the teacher. "Have the police been notified?"

"Yes, the principal called them. They're on their way," Adrienne said.

"Good. Is Hayden still at school?"

JP said, "Yes. They have him in the office waiting to talk to us."

"I'll bring him in for you, if you'd like," Adrienne offered.

The teacher returned with Hayden. JP and Sabre each gave her a card and thanked her for her help. Hayden sat down in one of the big, stuffed chairs. He looked so small sitting there, and his wide eyes looked like he might cry at any moment. JP tried to engage him while Sabre walked the teacher to the door, but Hayden didn't seem too responsive.

Sabre knelt down by Hayden so his eyes would be slightly above hers, hoping to give him a feeling of some power. He was a frightened little boy and she didn't want to make it worse for him. "Hi, Hayden. You know me, right?"

He nodded.

"We really need your help," she began, speaking softly. He just looked at her. "We need you to help Cole so he doesn't get hurt."

"He won't get hurt. He's big." Hayden said.

"Is that what he told you?" Sabre asked. Hayden didn't respond. "Yes, Cole is bigger than you, but he's still pretty young and he needs our help. Do you know where he is?"

Hayden shook his head back and forth.

"We know Cole came to see you today. Did he tell you where he was going?"

"Nope."

"What did he tell you?"

"I can't tell."

"We just want to keep Cole safe and we want him to be able to visit with you and your brothers and sister. You want that, don't you?"

"Mm ... hmm," Hayden muttered.

"Good, then it's real important that you tell us everything he told you."

"He said not to tell anyone he was here."

"What else did he say?"

"He said he ran away and he came to get me, but then the teacher came, and he said he'd come back and get me."

"Did he say when he would be back?"

"Nope."

Sabre looked him straight in the eye. "Are you sure?"

"I'm sure."

"What else did he say?"

"He said he was kinda hungry again."

Sabre took a deep breath. "Did he say anything else?"

Hayden shrugged his shoulders. "Nah ..."

Sabre and JP discussed what had just happened as they walked to their cars. "He's right under our noses. He's eight years old, and we can't find him. The police can't find him. Why is that?" Sabre asked.

"He's smarter'n a tree full of owls, that one."

"He is smart and seems to be pretty street wise, but every minute he's out there alone he's at risk. And how is he eating?"

"That's it." JP looked at Sabre. "If I was a kid out on the streets and I was hungry, I'd find a way to get food."

"But how?"

"I'd steal it. I'm not going to go fetch it out of trash cans like Mama T. I'd steal it before I'd do that."

"Since you put it that way, I guess I would, too."

"And he has to be hiding somewhere fairly close, so he's going to take the food from local stores. I'm guessing he's somewhere between the school, the park, and the bridge. He plans to come back here after Hayden, so he's not going far. I'll hit all the stores around here and see if anyone has seen him."

Bob was walking out of the courthouse when Sabre returned. She pulled into a parking space under a tree almost directly across from the door of the courthouse. Bob met her at her car and opened her door.

"Am I too late?" Sabre asked, as she exited the car.

"You're right on time. I just finished the case." Bob closed the door behind her. "Did you find Cole?"

"No, but he was at the school to see Hayden. So, he's alive and hasn't been abducted."

"That's a good thing."

"Well, at least he was alive an hour or so ago." Sabre jerked her head up. "Oh, no!"

"What?"

"What if he was abducted and someone is making him steal other kids, too? There are so many creeps out there." Sabre's voice escalated.

"How would someone have that kind of control over him? He hasn't been gone long enough to be loyal to someone."

"His abductor could have threatened to kill him, or his mother, or his siblings."

"Or maybe it's someone he knows, someone who would already have influence over him," Bob suggested.

"You mean like someone in the cult?" They walked over to a concrete planter that surrounded a small tree and served as a bench and sat down.

"I don't think there is a cult. I don't think Cole's mother is involved with satanic rituals. She just doesn't strike me as the type." Bob paused. He took a deep breath. "Do you think Cole could be involved in something like that? Could someone have him under some spell? He's young and impressionable." Bob removed a pack of cigarettes from his jacket pocket and took one out.

"I doubt it. I don't really know him that well, but he's like the 'little man of the house' and very determined to take care of his family."

"Which makes him that much more impressionable. Sabre, I'm not suggesting he's a bad kid. I'm just saying he could be under someone else's control." Bob put the cigarette in his mouth and lit it.

Sabre gave him her "I don't approve" scowl. "That's it. Maybe the abductor is not after just any kids, maybe he's just after the Johnson kids?"

"Their father," Bob stated. "That could explain why Cole would listen to him."

Sabre sighed. "I'd rather think that he was with his father than that he's out there all alone. It would have to be a better scenario. You'd think, right?"

"You'd think." Bob took a drag off the cigarette and then placed it down low to his right so the smoke wouldn't go in Sabre's direction.

Sabre thought Bob must know more about the father than had been reported, but she didn't really want to know that right now. "Can you talk to your client and see if she has seen anything strange that might indicate Cole has some involvement with a cult? I don't think he does, but we better check it out. He'd be in as much or more danger if it's an outside influence on him. And what about those chicken feet and goat blood?"

"It's just food," Bob replied, emphasizing the word food. "She got it from the guy up the street with the chicken farm. They were hungry. I don't think it has anything to do with satanic rituals." Bob raised his hand in dismissal. "That social worker is nuts. She's seeing Satan everywhere. Just because the police uncovered that house doesn't mean every juvenile case is involved."

"But the house was discovered after this case was filed," Sabre reminded him.

"I still think she's nuts. She hasn't found anything else that indicates any abuse, and absolutely nothing ritualistic."

"That's true, unless they have a hand in this ... this abduction."

Bob shook his head.

Sabre said, "I'm just saying we need to look at all possibilities. And in that vein, what else do you know about the father?"

"Not a lot. He was abusive to his wife, but Leanne says he never got real physical with the kids. He's an alcoholic and his abusive behavior had been escalating toward her and the children. She kicked him out before he could start hurting the kids."

"Where did he go?"

"She doesn't know. She says she hasn't seen or heard from him since." Bob put his cigarette out.

"Please find me anything you can on him and I'll have JP try to track him down. If he's behind this, who knows what he's into."

"Have you heard anything on Bailey?"

"Not a word," Sabre said. "How did the meeting go with her mother?"

"Fine. I told her to call if she hears from Bailey."

"Do you think she will?"

"Probably not."

"What happened with her case downtown?"

"She entered a plea to a misdemeanor. It's her first offense. She expects to get probation."

"That's good. If she cleans herself up, it'll be better for Bailey."

Bob didn't respond, but looked pensive.

"What is it? What are you thinking?"

"Do you know an attorney named Barry Betts?"

"That name sounds familiar." Sabre closed her lips tightly, moving them from left to right. "Hmm, I just heard that name recently, but I don't know where. Why?"

"He's Karen's attorney on the criminal case. He's in private practice and somehow he volunteered to take her case pro bono."

"That happens." Sabre stood up. "You ready?" She turned around and suddenly looked wide eyed at Bob. "I know where it was."

"Where what was?"

"The name . . . Barry Betts. I know where I heard the name. It was in court the other day on Collicott's case. She knows him from adoptions. That's his specialty. He was here representing the mother."

"What does he look like?"

"Kind of a sleaze. Tall, skinny guy, greasy hair. He was so thin his cheeks sunk in. You saw him come out of the courtroom. Remember? You called him Ichabod Crane."

"That was an attorney? I thought he was a parent. That guy was weird. I talked with him a few minutes out front that day. I went outside to get a little fresh air and . . ."

"You mean pollute the air."

Bob ignored her and finished his sentence. ". . . he starting talking to me."

"What did he say?"

"I only talked with him about five minutes, but he managed to tell me he was a Harvard graduate. He didn't say he was a lawyer, just that he went to Harvard. He had an odd twitch. He bobbed his head, kind of like one of those little, toy dogs that sit in people's car windows. It looked even stranger because he had such a long, skinny neck."

"Harvard?"

"Yeah. I just thought he was a client and he was making up crap. He asked me a couple of questions about procedure here, but he still didn't sound like an attorney, just someone wondering what was going to happen next. He was very odd. And then a cab pulled up and he got in it and left." Bob raised his hands, palms up. "Who takes a cab to work?"

"Maybe his car broke down or something."

"Maybe. But you know what's really strange. He offered to represent Karen Lecy in juvenile court . . . pro bono also. Why would he do that? No one in their right mind would do this work for free."

"Maybe he thought it would help her case downtown or maybe he's trying to get a foot in the juvenile door. Or maybe he's just a good guy trying to do some penance." But Sabre thought the same thing. Why would anyone do juvenile work pro bono? Every attorney knows it's the kind of law you need to do on a regular basis or you can't do it well, and it takes precedent over other courtrooms so you lose control of your calendar when you do juvenile work. "It's a little odd, I guess."

Chapter 16

The dawn had nothing on JP. He often arrived before it did. This morning was no exception and this time he had help waking up. His arm was hanging over the edge of the bed when he felt a warm, wet, rough tongue on his fingertips. He reached down and picked up his new roommate—a brown and white beagle puppy.

"Good morning, Louie," he said as he sat him down on his bare chest. Louie stuck his face right in JP's. JP turned his head but not before Louie got in a few good licks. "Wrong, Louie. Not on the face." JP grabbed Louie around the stomach with one hand, flung the covers back with the other, and stepped out of bed. Wearing nothing but his boxer shorts, he carried Louie out the back door, and gently sat the dog down on the grass. When he finished his business they both went back in the house to have some breakfast.

JP wanted to stay home and spend time with Louie. They were just getting to know one another, but he had a full plate and he was determined to find Cole before one more nightfall. In addition to locating Cole and Bailey, he needed to follow up on several other things for Sabre. He had appointments to meet with Regina Collicott, gather information on Barry Betts, finish canvassing the stores near Cole, and investigate Cole's father. But first he needed to find Cole. That awful feeling in his stomach wouldn't abate until he did.

The sun was coming up just as JP arrived at the park, his black Stetson in the front seat next to him. He picked up his hat and placed it on his head as he exited the car. Experience had taught him to wear the hat when he interviewed strangers, although he generally wore it anyway. But for some reason people seemed more willing to open up to a "cowboy." He made a quick trip around the park, checking all the places where a little boy could hide. He questioned the few people he saw, waking vagrants and stopping joggers, but to no avail.

After his search of the park, he made a round of all the stores where he thought Cole might try to steal some food. He had been to most of them yesterday, but today he brought copies of Cole's picture to leave at each store so clerks on different shifts might recognize him if he came in.

JP entered a convenience store on H Street and waited as the clerk finished ringing up a customer. JP introduced himself and handed the picture to the large, young man behind the counter. He stood about six-foot-four and had to weigh over three hundred pounds. His voice was deep but pleasant and JP could see the concern in his eyes when he told him the little boy was missing.

"What's your name?" JP asked.

"Mikey."

JP was a little surprised at the name. This little name didn't seem to fit such a big guy. Mike or Michael, maybe, but not Mikey. That was a kid's name—a pet name for a child—but then, he was someone's child. "This little boy has been missing for several days. Have you seen him?"

Mikey studied the picture for about thirty seconds and then shook his head. "I don't think so. I'm sorry."

"We have reason to believe that if he's hungry he might go into stores and try to steal something to eat. Do you know if you've had food missing off the shelves?"

"Stuff is always getting stolen here. It's hard to keep track. We get these scumballs that come in here and pocket things all the time. They're usually in groups and one or two will cause distractions while others heist stuff. I catch more of them than most of the clerks. I'm pretty good at it."

"But you've never seen this kid? He's nearly four feet tall, thin, and his hair is a little longer than the photo."

Mikey looked at the photo again. "Maybe."

"Maybe what?"

"When I came on my shift last night, a kid darted past me just before I came in the door. He flung the door open and took off running. It could've been him."

"Did you see his face?"

"Not really. I reached for the door just as it flew open. I was trying to keep from getting hit with the door so I didn't really look down. And before I knew it, he was past me."

"What time was that?"

"My shift started at ten o'clock. I was here about fifteen minutes before that."

"Did you see where he went?"

"He ran around the building." Mikey pointed to his left making a half circle motion. "By the time I turned around he was gone."

JP looked up at the surveillance camera in the corner. The light was on and it was moving from left to right scanning the store. "Any chance I could see the camera footage from last night?"

Mikey shook his head. "There's no tape in there. There's something wrong with the machine and it doesn't record. The boss leaves it on, hoping it will stop some thieves, but they don't seem to care anyway. I told him I could fix it for him. I know all about fixing things, but he doesn't want me to."

JP smiled, turning his head so as not to offend the young man. He recalled how nice it was to be young and know everything. He tried to remember when it was that he became stupid again. At seven or eight years old he felt stupid most of the time. But through his teen years, he thought he knew so much more than the adults around him. It was somewhere between twenty and thirty years old that things changed. It's not like he woke up one day and suddenly realized his parents, and most of the other adults in his teen years, actually knew what they were talking about. But somehow through the years he knew he started to heed their advice and even seek it out. Ah, to be young again. No, maybe not. Not in this world.

JP questioned Mikey a little longer and then handed him his card. "Thanks for all your help. Please call if you see him."

JP drove off to continue with his search. He turned around the side of the gas station where Mikey had indicated the young man had fled. He drove through the alley past the rear of a thrift store and out onto the street. He was several blocks from the park now and even further from where he was purported to be with Mama T. If it was Cole, he had covered a lot of ground assuming he came from the park. And what was he doing out so late at night by himself? JP circled around covering several blocks around the gas station while looking for Cole or some indication of a place where he might hide. He found nothing other than the standard dumpsters and rear entrances to stores with steps that might provide a bit of shelter from the night air. He questioned every bum and every store clerk within the circle but he didn't find one lead.

JP checked his cell phone for the time. He could make it to Regina Collicott's office in time for his appointment with about fifteen minutes to spare.

The law office of Regina Collicott was that of a sole practitioner. There was no receptionist to greet JP, nor was there a fancy lobby. JP didn't see a secretarial staff and he remembered that when he called to make the appointment Regina had answered the phone herself.

JP opened her office door. It seemed so private, he felt like he should knock, but he didn't. Regina remained behind her large, mahogany desk when he walked in. The light scent of perfume and cigarette smoke lingered in the air. The smoke scent wasn't very strong; she probably smoked outside and brought it in on her clothes. She motioned to a chair. "Please have a seat. And thank you for coming by this morning." Her words were spoken quickly but not abrasively.

"No problem. I was surprised you had me come by this time of day. Most of the juvenile court attorneys never have morning appointments. They're always in court, especially Sabre and Bob." JP sat down across from her in a gray office chair, one you might see in furniture rental places, not horribly uncomfortable but not a chair anyone would want to sit in too long. He wondered if they made them that way because it was cheaper, or if they were designed to keep meetings short.

"They both carry huge case loads. Only about a fourth of my calendar is dependency work. I spend the rest of the time on adoptions. There are a lot fewer court appearances." Regina handed him a juvenile court detention report. "I actually have two cases I'd like you to investigate, if you're willing, of course. I represent the children in this case and the case has been tagged as a 'ritual case' for lack of a better term."

"But you're not sure?" JP thought he detected some doubt in her voice.

"I certainly haven't ruled it out. The social worker points to self-mutilation of the seven-year-old girl as an indicator, which by itself could be many things. There are also the pictures the five-year-old boy has been drawing."

"What are the pictures of?" JP asked.

Regina reached into a file and removed a copy of a picture and handed it to JP. "Like this one."

"I don't get it," JP said.

"What do you see in the drawing?"

"I see geometric shapes. It looks like a math worksheet. There's a circle, a triangle, a rectangle, and what looks like a poorly drawn trapezoid, or maybe it's a bug. It's hard to tell."

"The social worker saw it quite differently and she found a therapist who seemed to agree with her. See how the triangle overlaps the circle."

"Yeah," JP said.

"The social worker thinks that's a pentagram."

"But it's only one triangle and it barely overlaps."

The social worker pointed to the rectangle shape. "And this she says is a coffin. The circle is a child."

JP raised his eyebrows. "And the bug?"

"That's the devil. See the two points on the end of it?"

"Yeah, they sort of look like antennae, but I really thought the little boy overlapped his lines."

"She thinks it illustrates a ritual commonly known as some kind of rebirth into Satan's world."

JP shook his head. He still thought it was a math paper.

"Were there any other 'satanic' indicators?"

"Just one. According to the report, when the social worker arrived to remove the children, the baby had feces smeared on his face and chest. But all the pictures show is a small smudge on the baby's cheek and I'm not sure anyone verified that it was even feces. It may very well have been chocolate since the five-year-old had a melted Twix bar in his pocket."

"Assuming it was feces, what does that have to do with anything?"

"It's another act that supposedly is performed by Satanists. They use excrement in rituals to defile the innocence of children and to humiliate them. This somehow puts them closer to Satan, I guess." Regina continued to speak quickly. At first JP thought she might be in a hurry, but after a while he decided she just spoke that way.

"What do you think? Do you think these are satanic rituals?"

"Personally, I think it's a stretch, but that's what I'd like you to find out."

"Anything you specifically want me to do? Or anywhere in particular you'd like me to start?"

"Talk to relatives, neighbors. Check the backgrounds on anyone you might find suspicious. Do another check on the parents. See if the department missed anything."

"Can I talk to the children?"

"Certainly. I'll set that up. I'll be there, of course. You do know how to interview children, don't you?" Before JP could answer, Regina continued, "Of course you do. I apologize for being so blunt. It's just that we've never worked together before and I don't really know how you operate. But you work with Sabre Brown and Bob Clark all the time and I trust their judgment."

JP was sure she was going to say more, but he jumped in. "If it'll make you more comfortable, you can do the talking. I mostly want to watch their body language. Sometimes I learn more from that than the actual words. It would probably be better for the children anyway."

Regina nodded her head as JP spoke. "That would be good," she said. "The social worker has the two older children in therapy, but I don't think we'll get much from the therapist yet. Therapy always takes a while. The judge ordered the social worker to have psych evals done for disposition. That's when they determine the placement of the children. The evaluations won't help us with jurisdiction, which is when the judge determines whether there should be a true finding in the case or not." Regina explained the legal terms to JP. He just listened carefully to what she said. He didn't interrupt her to tell her he had been working with the legal system almost as long as she had been alive. He wasn't insulted and he found her direct demeanor intriguing, although a bit exhausting. Regina went on. "We can, however, use the evals to help us with our fact finding. We just can't use it in court, for jurisdiction, that is. Make sense?"

"Perfectly," JP said. "Anything else I should know?"

Regina handed him a file. "This is everything I have so far on the case." She checked her calendar. "I'm meeting with the children tomorrow afternoon at 3:00 at Polinsky. If that'll work for you we can meet there." JP nodded his head. "The juris hearing is set for next Friday morning. I'll need your report by then."

"Okay."

"The other case I'd like you to look into is an older one. I represent a teenage girl at World of Hope. It's a facility for pregnant teenagers. Many girls are placed there through the dependency system, but it's a private organization so parents can pay to have their children there as well. My client, Mena, has been telling me some very interesting things about the group home. She's a very bright young lady of German descent, and she speaks both English and German fluently. Mena was born here but her parents immigrated. They came into the juvenile system several months ago on physical abuse allegations. The father used a belt on her. It was a very difficult case—an obstinate teenager and strict parents with strong disciplinary beliefs. We probably would've worked it out by providing services to the parents. But when the parents found out she was pregnant, all hell broke loose again and we all agreed this would be the best placement for her."

"And now you think there's a problem with the group home?"

"Mena claims there are strange things going on in this home."

"Like what?"

"She called me up the day before yesterday and said, and I quote, 'They want me to join their satanic cult.' She was whispering and I wasn't sure I heard her correctly. I asked her to repeat it and she said it a little louder. That's definitely what she said. Then she said, 'I've gotta go.' And hung up. I went to see her immediately, but they were on lock down so I couldn't get in."

"Can they do that?"

"Not for long. And a court order would allow me in to see her, but I didn't need that. I was able to see her yesterday afternoon and she recanted her earlier statements. So I don't know if there is something going on or if she's caught up in the satanic hysteria that has hit this city. There has been so much of it in the news, especially within the juvenile system." She pointed her pen at JP. "You have a very specific task on this one. Just find out, if you can, if there are any strange events happening in this group home."

"I'll get right on it."

JP stood up. Regina reached out her hand to shake and JP reciprocated. She had a nice firm grip. It seemed to be a trend with female attorneys. He was good with that. JP walked toward the door and Regina followed. "I'll be in touch," he said, as he tipped his hat and exited the door.

Before he reached his car his phone rang. "Hello, Sabre. I've been hunting for Cole most of the morning and now I'm on my way to try and find Bailey."

"Please hurry. I'm worried about Bailey. Scott Jamison, her mom's boyfriend, was found murdered this morning."

Chapter 17

Sabre hung up her phone and stuck it in her front pocket on her black slacks. She paced back and forth in front of juvenile court while waiting for Bob to finish his calendar. She removed her phone and dialed the social worker, but she only reached her voice mail. Sabre left a message for her to call if she had any new information on Bailey. She hoped to find Bailey before the police or the department did so she could find out if she was involved in Scott's murder. But her greatest concern was for her safety. If Bailey saw something or knew something, she could be in danger herself.

Bob walked out of the courthouse with an unlit cigarette in his mouth and his phone to his ear. He stopped when he saw Sabre, lit his cigarette, and then punched some numbers on his phone. "Voice mail," he mouthed. Sabre waited until he was finished listening. Bob closed the phone, took the cigarette out of his mouth, and blew out some smoke as he said, "They've arrested my client, Karen Lecy."

"For Scott's murder?"

"Not sure. They have her on a violation of her release, though. She was higher than a kite when they found Scott. Apparently, she was passed out on the bed and his body was found in the living room. That's about all I know."

"Are you going to see her?"

"She's not my problem. Stupid woman. She just can't stay away from the drugs. I knew she'd been using when she met me last time." He paused. "I suppose out of professional courtesy I should call Ichabod Crane and let him know."

Sabre raised her eyebrows at Bob. "His name is Barry Betts, not Ichabod Crane."

"He's Ichabod to me. Let's see ... How would JP describe him?" Bob spoke in a Texas accent. "He's so ugly his mama takes him everywhere so she doesn't have to kiss him good-bye."

Sabre laughed. It lightened the load for a second. While Bob called Betts, Sabre called JP. "Any leads on Bailey's whereabouts?"

"I haven't found her yet, but I did speak with the detective on the murder investigation and they have several suspects. Not the least of which is Bailey and her boyfriend, Apollo."

"What?" Sabre said loudly.

"It seems some neighbor identified them running from the house. The police think it was around the time Scott was killed. At least the description the neighbor gave fit them. The neighbor didn't know her name, but he was sure it was the 'girl who lived there' that he saw running away. The boy with her fit Apollo's description. There's an APB out on them both."

"There's already something out on Bailey. So far they haven't been very quick to catch her."

JP responded. "Yeah, but now they're really looking. She's not just a runaway any longer. She's a suspect."

Bob finished his call, walked over to Sabre, and listened to her side of the conversation. "Do they have other suspects?"

JP said, "They're questioning Bailey's mother, Karen Lecy, and they have a number of druggies they're talking to. But they think it was something more personal because whoever did it beat him up pretty good and bashed his head in. I can think of several people who would want to do that to him, including me, for the way he treated you and for who knows what he has done to Bailey and any number of other young girls."

Sabre could hear the anger in JP's voice. "He was a creep, for sure, but he's a dead creep now and although I don't wish that on anyone we need to really concentrate on finding Bailey. If you find her before the authorities do, make sure she doesn't talk to anyone. And call me right away. I'll try to convince her to go in voluntarily."

"I know the drill. I'll call you as soon as I know something."

Before Sabre could hang up, Bob was asking what happened. "Was that JP?"

"Yes." Sabre's shoulders dropped. "He says Bailey and Apollo are the prime suspects in Scott's murder. Someone saw them running from the house last night."

Bob put his arm around Sabre's shoulder. "I'm sorry, Sobs. Anything I can do?"

"No, but I think I'll skip lunch. I want to go back to my office and read through the reports. Maybe I can find something that will lead me to Bailey and/or Cole." She looked up at Bob. "Do you mind?"

"Of course not. I don't have a trial this afternoon so I think I might leave a little early and pick my son up from school, maybe hang out with him a little."

"I'm sure Marilee would appreciate it as well," Sabre said.

"Yeah, she's been after me to spend more time with him. Always nagging about how fast they grow up. But she's right. Today's the day."

Sabre returned to her office and rifled through the Lecy file trying to find anything that might help find Bailey. She found nothing that JP hadn't already followed up on. Sabre knew full well JP would call her as soon as he had anything to report, but she called him anyway. "Anything new?"

"I just hung up with Shellie Ingraham, Bailey's best friend, again. Shellie swears she hasn't seen her, but she did give me the name of one of Apollo's friends whom she met once. His name is Josiah. It's only a first name but I'm going to Apollo's school right now to see if it leads me anywhere. Oh, and by the way, after I left the other day Shellie told her stepdad, Jim Boller, about Scott hitting on her. I hope he didn't decide to hit back."

"Do you think he might have killed him?"

"He didn't strike me as the kind to go bash someone's head in—although Shellie told me she didn't tell Jim before because she was afraid he would kill Scott. I just assumed it was a figure of speech."

"It's good information if we ever need it. Thanks. And, JP, please call me if you learn anything from Apollo's friend."

JP drove to Kearny High School and parked in the only spot he could find. It was located at the far end of the parking lot. When he walked through the big wrought iron gates and saw the locks and chains, he wondered when schools had started to feel more like prisons than schools. It was so different thirty years ago. There were a lot fewer students crowded into the hallways, not nearly as many gangs, and drugs were available but only to those who really knew where to look. Now it seemed that you could almost buy them from the vending machines.

JP walked into the office. He wore his best smile and his Stetson as he approached a young woman who appeared to still be in her teens sitting in front of a computer. "Howdy, ma'am," he said accentuating his Texas drawl.

She smiled and said, "Howdy."

He continued to speak in a heavy accent. "My name is JP Torn." He reached his hand out to shake hers.

She blushed as she reciprocated. "I'm Helen."

"I'm hoping you can provide me with a little information. You see, we're looking for a missing girl." He took her photo out of the file he was carrying and showed it to the clerk. "She's been gone from foster care for nearly a week and we're real concerned for her safety."

"I don't recognize her. Is she a student here?"

"No, but we have reason to believe a student here might be privy to her whereabouts. I would like to speak to that gentleman, if at all possible."

The clerk stared at JP, almost mesmerized by his charm. "Do you have a name?"

"That's a bit of a problem. I only have a first name, but it's a little unusual, if that helps. His name is Josiah."

"Let me check the computer and see what we have." She typed something on the keyboard that pulled up a list on the screen. "We have three Josiahs in this school—one freshman and two juniors."

"That's amazing. I've never even met a Josiah and you have three of them here in this school." JP shook his head. "Hmm ... well it's most likely not the freshman. And he has a good friend named Apollo Servantes. Do you happen to have any classes that have both Josiah and Apollo in them?"

"Let me check." She smiled up at JP. "Here you go. There's only one Apollo in this school and he and Josiah Little have three classes together. But Apollo appears to have been absent for some time now."

"Where could I find this Josiah Little?"

She looked back at her computer, entered more information, and said, "He'll be leaving Mr. Huddleston's class in just a few minutes. Room 204."

"Helen," a tall, heavyset woman in a suit spoke loudly as she approached the desk. "I need you to take these files to Room 812." She turned to JP. "Is there something I can help you with?"

Helen reached for the files and scrambled to get up and around the counter. JP spoke as he stepped toward the door, glancing back at Helen with a wink. "I'm here to meet with Mr. Huddleston about my son and I forgot the room number. I'm good now."

"It's down the hall to your right. Second row of rooms."

"Thanks."

JP reached the room just as the class was letting out. He looked into the group of students and yelled, "Josiah." A young, black man whose head already towered above the rest turned his head toward him. JP nodded to him. He walked out of the classroom and up to JP.

"Yes?"

"Hi, Josiah. I'm JP. You got a minute?"

"For what?" He responded politely, but his body language said he was skeptical.

"I'd like to ask you a few questions about Apollo."

"You the police?"

"No. I'm a private investigator. We're looking for a girl named Bailey Lecy. I work for her attorney." He looked up at Josiah, who stood at least two inches taller than him. "Do you know her?"

"I've seen her a couple of times." He paused. "But not lately," he added quickly. "It's probably been a month or more since I saw her."

"When did you last see or talk with Apollo?"

"He called me last Saturday and wanted me to let him and his girlfriend, Bailey, crash at my house."

"Did you let him stay?"

"No, my parents would've been furious."

"And you haven't had any communication with him since?"

"Nope."

"I understand you and Apollo are pretty good friends. Is that right?"

"We used to be. We took a film class together. That's where we met. Apollo was new in town. He came here from Nebraska or New Hampshire or someplace like that. He believes he's going to be a big-time movie director some day. He's always filming stuff, and he's real good at it. But a few months ago he became real serious about some secret project he was working on. He started spending all his time either on the project or with Bailey. I didn't see much of him after that."

"Do you know what the 'secret project' was?"

"No, but Apollo started dressing all in black, kinda Gothic-like, but not really. I thought maybe he was filming some kind of underground Gothic-Rock thing, but he never would say what it was. And I don't really dig that kind of music anyway so I wasn't that interested."

"Do you know who else Apollo hung out with?"

"He never had a lot of friends. Like I said, he was new here when I met him and we hung out a lot until he met Bailey."

"Did you ever meet any of Bailey's family? Ever go to her house?"

Josiah shook his head. "No."

"Have you ever known Apollo to be violent?"

"No. Never. He's the most easy-going guy I've ever met. I used to tease him about being a country hick. The only time he was ever excited was when he was filming something. Why? Did he do something?"

JP took a deep breath. "I have reason to believe the cops are looking for Apollo and Bailey in connection with a murder." JP noted the surprised look on Josiah's face. "Bailey's mother's boyfriend was beaten to death. Do you think that's something that Apollo could do?"

"That's not Apollo. Something really awful would've had to happen for him to do something like that." He paused. "Maybe it was Bailey."

"Do you think she could do it?"

"Like I said, I've only seen her a couple of times, but she has a temper. The first time I met her she was screaming and cussing about someone. I thought it was her mom, but I'm not sure. But she was real mad."

JP handed Josiah his card. "Please call me if you hear from him. It's real important that we find them. Both Bailey and

Apollo could be in danger, and if the cops reach them first it'll be a lot harder on them."

Chapter 18

The sun was just beginning to stream into Sabre's bedroom through her window and the first thing it touched was the photo of her brother. "Good morning, Ron," Sabre said aloud to her brother. He had found a permanent place on the nightstand by her bed. She had made a habit of saying "good morning" to him every morning as she first woke up and "goodnight" every night before she went to sleep. He left almost six years ago, exactly six on her upcoming birthday. She still missed him so much. He was her rock and her protector.

The nightstand next to her bed housed the little red notebook Ron had given her for her sixth birthday. She reached into the drawer and removed it. She opened the book and read the last couple of entries.

Sabre stepped out of bed. No running this morning. It was Thursday and that meant breakfast with Bob. They had started meeting every Thursday because Bob's son, Corey, had band practice and had to be dropped off by 6:30 in the morning. Bob had nothing to do between the drop-off and court so they filled it with breakfast and conversation.

Sabre showered, dressed, and arrived at IHOP before Bob. The weather was still nice enough to sit outside, so she chose to sit outdoors on the patio. She was seated and had two pots of coffee delivered, one decaf and one regular, when Bob walked in.

"Morning, Sobs."

"Good morning." Sabre opened four of the little containers of half-and-half and poured them into her cup. Then she filled her cup with decaf coffee.

"Hey, did you see in the paper this morning about all the graffiti they're finding in San Diego?" Bob asked as he poured his coffee. "They think it's connected to the 'Devil House' because there's a lot of sixes. There's been some tagging of trees similar to the one on the news, as well."

"What is going on? Do you think there is some cult trying to take over the city?"

"I think the tagging is just kids trying to jump on the band wagon, and satanic stuff can be pretty intriguing to teenagers. The media has really tried to sensationalize it."

"That's true. 'The devil made me do it' is a great excuse to act badly. But what about all the cases we're seeing in juvenile court? And that house? Someone is doing something."

Bob spoke in a creepy, quiet voice, hissing as he said Satan, "Do you think S-s-s-atan is behind it all? Is he building his empire so he can control everyone and rule the world?"

"No, I think some creep is out there trying to make a name for himself and destroying people's lives as he does it, and I think others are getting caught up in the hysteria."

The waitress approached the table and took their order. Two eggs, hash browns, bacon, and white toast for Bob. The crepes, or Swedish pancakes, as they called them here, for Sabre. After Sabre placed her order, she said, "I'm getting as bad as you. I order the same thing every time we come here."

"No, sometimes you order the French pancakes."

"Yeah, I change the topping. Big deal. But I guess that is more than you'd ever do."

Bob wrinkled his brow and then nodded as if he had a brilliant thought. He said, "We need to look at all the cases at juvenile court and see what they have in common. Maybe we can figure this out."

"We can't look at all the cases. We don't know which ones are ritual cases and they're all confidential."

"We can talk to the other panel attorneys and see who has an unusual case, anything that might fall into a 'ritual abuse' case. There's nothing wrong with consulting on the cases."

"That's true."

"And I can steal the new detention and disposition reports as they come in. I'll make copies, of course, and return then."

Sabre shook her head. "Bob, you can't do that."

"Sure I can. I'll gather the information and give it to you. You can make a chart."

"Why don't you make the chart?"

"You do charts. I don't do charts. And you know I'll never get it done. So that's the plan."

"It's not a very good plan."

"It's a great plan. We'll record everything we know about these cases, put it all on a spreadsheet, and see what they have in common. Maybe they all belong to the same church, or maybe it's a political thing."

"A political thing?"

"I'm just saying there must be some connection between these cases."

The waitress arrived with their food.

After she left, Sabre said, "I heard Underwood got a new ritual case yesterday."

"I bet he was all excited about that. That guy is weird. He probably gets off on that kind of thing."

"You were excited to get one, too, remember?"

"Yeah, but I was glad to have something that wasn't so routine. Underpants will probably use it in one of his crazy comic books."

Sabre laughed. Bob had a nickname for just about everyone at court. "They're graphic novels," Sabre said, imitating Underwood's previous statement.

"They're damn comic books. They look like comic books, they feel like comic books, and they're even the size of a comic book. They're comic books."

Sabre laughed. "They look like comics to me, too."

Bob and Sabre ate their breakfast, occasionally talking about other things in their daily lives. They talked about Corey and Marilee. They discussed the progress on the Lecy case and the lack thereof on Johnson. But Bob couldn't let go of the plan he had come up with. "We'll make some categories to compare. So here, write this stuff down."

"Why don't you write it down?"

"Because I don't have a pad of paper with me and I bet you do." Sabre looked up at him sheepishly and took a yellow pad out of her bag. "And besides, you always complain that you can't read my handwriting."

"You're impossible." She smiled. "Okay, shoot."

"A common church would be the most likely thing."

Sabre wrote down Churches. "How about the area they live in?"

"That's good. We need to look at any organizations they may belong to."

"What kind of organizations? Most of our clients aren't exactly 'Rotarian' material."

"I know, but they could belong to some community groups or something," Bob said. "But, you're right. Let's look at other stuff like who the social worker is, stuff like that."

"And indicators."

"Huh?"

"The things that make it a ritual abuse case. They vary from case to case. We'll assess what's alike and what's different. It might tell us something."

Bob nodded. "That's a good one. And let's check to see if these cases are coming out of drug related cases. Maybe it's a drug culture thing."

"Most of our cases are drug related. I don't think that will narrow the search much."

"True, but if there are cases that don't have drugs involved, it'll tell us something."

They continued to compile and refine a list until it was time to leave for court. Sabre paid the check since it was her turn. On the way to the car, Sabre said, "You know, this just might help us to understand what's going on. Who knows? We might crack this thing wide open."

"Yeah, it's a great plan."

"Ahh ... It's an okay plan," Sabre said. "And my secretary can help me."

All morning, between cases, Bob would bring Sabre sheets of paper with information on other ritual abuse cases. He gathered it from Underwood, Wagner, Collicott, and several other panel attorneys. By noon, Sabre had information for eight cases, or nine if she included the one she was working on. She skipped lunch and returned to her office to have Elaine create the spreadsheet. She also needed to spend a little preparation time for her afternoon trial, although she was pretty certain it would settle.

She returned to court around 1:15 p.m. Bob was still there. His morning calendar had run late and he had to meet with his client who was produced from Las Colinas for his trial. Sabre walked up to Bob and handed him a file.

"What's this?"

"The ritual abuse spreadsheet."

"That was fast."

"Of course. You want a job done, you give it to a woman." She smirked at him. Sabre was organized and efficient almost to the point of being anal. Her files were all color coded, and every bit of information gathered on a case was attached inside her files with metal fasteners. Sabre knew she couldn't control certain things in her life and they often became chaotic. But she could keep order in the little things and she counted on that to make it through the day.

"So did you see any glaring clues?"

"Nothing jumped out at me, but I just glanced at it. I haven't had time to study it yet. There are still a lot of blanks we need to fill in, and we might want to add more categories, but it's what we have so far."

Bob reached down and kissed her on the forehead. "Thanks, my post-pubescent nugget of love and carnality."

Sabre laughed and walked away. "I need to go do my trial. See you later."

Sabre's trial took about forty minutes to settle and to put it on the record. When she walked out of the courtroom, Bob was still waiting for his trial to start. "How did it go?" he asked.

"Fine, no surprises." She shuffled her files to place them more comfortably in her arms. "And that's a wrap."

"My trial won't start for another half hour at least. Come on. I'll walk you to your car."

They left the building and started across the parking lot. Sabre handed Bob her files. "Hold these a sec. I need to turn my phone back on and check my messages." She took her phone out and turned it on. "I'm always hoping I'll receive some news on Cole. Oh, there's a message from JP." She listened. Her mouth turned down with concern.

"What is it?"

"Apollo was arrested for Scott's murder." Sabre hung up her phone.

"And Bailey?"

"She's still on the loose."

Chapter 19

JP entered Sabre's office building through the back door. It opened into the copy room, which doubled as a lounge area. The small room had once been a porch on this old Victorian home. An attorney, Jack Snecker, had purchased the building some time ago and turned it into office space. The house sat directly across from the family law court so it attracted primarily divorce lawyers. Sabre had been handling domestic cases when she first rented the office space from Jack, but shortly thereafter she found her calling in juvenile court, which was located about ten minutes away. It was an easy decision to remain in the building.

Jack's office was on the bottom floor, as was another family law attorney who spent most of his time working with his wife in an ice cream business. Sabre had the third office downstairs. It was meager, but comfortable, and remained the way she had decorated it over the five years she had been there. She often thought about redecorating but it never seemed to be a priority, so the cheap furniture, the simple gray blinds, and the one picture of a single flower remained. Other attorneys occupied the rooms upstairs. They came and went through a different entrance so she seldom saw them.

Sabre smiled at JP as he stepped inside the copy room through the back door. He seemed to fill the room, although there was admittedly little space left. She stepped forward just as he did, accidently brushing against him. She felt a little awkward, but JP made her laugh when he quickly said, "I'll give you an hour to quit that."

JP stepped back and waved his hand toward the door, allowing Sabre to go first. He followed her into her office, closing the door behind him. Sabre always insisted on privacy when they discussed cases. One of her colleagues had been sued once for something she said in the courthouse restroom. She knew one couldn't be too careful.

"So what's new on Cole and Bailey?" Sabre asked.

"I keep receiving reports of sightings on Cole, but I'm not sure it's even him. If it is, that kid is slicker than a wet weasel on a linoleum floor. He's gone before I can smell the scent." He rubbed his chin. "I hate being outsmarted by an eight-year-old, but I'd rather think that than to think some pervert has him."

"I know. The alternatives are unbearable to think about." Sabre took a deep breath. "He's been gone for five days now. What are the chances that he's even still alive?"

"The police haven't found a body, so there's still hope. And I can't help but believe he's out there, but we're missing something. I just don't know what it is."

Sabre sat for several seconds without speaking. Then she asked, "What about Bailey? Anything?"

"I've been talking to her friends. Or should I say previous friends? She doesn't seem to have many any longer. I hear the same story from them all. She just sort of dropped out of everyone's life. She was missing a lot of school, attending only a couple of days a week, and then she often showed up late. She apparently dropped out completely the last three or four months of the last school term. Until recently, no one saw her after that."

"No one?"

"I think maybe Shellie did. In fact, I think she knows a lot more than she's saying, but she's not giving it up."

"Do you think she knows where Bailey is?"

"That I don't know. But it might be worth tailing her for a while, especially now that Apollo has been picked up. Bailey might call on Shellie for help."

"That's a good idea. If she doesn't have anywhere else to go or anyone to turn to, she may seek out Shellie. God knows, she's not going to call me. She doesn't even like me. We never had the chance to bond." Sabre made quotation marks in the air when she said the word bond. "Maybe you can convince Shellie that I can help Bailey and maybe she'll be able to convince Bailey to at least call me." Sabre's eyes lit up with hope.

"Not a bad idea, kid. I'll see what I can do," JP said. "And by the way, I met with Collicott's minors on her case and I did some investigation for her. I haven't had a chance to write the report yet but she said I could share the information with you, for what it's worth."

"So what did you find out?"

"It's a single mother caring for the children, deadbeat dads, a different one for each child. The first one disappeared when Mom filed domestic violence charges against him. He was in and out of the joint a few times, nothing long term. He's apparently on the lam now. The second father is unknown, or at least she's not telling who it is. There's no name on the birth certificate."

"What about Mom?"

"She has no drug or employment history and receives state aid for the children. She was pretty young when she gave birth the first time, fifteen or sixteen. I'd have to check my file."

"Does she have family support?" Sabre asked.

"She lives with her alcoholic mother. There are other relatives around but they're all marginal. Frankly, I think the mom is the best of the lot. She seems to really care for her children. She's just so young, but she seems to be pretty protective. In fact, she kept her baby from being kidnapped."

"What?"

"She was leaving the grocery store with the two kids. The older one had been begging for something and wouldn't let up. When she knelt down to talk to him, a man tried to steal the baby from the cart."

"Oh my God. What did she do?"

"She attacked him. Hit him with her purse, kicked him, and bit him. He apparently didn't have the baby all the way out of the basket. The man started to fight back, but then some people came out of the store and he ran off."

"Good for her."

"That's what I thought, but DSS is using it against her. They're using it as an example that the children are at risk."

Sabre shook her head. "Did you find anything that would help us?"

"Not really. No strong religious ties, but they all appear to believe in God. I didn't find any suspicious activities or unexplainable behaviors. Admittedly, I didn't have a lot of time to investigate, but I have nothing so far. Nothing except the social worker's interpretation of the pictures the children drew."

Sabre nodded as she listened.

JP continued, "And Collicott has another case where a teenage girl is in a group home and previously claimed they wanted her to join a cult."

"Claimed? Past tense?"

"Yeah, she has since recanted. I visited the home, and although I haven't found anything yet, I felt a real strange vibe—like everyone was walking on eggshells. I'm still investigating, running background checks on the employees and owners, etc. But for now, I have nothing."

"Sometimes nothing is something."

Chapter 20

JP had no more than walked out of Sabre's office when Bob stepped into it.

"Hey, you just missed JP," Sabre said.

"We 'howdied' outside," Bob said, imitating JP. Does he have any news on the kids?"

"No, but we're trying a new approach on Bailey. By the way, do you think your client, Karen Lecy, can be convinced to have her daughter call me if she hears from her?" Sabre waved her hand from side to side. "Never mind. I forgot; she's locked up. She's not going to hear from Bailey."

"No. She's back on the streets. They released her."

"Already?"

"I guess they don't think she committed Scott's murder and there's no room at Las Colinas to house the druggies right now. But as for convincing her of anything, that's doubtful. She's dumber than dirt. She's fried her brains with all that crap she's been using. When something about Bailey comes up, she vacillates between blubbering about how Bailey will never forgive her and yelling about what a pain-in-the-ass she is."

"Forgive her for what?"

"For being such a crappy mother? For bringing her into this world? Hell if I know. I'm sure the kid has plenty of reasons to be angry at her mother and vice versa. But my client isn't exactly June Cleaver material."

"June who?"

"Beaver's mother." Sabre's face was blank with lack of recognition. "You know, Leave It to Beaver." Still no response from Sabre. "You don't watch enough late night television."

Sabre tilted her head to one side and rolled her eyes.

"I'll talk to her, but I wouldn't count on much," Bob said.

"Just do what you can."

Bob opened a file folder, removed the spreadsheet they'd been working on for the ritual cases, and handed it to Sabre. "I have a little more information for you."

Sabre looked at the sheet. "Wow. You dug up a lot more. You've added three more cases on here and filled in lots of blanks. Where did you get these?"

"You don't want to know."

"Bob," Sabre said in a reprimanding voice. "This looks like County Counsel stuff.... Did you snoop in someone's files?"

"Would I do that?"

"Yeah ... if you had the chance."

"Look, I obtained it legally. Well, sort of." He waved his hand making a gesture of dismissal. "Just take the information to Elaine so she can type it up and we can start sorting through it."

Bob threw three disposition reports on Sabre's desk. "Oh, and I have these. They should be helpful," he said.

"Now you're stealing reports?"

"Don't worry. I made copies. The originals are still in the folders at court."

Sabre smirked as she walked out of her office to take the spreadsheet to Elaine. She returned shortly to find Bob reading through one of the reports, his glasses down on his nose so he could see over them. Most people she knew looked over their readers to see distance, but Bob's nearsighted vision allowed him to see up close. Without his thick glasses, everything in the distance was blurry.

"Look at this one," Bob said. "The child's therapist wrote, *The victim reported the sexual abuse by her grandfather included such things as tying her to a table, smearing blood from a dead rabbit on the child's face and body before ...*"

"Enough already!" Sabre grimaced. "What is this? Are we back in the eighties when we had the mass hysteria about satanic ritual abuse? I thought all this was laid to rest after that fiasco with the McMartin trials. If I remember right, the FBI came out with a report in the late eighties or early nineties saying that organized satanic ritual didn't exist."

"Is that the same FBI that once denied the existence of organized crime?"

"Good point, but don't tell me you believe there's actually a satanic movement going on."

Bob smiled. "I'm just saying." Then in a serious tone, he said, "Naw. I think it's all a bunch of malarkey. Besides, there really hasn't been anything suggesting satanic involvement."

"That's true. The numbers have only been two sixes, not three. And we saw a circle in the house around a hospital bed. What is that? There's been no mention of the devil in anything except some overzealous social worker's interpretation. And a tree, what does that have to do with ritual abuse? It's all very strange."

"I think it's just another excuse for these imbeciles to abuse their children, just like those strong religious zealots who beat their children in the name of God. They believe in this almighty, omni-benevolent being who is their source of all moral obligation, and yet they can justify a behavior, in His name, that cripples a child for life, causes brain damage, or leaves welts and bruises on one of His precious little creatures. It just makes no sense to me."

"What wound you up?"

"Sometimes I just get so sick of the people we work with. Half the time I work harder than they do to get their kids back."

A knock on the door interrupted the rest of Bob's rant. Elaine stepped inside and handed Sabre several copies of the spreadsheet. "Here you go," she said, and walked back out.

Sabre gave a copy to Bob and they both read through it looking for some common ground. "There are a lot of pentagrams and 666's, but other than that the behaviors or indicators really vary," Sabre said.

"No connection on the churches. Only two of them attend any church at all, one Catholic and one Baptist. No community organization connection. Even the neighborhoods are spread out. Aside from the one case in North County, the rest are in the San Diego area, which makes sense because otherwise they wouldn't be filed in this court." Bob looked up. "Do we know if the other juvenile courts in the county have filed any of these cases?"

"I don't know, but I'll see what I can find out. Or better yet, you do it. You seem to have better connections than I do." She gave Bob a stern look. "But please try to do it without breaking any laws or moral codes."

"Hmm . . ."

"I can't tell how close in proximity these cases are without running the addresses. I'll have JP do that." Sabre jotted herself a note on a yellow pad. "He can also check to see if any of them are in close proximity to the 'Devil House' that aired on the news."

"Nothing else seems to be connected. Eight of them have drugs involved in some fashion, the ages of the kids range from infants to teenagers, and the ethnic backgrounds vary."

"Maybe we need more categories? There have to be some similarities. Let's check who the social workers are on the cases."

Bob took his pen out of his pocket and wrote Social Worker in one of the columns at the top of the spreadsheet. "And therapists," he said, as he labeled another column.

"Why therapists? They aren't usually even on the case until after it's already filed."

"You don't watch enough movies. Therapists are always involved in this stuff."

Sabre shook her head. "Why do I put up with you?"

"Because you love me, snookums," Bob said in a baby-talk tone.

"Okay, you take care of the list. And while you're at it, add the names of the attorneys on the cases so we know who to talk to if we have any questions." Sabre stood up. "And now, I don't know about you, but I'm ready to get out of here."

She started to stack her folders to take with her when her phone beeped from Elaine. Sabre hit the speaker button and Elaine said, "You have a call on line one. She says her name is Bailey."

Chapter 21

"Hello, Bailey. This is Sabre. Are you okay?"

"I'm fine. You need to help Apollo. He's in jail."

"I know. They'll appoint an attorney to help him. It's you I want to help." Sabre reached for a pen and yellow pad in case she needed to write something down.

"I don't need your help. I need you to help Apollo," Bailey pleaded. "He didn't kill Scott."

"How do you know that, Bailey?"

"I just know. He didn't do it." She spoke a little louder.

"Bailey, where are you?"

"Are you going to help Apollo or not?"

Sabre feared Bailey would hang up and she wouldn't hear from her again. She tried to choose her words carefully. "I'm not sure what I can do for him, but I'll try. Listen, Bailey, what you tell me is confidential. Remember, I'm your attorney so I can't tell anyone, but I need to know what happened so I can help you."

Silence ensued. Sabre hoped that meant she was getting through to her. But when she didn't respond after several seconds, Sabre asked, "Bailey?"

"Yeah. I'm thinking."

"Tell me where you are and I'll come meet you."

"I can't do that. Are you going to help or not?"

"Yes. I'm going to help. I'm going to help you and I'll see what I can find out about Apollo. But I can't represent him because there may be a conflict of interest. You're my client and the police are also looking for you in conjunction with Scott's murder. Please, let me help you."

"I've gotta go."

"Bailey, wait! Take my cell number." Sabre gave her the number. She could only hope she wrote it down. "How can I reach you? Give me a phone number or some ..." Sabre heard a dial tone.

She jumped up and dashed into the reception area, still carrying her pen. "Elaine, check to see what number Bailey called from."

Elaine picked up the phone and tapped the CID button on the phone three times. She shook her head. "Sorry, it was a blocked number."

Sabre walked back to her office where Bob was waiting. "Damn it! I blew it."

"What did she say?"

"She wants me to help Apollo. She said he's innocent."

"Do you think she did it?"

"I have no idea. She wouldn't tell me anything." Sabre threw her pen on the desk. "Damn! I should've said something else."

"Like what?"

"I don't know. I should've convinced her I was going to help Apollo. Then she would at least call back to find out what's going on."

"You said enough to get her to do that. You told her you would try." Bob walked over to her and put his arm around her shoulder. "She's going to call back. You're all she has to connect her to Apollo, and she has your cell number now. She'll call."

"So how am I going to find out anything about Apollo? He'll be lawyered-up soon, if he isn't already. And I really don't know anyone that well downtown who would provide me with information."

"Isn't he a minor?"

"That's right." Sabre looked up, her eyes opened wide. "He'll be in juvey. They'll probably attempt to try him as an adult, but he has to start in kiddie court." Sabre stood up, shuffled through a few files, picked out the one she wanted, and stepped out from behind her desk. "I have to go."

"To court?"

"Juvenile Hall if I can get in."

"It's getting late," Bob said.

"I know, but it's worth a shot. I need to talk with him, or at least see if I can get any information. It'll be a lot easier before he's appointed counsel."

"Don't you have to be a person of interest to interview a minor in the Hall?"

"I am a person of interest." Sabre picked up her briefcase and looked around to see if she had forgotten anything.

"That's cool. So, you're going to go in there and pretend you're his attorney?"

"No. I'm not going to pretend anything."

"That's what I would do. Say you're an attorney and you're there to see Apollo. They'll probably just let you in. They don't usually ask if you're his attorney."

Sabre smiled. "I'm sure you would." She walked toward the door. Bob followed.

"So what are you going to tell them?"

"The truth." Just as they reached Sabre's car, she clicked her keys and unlocked the trunk and her door. She put her briefcase in the trunk and walked to the driver's side of the car. Bob opened her door for her.

"What if the truth doesn't work?" Bob asked.

"It'll work. If necessary, I'll obtain a court order."

"I'd do it my way."

"I know." Sabre stepped inside and sat down. "See ya. I need to get there before they shut down for dinner." Sabre drove off.

She arrived at the Kearny Mesa Juvenile Detention Facility at 4:30 p.m. It was located directly behind the San Diego Superior Court Juvenile Division and was connected by a long tunnel that had access through the courthouse. Sabre had represented enough delinquents to be familiar with the system and, more importantly, for the probation officers to know her. She hoped she could gain access through the tunnel because it would be a lot simpler and there would be no form to fill out. But it was too late by the time she arrived. The tunnel had already been shut down.

Sabre went back to her car, drove around the building, and parked in the parking lot in front of the Hall. The old building had housed juvenile offenders for over fifty years. Suddenly Sabre realized he might not be at this facility. He could be at the new Hall that had been built a few years back in East Otay Mesa just north of Brown Field. What if they took him there? She seldom dealt with that facility so she often forgot about it, but if that's where they took him she knew she wouldn't be able to see him until tomorrow and by then he could have a lawyer.

Sabre stepped into the lobby of the old Hall, a stark room with off white walls that needed paint. It contained a row of uncomfortable chairs and a trash can. A small stand with some reading material about the rules and regulations for visitors leaned against the wall. A Mexican-American man and woman, approximately sixty years old, sat next to one another near the door. They both looked frightened and concerned. Sabre wondered if they were the grandparents of another rebellious teenager. She nodded to them as she walked by. There was no one in line when she reached the window. She presented the receptionist with her bar card and California driver's license, explained who she was, filled out the required form, and then sat down near the door and waited to be called.

About five minutes later a woman opened the door and called Sabre's name.

"That's me," she said, stepping up to meet the woman.

The woman reached out her right hand. "Hi Counselor. I'm Coleen, the Watch Commander on duty. I understand you want to speak to someone in the 1400 Unit." She looked at the paper she carried in her left hand. "Apollo Servantes?"

Sabre reciprocated, shaking her hand. "Yes, that's correct."

"There's no attorney of record yet, but I understand you're not his attorney, so what is your interest in the minor?"

"I represent a fourteen-year-old in the dependency system who is apparently Apollo's girlfriend. There's a Pick Up and Detain Order on her. She ran away nearly a week ago and we have every reason to believe she's been with Apollo the entire time. I want to talk with Apollo to see if he'll help us find her. I'm sure he knows where she's hiding. I'm not here to discuss the pending murder case with him and I will not. It's urgent that we find her before something happens to her, especially now that she's on the streets alone."

"Do you have a court order?"

Sabre reached in her file folder and took out some papers and handed them to her. "Only the Pick Up and Detain. I'm sure I could get a court order in the morning, but I hate to leave her on the streets for another night if there's a chance we could find her."

"Come on in," Coleen said, as she opened the door further. "I'll send a probation officer to bring him up. He'll wait outside the interview room until you're finished. You know your way to the unit, right?"

"Yes, I do. Thanks."

Sabre walked down the austere hallway and past rooms with heavy doors that contained one small window centered about eye level. At the end of the hallway she pushed the intercom button, gave her name, and the door buzzed open. She checked in at the next desk and was escorted the rest of the way to the 1400 unit, where they housed the delinquents with violent felony charges. This delinquent facility had a capacity of about 350. Sabre wondered how many of them were housed in the 1400 unit. Far too many, she surmised.

She often heard people say, "How did those kids get there?" But she knew how they got there. She saw it every day in the dependency system. So many of them didn't stand a chance with the parenting they received. Sabre was actually more surprised that the numbers weren't higher. These children lived in an environment of drugs, alcohol, and domestic violence. They learned to deal with all their problems by fighting or running. They dodged responsibility because they had never had a good role model. They dished out abuse because they were abused. When they couldn't deal with the craziness that afflicts every teenager—the raging hormones, the peer pressures, the need to be a part of the group—they tried to escape either into a bottle or some other drug. They formed bonds with others who suffered from the same afflictions, and sometimes the only "family" that seemed to fit was the neighborhood gang. They found a place where they felt like they belonged and they did whatever it took to be accepted.

They reached the interview room, where her escort left her after indicating Apollo would be there shortly. The room contained only a table with a bench on one side and a chair on the other. It had a glass window where one could watch from the hallway. Sabre sat down in the chair and waited.

Within about three minutes, the door opened. A probation officer walked in with a young man who was about five-foot-eight with soft features. Apollo was wearing Harry Potter style glasses and his dark brown, curly hair was in serious need of a haircut. Although most of the hair was only about an inch in length and clung closely to his scalp, the remains of his Mohawk hung down in uneven waves. His body was muscular, not overly so, but there was evidence he'd been working out for some time. Everything else about him would lead one to believe he was bucking for vale-dictorian. Sabre thought nerd. She was dealing with a nerd with the remains of a Mohawk, charged with murder. It didn't compute.

The probation officer instructed Apollo to sit on the bench and then turned to Sabre and said, "I'll be right outside watching and waiting. Just let me know when you're fin-ished."

"Thanks," Sabre responded. She looked at the young man across from her. "Hello, Apollo. I'm Attorney Sabre Brown. I represent Bailey. Before you say anything, I want you to know I'm not here to talk about the murder charges." Apollo didn't respond. "Do you understand?" Sabre asked softly.

Apollo nodded his head.

"I know Bailey has been with you since she ran away from the foster home. I need to find her. She isn't safe out there alone. Will you help me?"

He shook his head. "I can't."

"Can't or won't?"

"I promised her I wouldn't tell anyone where she is."

"Listen, Apollo, I'm really grateful to you that you were with her to help keep her safe, but now she's alone. So many awful things could happen to her."

"They already have," he said.

"What do you mean?"

"Nothing." Apollo's eyes were not on Sabre. He wouldn't keep eye contact for more than a second or two at a time.

"Apollo, I just want to help her." He didn't respond, so she tried another approach. "Do you know the police are looking for Bailey for Scott's murder?"

"She didn't do it. She didn't kill him." He spoke louder and for the first time looked directly at Sabre when he spoke.

"She said the same about you."

"You've talked to her?"

"Yes, she called me a couple of hours ago. She wanted me to help you, to represent you. I explained I couldn't because there is a conflict of interest since she is a suspect in the murder as well. But you're both tying my hands and it won't be long before the police pick her up. It would be so much better for Bailey if I could find her first." Apollo didn't respond. His eyes fixed downward toward the floor.

Sabre let him reflect for a few seconds on what she said. "She's not safe out there alone, Apollo. She needs you, but you're not there to help her. Who else does she have that can protect her?"

He shook his head from side to side.

"Apollo, does she have anyone else?"

Again he shook his head, but no response.

"That leaves me, Apollo," she pleaded. "Please let me help her. Tell me where she is."

He just kept shaking his head. "No. I can't. She'll be okay. At least Scott can't hurt her anymore."

Sabre leaned over so she could look more directly at this scared young man. When she caught his eye she said, "But he's not the only one who wants to hurt her, is he?"

"No," he replied in almost a whisper.

"What's going on? Who's she afraid of?"

"Nobody. Nothing. She'll be fine."

Chapter 22

Darkness was setting in as JP watched Shellie and a brunette girl leave the school and walk south. When they turned onto Date Avenue, he dropped back a bit. The girls stood in front of the corner house chatting until the brunette went inside. Shellie continued walking toward her house. JP waited about five minutes and then walked up to the front door of the brunette's house and knocked. The girl came to the door.

"Excuse me," JP said. "I'm working with an attorney in the juvenile court system and we're looking for a missing girl. She's been missing for a while and we need to find her and keep her safe." He showed her a picture of Bailey. "Do you know this girl?"

After a quick glance at the photo she said, "Yes, she goes to my school. Her name is Bailey." She paused. "Bailey something. I don't know her last name. She was in my English class last year."

JP was frustrated that this young girl was even talking to him. She shouldn't be. She opened the door for him and didn't ask for a badge. She must've assumed what he had implied, that he was with law enforcement, but nevertheless she shouldn't have. He didn't go inside, but he thought how easy it was for deviants to get what they want. "What can you tell me about her?"

"Not much. She dropped out of school last year and she hasn't been back."

"So you haven't seen her recently?"

"No ... yes ... maybe ..." she looked up and wrinkled her nose.

"What?" JP asked.

"I think I saw her one day by my friend Shellie's house."

"But you're not sure it was her?"

"The face looked just like her, but with pimples. She never had pimples before. And she was thinner. Bailey was always kinda ... plump."

"Did you get a good look at her?"

"Yes. I think I surprised her. I was going toward the back door of the house because it's a lot closer to Shellie's room. She came from around the corner of the house so we were face to face for a second."

"Did you talk to her?"

"No. I started to say something but she didn't answer. She just took off."

"Did you ask Shellie about her?"

"I did, but she acted like she didn't know what I was talking about."

JP thanked her for her help, but before he left he said, "You need to be more careful with strangers. I've worked with the law for many years and I know how bad it is out there. Please, don't open your door for strangers and if someone identifies themselves as law enforcement, ask for their badge." She pulled the door closed and locked it. JP was a little upset at himself for saying what he did, but these kids need to be more careful. He hoped he hadn't scared her too much, just enough to make her think next time.

He drove directly to Shellie's house. No one answered when he knocked on the front door. He wondered if she had left or if her friend had already called her and warned her. As he walked around to the back door he could hear music blaring, although he didn't really consider "loud noise with someone yelling in the background" as music. Apparently the record companies did because they seemed to make a lot of money from it.

Surprisingly, Shellie opened the back door. "Oh, it's you," she said.

"Yes, it's me. Your friend called you, didn't she?"

"She texted me. I thought it was her coming over."

"Is your dad home?"

"No and he doesn't need to know about this. Anyway, she's wrong. Bailey hasn't been here."

"Shellie, I know differently. And you need to help her."

"I am helping her."

"You're helping her commit a crime. You're helping to keep her in danger. You're helping to make her prey for every sick pervert that walks the streets looking for vulnerable young girls."

"Bailey can protect herself."

"No." JP shook his head. "She can't. How's she going to do that? Does she have a gun?"

"No," she snapped. Then she looked up at JP. "I don't think she does. No. She wouldn't have a gun."

"Shellie, listen to me. Bailey is not safe and neither are you if you know where she is. First of all, you're breaking the law by hiding her."

"I'm not hiding her."

"If you know where she is and you're not telling, then you're committing a crime. And who knows who may be looking for her besides the police? If I can find you, so can someone else."

Shellie started to cry. "I don't know where she is. She wouldn't tell me." She sniffled. "Do you think they'll come after me?"

"Who?"

"The ones who are looking for Bailey?"

"Do you know who's looking for her?"

"The devil worshippers."

JP tried not to show his surprise, but he was caught off guard. This was the only case he had received recently that was not connected to the devil—and now it was. He continued to ask more questions but was unable to gain any more information from Shellie. She must've sensed she had already said more than she should have.

"Shellie, please call me if you hear from Bailey again. She could die out there." He hated to sound so dramatic, but it was the truth. Before he handed her another card, he wrote a phone number on the back. "If you can, please try to convince Bailey to call her attorney. I've written her cell number on the back of my card. Sabre can help her if she will just let her. Can you do that?"

She nodded her head.

"Oh, and when you talk to Bailey, please tell her that her attorney is meeting with Apollo just as she asked her to do."

JP called Sabre when he returned to his car. He had resisted buying an earpiece, claiming one shouldn't talk while driving. But he had to admit there were times he could accomplish a lot more if he made his calls while on the road. Maybe this weekend I'll pick one up.

Sabre answered her phone on the second ring. JP said, "I have some things to go over with you, but I want to follow up on Cole first. Can we meet in your office tomorrow?" He listened as she responded. "Eleven-thirty it is." He hung up the phone, started his engine, and drove off.

It was nearly six o'clock when he pulled up in front of Hansen Plumbing where Cole's father was last employed. He had called ahead to make sure someone would be there, but they closed at six, so JP was concerned. As he parked, he could see the sign still read "Open." He walked in and approached a gray-haired woman behind the counter who appeared to be in her late sixties. She looked up from where she was gathering her things. "Can I help you?"

"Yes," JP said. "Are you the owner?"

She nodded her head. "My husband and I own the business. He's the plumber. I take care of the books."

JP handed her a card. "I'm JP Torn. I'm working for an attorney in juvenile court who's looking for a missing eight-year-old child."

"What can I do for you?"

"The child's father is Dean Johnson. I understand he was an employee of yours."

"He used to be. It's been over a year. We hated to lay him off with all those kids, but times are tough. The plumber's assistants had to go. We had three of them then. Dean had been with us for six years. The next assistant was laid off about six months later, and if things don't improve soon, the last one will be going. It's hard, though. My husband's getting too old to do all the work himself, but we're just not getting the calls. I guess people are buying their own snakes and doing their own work, or the big companies that can afford to advertise are getting the business. I just don't know."

JP wondered if she'd ever stop talking. It seemed like a good place to cut in. "Do you know if he was hired anywhere else?"

"Not anywhere around here in Vista. I'm pretty familiar with the plumbing community. I'd know if he is working anywhere close. He could be in San Diego, but he's not here in North County."

"Was he a good employee?"

"He was a good worker."

"Did you ever have any problems with him?"

"Sometimes he came in a little late on Monday mornings smelling like liquor. Between you and me, I think he was a weekend drunk. He never smelled like that any other day of the week and he never missed work. I think it was just a weekend thing. But that's what made us decide to let him go first. We figured the weekends would eventually turn into more and we couldn't risk it. My husband hated to let him go.

Said he was by far the best worker of the three, but he agreed that if times got worse so would he. People with that sort of problem just can't help themselves. My father was like that. He just couldn't stop drinking. Went to his grave with a bottle in his hand. That's why I don't drink. Oh, I have an occasional glass of wine with dinner, but that's all."

JP wondered how he was going to get her to stop talking so he could leave when she picked up her purse and stepped out from behind the counter. "If there's nothing else, Mr. Torn, I'll be closing up."

"That will be all. You've been very helpful," he said, as he turned and walked quickly toward the door before she could say anything else.

JP drove to the Vista Station of the San Diego County Sheriff's Department on Melrose. He had never worked out of Vista. Usually he had been stationed downtown and in east county, but he had some close friends at this station. It didn't take him long to find his friend, Ernie Cook.

"Hey, JP. How are you, brother?" Ernie greeted him with a big smile.

"I'm good. And you?"

"Life is good. The scouts are out in full force this year. It's my boy's senior year, you know. And he's really hot this year, already beating last year's records. I think he grew a half a foot over the summer."

"Any word from Michigan?"

"Oh yeah, and he had about twenty other offers as well."

"You've come a long way with that boy."

"So, what brings you into my neighborhood?"

"I'm working on a juvenile dependency case. We have a missing eight-year-old boy that lived in this area. I'm sure you've seen the photos. There's been a Pick Up and Detain Order out for nearly two weeks." JP took the photos of Cole and his father out of his file. "This is the boy, and this is his father, Dean Johnson. I don't think Cole is anywhere around here, but I was hoping I could track his father down."

"Do you think his father has him?"

"It's a long shot, but one worth checking out. The father left Mom and the five kids over a year ago and no one seems to have heard from him since." Ernie turned toward his computer and started to input his name when JP said, "I've already run a criminal check on him. All I could find was a really old drunk-driving charge. According to his wife and his last employer he still has a drinking problem, or at least did when they last saw him."

"You checked his work record?"

"I haven't found anything for the last year. He formerly worked at a place called Hansen's Plumbing as a plumber's assistant."

"Any other family?"

"Not here. They're somewhere in Arkansas and so far I haven't found any evidence of him showing up there, but he could be anywhere."

"So what can I do to help?"

"The guy lost his wife, his kids, his job, and he has a drinking problem. I'm thinking it may have been too much and he hit the streets."

"I can make copies of his photo and pass it out to the guys working the beat. They'll ask around. I'll let you know if I hear anything."

JP reached his hand out to shake Ernie's. "It was nice seeing you."

"You too, brother. Maybe next year we can take a trip to Michigan and watch my boy play."

"I'd like that."

JP drove back to Cole's neighborhood on the outside chance that he would spot him. It was a pattern he had developed ever since Cole went missing: A couple of times a day he would canvas the area hoping for some sign of little Cole. He drove up and down the streets between Cole's and Hayden's foster homes. He drove around the park and made his way to the gas station where he stopped and spoke with Mikey, the clerk. From all of the reports that Mikey had collected from his fellow employees, the boy had not returned to the store. And JP found no visible signs of him anywhere on the streets.

It had been nearly forty-eight hours now since anyone had reported seeing Cole. The thought of what that might mean made JP's stomach turn.

Chapter 23

"I thought you didn't have court this morning," Bob said to Sabre as she walked into juvenile court.

"Good morning to you, too," Sabre said, smiling at her friend. "I don't, but I just received word they have Apollo's arraignment on calendar this morning."

"Already? Isn't that kind of quick?"

"It is, but the law says they have to have the hearing no later than seventy-two hours after they pick the minor up. There's nothing saying they can't do it sooner. I'd be curious to know who's pushing this one through, though."

Bob put his arm around Sabre's shoulder. "Sobs, I don't do delinquency cases so I haven't seen it first hand, but isn't it like dependency? Don't they exclude everyone from the courtroom?"

Sabre shook her head. "Not the other attorneys. Most of the judges want them sitting in there so they can complete their calendars. They're afraid they'll lose them to a dependency courtroom. Judge Scary Larry calls it the 'black hole.' Remember, it used to be like that in dependency too."

"That's right. It was that way until our presiding judge, Judge Jerk-off, took over and then embarrassed himself when he thought two of the attorneys were the parents on the case and kept speaking to them as if they were."

Sabre laughed at Bob's play on Judge Shirkoff's name. "He deserved to be embarrassed. He'd been here over a year and he still didn't recognize the attorneys who work here every day."

"That's because he never talked to anyone. He came in here with all the hype about working together as a team and then he hardly ever took the bench, never showed up for any kind of functions, and basically hid out."

"Anyway, I want to see who's appointed to represent Apollo. Hopefully, it's someone who'll be easy to work with and will help us find Bailey. I checked the calendar. It's in Department Five, Scary Larry's department."

"Why do they call him that? Is he mean?"

"No, he's just a wild card. You never know what he's going to do or how he'll rule on a case. He's very unpredictable and he has a sarcastic sense of humor. If you have a losing case you may as well be in his court because then you at least have a chance. But when you have a case you should win, you really don't want to have Scary Larry on it. When he doesn't follow the law and you call him on it, his standard response is, 'That's what appellate courts are for.' Oh yeah, and he yells a lot."

"At who?"

"Attorneys, defendants, parents, anyone who happens to cross him that morning."

Two sheriffs walked past Bob and Sabre and exited the front door. Another walked up and stood close to the metal detector. Sabre looked out and saw a crowd gathering near the entrance. A news van pulled up and a man stepped out carrying a huge camera, along with a woman carrying a microphone. They appeared to be filming and questioning a middle-aged Mexican-American man and a blonde woman about the same age. The couple kept walking toward the courthouse, not responding to the questions. When they neared the door, the sheriffs stepped up and let the couple enter, keeping the news crew outside.

"Who's that?" Bob asked.

Sabre shrugged her shoulders. "I don't know. There must be some high profile case on calendar this morning. I haven't heard about anything, have you?"

"No. That's strange."

"I'm going into the courtroom. I'll see you later. Do you have anything on calendar this afternoon?"

"I have a continuing trial. How about you?"

"I'll be here for an adoption. One of my minors has been waiting a long time to have this finalized. She wanted me there. So I'm going."

Sabre went directly to Department Five where two other delinquency attorneys were also in attendance. The judge looked up as she walked in. "Good morning, Your Honor," she said. He nodded and seemed to force a smile. Uh, oh, Sabre thought. He must be in a bad mood. She was glad she didn't have a case before him this morning. She sat down in the back of the courtroom.

Sabre sat patiently as they called the morning calendar. Attorneys and parents went in and out of the front door. Defendants ranging from twelve to seventeen were escorted by the sheriffs through the back door from Juvenile Hall. Approximately forty-five minutes later the Apollo Servantes case came up. A different assistant district attorney, a tall, thin man about forty-five years old, came into the courtroom to prosecute his case. Sabre wondered why it was given special attention.

The judge spoke. "Who's representing the minor, Apollo Servantes?"

A panel attorney, Roberto Arroyo, stepped forward. "Your Honor, the public defender has a conflict on this case. I'm on detentions this morning and I'll be requesting to be appointed."

The assistant D.A. stood up. "Your Honor, the state asks that the courtroom be cleared for this hearing."

The judge didn't ask for a reason and Arroyo didn't object. "So ordered," the judge said. The three remaining attorneys and Sabre exited the courtroom chatting about why they had to leave. They assumed the reason must be related to the news vans outside.

About five minutes later, Attorney Roberto Arroyo came out of Department Five and escorted Apollo's parents, the Mexican-American man and blonde woman, into the courtroom.

Sabre was pleased Roberto had the case. They had been friends for a long time. They first met when Sabre came to work at juvenile court. Both were members of the juvenile court panel and consequently had many cases together. At the time, Roberto was newly divorced with a three-year-old daughter with a hippopotamus collection. Roberto was always buying her a new stuffed animal. They easily became friends and even tried to date once. They went to see "Of Mice and Men" at the Old Globe Theater in Balboa Park. The date was nice, and Sabre couldn't remember why there wasn't a second date. The best she could remember was that they both opted for friendship.

Roberto's daughter was now about nine years old, making him even more apt to help Sabre find Bailey. She knew he'd be reasonable to work with and would help her as long as it didn't conflict with his client's interest. She'd talk to Roberto after the hearing and hopefully Apollo's parents as well.

The hearing lasted about twenty-five minutes, which was rather long for a detention hearing. Sabre became bored and then anxious while she waited. Finally, Roberto came out with the parents. Sabre approached him immediately.

"I'd like to speak to you and Apollo's parents if you can give me a minute."

Roberto smiled. "What's up, Sabre?"

"I represent a minor in a dependency case. Her name is Bailey. She's purported to be Apollo's girlfriend and has been absent from her foster home for over a week. We know she was with Apollo the majority of that time." Sabre turned her head from Roberto to the parents. "Do you know Bailey?"

The father looked at Roberto who nodded and said, "You can tell her anything you know about Bailey."

The father said, "We knew he had a girlfriend, but we never met her. Other than her name, we didn't really know much."

Sabre looked at Apollo's mother. She was a tall, big-boned woman but not overweight. She wore no make-up except for a little mascara. Her chiseled nose matched the rest of her perfect features. Sabre couldn't help but think how attractive she was. In the right clothes and the right setting, she could compete with the best of them. But today she looked frightened and vulnerable. She fought back tears when she spoke. "I never met her, either. Apollo is such a good boy. He's never been in trouble and until this last week, he never missed school. Even then, when he was running with her, he called every day to let us know he was all right. I know he didn't kill that man." Mr. Servantes put his arm around his wife and they stepped off to the side.

Roberto said, "I don't think they know anything about her. Let me talk to them a few minutes and then you and I can talk."

Sabre walked outside into a crowd of people and waited against the wall while Roberto finished his conversation with Apollo's parents. She took out her cell phone and checked the time. She still had another hour before her appointment with JP at her office.

A few minutes later Roberto walked out with the couple, shielding Mrs. Servantes in the middle. The reporter Sabre had seen earlier was waiting and in their face before the door closed behind them. She heard Roberto advise them. "Don't say anything. Just keep walking."

The reporter held the microphone up in front of the father and asked, "Did your son kill Scott Jamison?"

The father didn't respond. Roberto pushed his way ahead and escorted the parents to their car. The cameraman and reporter followed, still filming and asking questions.

When Roberto returned, the crowd had dispersed. "Why is the press interested in this case?" Sabre asked.

"I'm not sure exactly. Hopefully, I'll be able to find out from my client."

"I met with Apollo yesterday in the Hall. I explained to him that I was only there about Bailey. I advised him not to talk about anything else and he didn't, but I wanted you to know that."

"I take it you didn't get any information about Bailey's whereabouts."

"That's right, but I'd like to try again, if you don't mind."

"I'll be glad to help in any way. Let me talk to Apollo and make sure it's not going to hurt his case and if not, we'll set up a meeting for the three of us as soon as possible. Will this afternoon work for you?"

"Absolutely. I'm here for an adoption hearing anyway. Just let me know what time and I'll work around it. Thanks, Roberto, you're a sweetheart."

"That's me, a real sweetheart." He winked at her. Then, in a serious tone, he said, "I know you'd do the same if I had a minor on the streets. I don't want her there, either."

The mirror in Sabre's office bathroom reflected back at Sabre as she fluffed her hair and checked her make-up. She walked back into her office and sat behind her desk. JP would be there any minute. She picked up the ritual abuse spreadsheet and glanced through the columns. When she looked up, she saw a handsome cowboy standing in her doorway holding some papers.

"Hey, kid." The sound of his voice made her feel safe. During the last year, he had always been there to protect her when she most needed him.

"Good morning. It is still morning, isn't it?"

"The roosters hollered nearly seven hours ago. Seems like evening to me."

Sabre laughed. "Well, good evening to you, JP."

He approached her desk and handed her a copy of the spreadsheet. "I've added another case to this list—the Lecy case."

Sabre's mouth dropped open. "What?"

"Shellie said Bailey is afraid of the 'devil worshippers.'"

"What the hell?"

JP reported on his visit with Shellie and her friend.

"That explains the media coverage." JP wrinkled his brow. "There was a reporter and a cameraman at court this morning. They tried to question Apollo's parents. I bet it's because of the satanic angle. Why else would they be interested? There wasn't anything that newsworthy about the murder. Nothing unusual anyway."

"I'll bet you're right. There's been a lot of buzz since the 'Devil House' was discovered."

"Have you heard anything new on the 'House?'"

"Not a word." JP said. "By the way, I left my card and your cell phone number with Shellie and encouraged her to convince Bailey to call you. I also told her to tell Bailey that you were in contact with Apollo. I thought it might be enough to get her to call."

"Thanks, that was a good idea. I hope it works."

Sabre read the spreadsheet, noticing where JP had very neatly handwritten the name Lecy in the first column. In the column titled Indicators he had written Fear of Devil Worshippers. Neighborhood, Age, and Ethnicity were completed. Sabre filled in the spaces for the social worker and the attorneys. "What does this mean?" Sabre asked, expecting an opinion rather than a real answer.

"I don't know. I've run the demographics for the Neighborhood column. They seem to cluster around two areas, Tierrasanta and Downtown, but not entirely because then you have your Johnson case in Vista, thirty-plus miles north, and one case about the same distance to the east. I've tried looking for a pattern, but I can't come up with anything that seems to matter." JP handed Sabre a map. "I've marked the map where we have strange cases. The black numbers indicate the order in which they came into the juvenile system."

"What's this?" Sabre asked as she pointed to a large red X on the map.

"That's the 'Devil House' that was on the news." JP moved his finger around the map pointing to other red marks. "And these are all places that have been reported by agencies outside of juvey—police reports on taggers mostly. Just something different to graffiti."

"They're all over the map."

"I know. I really don't think they have anything to do with our cases. I think it's just teenagers jumping on the band wagon—wannabes with too much time on their hands." JP handed her another map. "Here's a map without the graffiti. I left the 'Devil House' on there."

Sabre started to stand up. "I'll make copies."

JP touched her arm. "Sit, kid. Those are your copies. I have mine."

Sabre felt a sweet tingle from his touch, and it made her uncomfortable. She wasn't sure why. She shook it off. "Thanks. What other good news do you have for me today?"

JP told her what he had found out about Cole's father and his latest uneventful search for Cole. Sabre knew JP searched the neighborhood a couple of times a day even though he didn't bill her for it. Sabre had been doing the same thing. After court this morning, she had driven around the park and past Cole and Hayden's foster homes before she returned to the office to meet with JP.

JP continued, "We haven't had any sightings of Cole since Tuesday night. That's over forty-eight hours."

Sabre saw the tension in JP's face, how his forehead wrinkled, and she was certain she spotted a little extra gray at his temples. She knew what he was feeling. She felt it, too—the helplessness, the concern, the fear of what Cole might be going through.

Chapter 24

Friday afternoons at juvenile court were different than any of the other days. The courthouse was filled with families wearing smiling faces, little boys and girls dressed in pretty clothes, and there were far fewer attorneys walking the halls. The adoption calendar brought in a different class of client. Parents and children were anxious to finalize a process that had often taken years to achieve, especially the cases that had commenced in the dependency court.

When a child was removed from a parent, the parent had six months to reunify. If they were close to reunification they were given another six months. If by the end of the twelfth month they still had not made enough progress toward reunification, a .26 hearing was held and parental rights could be terminated. If the rights were removed, the Department of Social Services worked diligently to try and find an adoptive home for the child. Often the minor was already placed with foster parents or relatives who wanted to adopt. The process generally took several years and if a home wasn't found, the child remained a legal orphan.

Whenever Sabre had a Friday afternoon trial and she had some downtime, she'd slip into Department One where Judge Shirkoff was handling the adoption calendar and watch the happy people as they legally committed to their new families. It helped her balance all the pain and suffering she saw the rest of the time.

Sabre ducked under a bunch of bright pink balloons and stepped around a family of about twenty, all dressed in church clothes, as she worked her way toward the courtroom. Once inside she took a seat at the back of the room. She had prearranged a visit with Roberto and Apollo. As soon as Roberto finished his court calendar, he would text her and they'd walk through the tunnel to the hall and meet with his client.

In the meantime, she would be present in court for Addison, a seven-year-old girl who was once her client. She hadn't represented her since the .26 hearing when the parents' rights were terminated. Back then her name was Tiffany, but her name would be legally changed when she was adopted. Her new parents let Tiffany choose her own name and for the past six months she went by Addison.

Sabre had come to be quite close to Addison over the past two-and-a-half years. As she watched her move from foster home to foster home, therapist to therapist, Sabre seemed to be the only constant in her life. When Addison was finally matched with an older couple interested in adoption, Sabre had to let go. She remembered how difficult that was for her. Of all the children she worked with, she had become the most attached to Addison. Bob had even encouraged her to adopt Addison herself, but Sabre knew she couldn't give her the attention she needed.

Now, Addison walked into the courtroom wearing a pale green dress with life-size pink lilies scattered throughout the fabric, a pink ribbon in her soft brown curls, pink anklets, and shiny white, patent-leather ballet flats. She seemed calm and almost angelic, quite different from the hyper little girl she had first met. She was no angel, but Sabre was confident her new parents were a good fit for her. When Addison spotted Sabre, a huge smile crossed her face, her eyes opened wide, she held her head up tall, and said aloud across the room, "I'm getting adopted today!"

"Indeed you are," Sabre responded. The judge, the bailiff, and the court clerk all smiled as they watched this seven-year-old girl walk up to the table and take part in one of the most significant events in her life.

Sabre felt herself choke up as she watched the adoption proceedings. Addison had a family. Today, at seven years, three months, and four days old, Addison Sabre McLaughlin started a new life with the new name that she had chosen.

Sabre missed her own family. She missed her brother and her father. Most of her aunts, uncles, and cousins were too far away. She had a decent, yet somewhat strained relationship with her mother. They were never as close as she had been with her father or her brother. Her mother lived about an hour from her and she hadn't seen her in almost two months. Her mother had a busy social life. She had lots of friends, played bridge twice a week, and was always involved in charitable work. But still, she knew her mother enjoyed her visits. Sabre made a mental note to visit her mother as soon as things settled down on these cases.

Right now, she needed to find her missing clients.

Sabre lingered in the courtroom after Addison's hearing, watching some of the other adoption proceedings and waiting for a text from Roberto. The sound on her phone was shut off but she felt the vibration in her hand when it dinged. *Meet me by the info counter.* Sabre stood up and quietly left the courtroom. Gillian, the social worker on Bailey's case was going into Department One just as Sabre was leaving.

"Any word from Bailey?" Gillian asked.

"Not a word," Sabre said and walked on.

Roberto greeted her with a smile and a hug. "How's the silverback?" Sabre asked. It was a nickname she had for him. She tried to remember when it started or where it came from, but she couldn't.

"Couldn't be better," he said. "I talked to Apollo and he's willing to meet with you again. He wants you to send a very specific message to Bailey and he implied the message will in turn get her to contact you. I'm not sure exactly what that means, but it's something."

"Whatever it takes. I think I can get Shellie to pass on a message to her but I don't know how long it'll take."

"According to Apollo, Shellie will get the message to her quickly."

Sabre felt a little better. At least there was a chance of reaching her client.

"You ready?" Roberto asked.

"Let's go."

"By the way, just so you know, Apollo claims neither he nor Bailey killed Scott."

"Do you believe him?" Sabre asked.

Roberto tilted his head to one side. "It doesn't matter if I do or don't."

They walked toward the door leading to the back room and the tunnel to the Hall, but before they reached the door Barry Betts approached Roberto. "Hi, Barry," Roberto said.

"Hello," Betts said. He turned to Sabre and nodded, "Counselor." Betts handed Roberto a piece of paper.

"What's this?" Roberto asked before he looked at it.

"I've been retained to represent Apollo Servantes." His head nodded up and down on his long neck and the last word in each sentence raised an octave. "You're no longer on the case."

Sabre said, "We were just going to see him. He's going to help me find a missing minor in a dependency case."

Betts shook his head from side to side. "No. No. You can't do that."

"Will you please talk to him and see if he's willing to help us?"

"Already have. I'm afraid I had to advise him not to talk to anyone."

Sabre started to speak, but Betts kept shaking his head. "No. No. Sorry. I have to protect my client."

Roberto handed the court order back to Betts and he walked off. "That guy's weird. Ever notice how his head bobs around and the whole time his eyes don't move—like they're not connected or something?"

Sabre chuckled in spite of her frustration. "Dang. Now I'm back to square one."

They turned and walked back up the tunnel toward the courtroom.

"At least you know that Shellie has more information than she's giving."

"That's true. I'll put JP right on it." Sabre reached her hand out and touched Roberto on the arm. "Thanks for trying, Silverback."

He winked at her. "Anytime, Sabre."

They exited the tunnel door and stepped into the hallway of the courthouse. Sabre turned to leave and then turned back, "Oh, so what's the message?"

Roberto opened his file, took out a legal pad, tore off the top sheet, and handed it to Sabre. She read it aloud. *Show the second one to someone you can trust. Keep the third one hidden.*

Chapter 25

Sabre reached for her feather pillow, fluffed it, and laid her head down. More tired than usual, she closed her eyes and started to drift off to sleep. Her cell phone rang. At first she thought she was dreaming. She turned over in her bed and looked at the pyramid-shaped clock on her nightstand. She tapped the point of the pyramid and a robotic voice said, "Eleven-fifty-two p.m." She had been in bed less than twenty minutes.

Sabre stepped out of bed and took the three steps to the counter where her phone was plugged in. By the time she reached her cell it had already rung three times. The number was blocked.

"Hello." For a couple of seconds no one responded. Sabre pulled the phone back from her ear, checking to see if she had missed the call. She was still connected. "Hello," she repeated.

"Hello," the young voice was tentative. "Is this Sabre Brown?"

"Yes. Who's this?"

"Bailey."

"Bailey!" Sabre said. "I'm so glad you called. Are you okay?"

"Yes."

"Where are you?"

"I need to meet with you. I need to give you something. But first I need to know that you won't turn me in."

Sabre hesitated for just a second. She wanted Bailey off the streets but she also didn't want her arrested. She had an obligation to protect her minor client, but she also had to honor her confidentiality. It was more difficult with children. The law was a lot clearer with adults.

"Of course. I won't turn you in. Where can we meet?"

"And you won't bring anyone with you?" Bailey asked.

"No. I'll come alone."

"You promise?" Bailey sounded even younger than her fourteen years. Sabre could tell Bailey wanted to believe her, but anyone would've told her those words. Sabre knew that many people had probably already made her lots of promises they didn't keep.

"I promise."

"And you won't tell anyone?"

"I won't tell anyone. Where are you?"

"Do you know where Tecolote Canyon is?"

"Yes."

"There's an entrance to the canyon and the golf course. Just pull into the driveway there and wait for me. I'll be there soon."

"Off of Mt. Acadia?"

"Yes."

"Okay. It'll take me about ten minutes to get there."

"Can I trust you?" Bailey asked.

"Yes, you can. I'm your lawyer."

"That doesn't mean you can be trusted." She sounded more like the Bailey she had encountered earlier, but even through the sarcasm Sabre could hear the fear in her voice.

"Well, you can trust me. I just want to help you." Sabre spoke with sincerity. She hoped Bailey believed her. But before Sabre could say anything else, she heard a dial tone. She wasn't entirely certain what that meant. Was Bailey still going to meet her or had she changed her mind? Did someone interrupt her? Either way, she still had to go and find out.

Sabre dressed quickly, grabbed her keys, and jumped in her car. She plugged her phone into her earpiece in case Bailey called back. She was tempted to call JP, but she had promised she'd go alone and she knew JP wouldn't let her do that if he knew she was out at midnight meeting with a teenage runaway near a canyon. When she thought of it that way, it didn't sound like such a good idea to her, either. But she had promised.

Sabre turned onto Mt. Acadia, driving around and up and down the hilly street until she reached Snead Ave. and the entrance to Tecolote Canyon. A yellow caution light blinked on and off about thirty feet before the turn. She turned onto Snead, the street that led into the canyon and up to the golf course. It looked more like a long driveway than a street and the golf course, which was situated inside the canyon, wasn't visible. All one could see, even in the daylight, was brush, hills, and trees. Tonight the sky was too dark to even see that.

There were no other cars around. She flipped a u-turn and faced her car toward the street instead of the canyon, just in case she needed to leave in a hurry. She left her car running, double-checked her doors to make sure they were locked, and shut off her lights. She felt more and more uneasy as she waited there in the complete darkness. Sabre regretted she hadn't called JP. After all, he was her investigator and had the same obligation to not break their client's confidentiality. But she again decided not to call him.

Sabre waited for what seemed like an hour, checking her watch every few minutes. Six minutes had passed, then seven, eight. . . . No Bailey. The silence was deafening. A noise in the darkness startled her. It took her a second to realize it was the hoot of an owl. After all, she was in "Owl" Canyon. Another two minutes passed. The warmth inside the car competed with the colder outside air and the windows began to fog up. Sabre turned the defogger on and ran her windshield wipers to help clear them. Very little was visible outside. It was completely dark behind her car, some light from the partial moon shone down in front of her, and the lights on the hill from houses far above her brightened the top of the hill. Off to her left about thirty yards away sat one lone street lamp offering a little light in about a ten-foot circle below it. She continued to look out her windows without rolling them down, but to little avail.

Eleven minutes had passed since she arrived. She wondered how long she should wait. She may not even show up. Car lights approached from the left along Mt. Acadia. She watched the car speed down the hill and around the curve. A man's voice bellowed, "Yahoo!" Sabre saw an upper body, head, and arm reach outside the passenger window and fling what looked like a bottle into the canyon about fifty feet from her car. He continued to hoot and holler as they passed her car and disappeared into the night.

Sabre checked her watch again. Thirteen minutes.

"Ahh . . ." Sabre put her hand over her own mouth to stifle the scream brought on by the face she saw in her passenger window. Then a knock. She couldn't tell for certain who it was. She waited for a second.

"It's me," Bailey said.

Sabre unlocked the door and Bailey stepped inside the car. "Brr . . . It's cold out there."

"How long have you been here?" Sabre asked.

"Not long."

Bailey was dressed in jeans and a dark, long-sleeved shirt; a knit cap was pulled down below her ears. She held a small paper bag in her hand. Sabre turned the heat up, then glanced around the car. She spotted what she was looking for, reached behind Bailey, and picked up a sweatshirt from the back seat. She handed it to Bailey. "Here. Put this on."

Bailey pulled the sweatshirt over her head and stuck her hands and her package inside the front pocket. Her knit cap fell off, and before she could put it back on Sabre saw her blond roots reaching out from her scalp to meet the black dye on her hair.

"Bailey, I want to help you any way that I can, but first I need to know if you're safe."

"I'm fine." Bailey didn't sound as hostile as she had the first time they met, but she did remain cautious.

"I'm not asking you where you're staying, but just tell me if you have a house to stay in or if you're living on the streets."

She nodded. "I'm fine," she repeated.

"Do you have food? Do you need anything?"

"I'm eating okay. I want to know about Apollo."

"I saw Apollo yesterday. He seems like a good kid. And he's very protective of you."

"He didn't kill Scott." She said in a louder voice.

"Do you know who did?"

Bailey shook her head from side to side but didn't verbally respond. Sabre waited for a few seconds in the silence. "The police have a witness that saw both you and Apollo running from the house around the time Scott was killed. Were you there? Did you see Scott or who killed him?"

"He was already dead when we got there. We stopped in to pick up a few things. Mom told me Scott wouldn't be there, but we got there a little later than we planned. He was lying on the floor in a puddle of blood when we came in the room."

"Was your mother there?"

"She was passed out on the bed as usual." She spoke calmly, and no anger showed in her voice. To Sabre it sounded more like resignation.

"Did you see anyone else?"

"No."

"Bailey, who do you think killed Scott?"

Bailey's brow wrinkled and she stared for a moment at Sabre, either surprised or confused by the question. Then she quickly looked down and mumbled, "I hoped it would all be over when Scott was killed."

"All what would be over?" Sabre asked.

Again Bailey shook her head but she didn't answer the question. She reached in her pocket and pulled out the little bag she had been carrying. She handed it to Sabre. "Apollo said to give this to someone I can trust. I think that's you."

"What is it?"

"It's a video Apollo took. It's at the 'Devil House.' Please use it to help Apollo."

"Did Apollo take the video that the police have? The one that was on the news?"

Bailey nodded affirmatively.

"How are you and Apollo involved?"

"I can't tell you that."

"Bailey, I want to help you."

"Just take the disc and use it to help us."

"What's on it?"

"You'll see." Bailey reached for the door handle.

"Bailey," Sabre said. Bailey turned and looked at her, keeping her hand on the door handle. "I'll keep my promise to not go to the authorities but I have to try and convince you to turn yourself in. It'll be a lot better for you if you do."

"I can't." She opened the door. "Please help Apollo."

"I'll do what I can, but you know I can't represent him." Bailey started to close the door. "Wait," Sabre said. "Can I drop you off somewhere?"

"No, thanks. I'm fine. I'll leave after you do."

Bailey stepped out of the car, and as the door was closing Sabre said, "Keep in touch with me, please."

The door closed. Sabre didn't want to leave until she knew Bailey was safe. She was concerned that she might be staying somewhere in the canyon. It was a dark, scary place. Sabre had hiked there one afternoon with a friend, and even then it was dark from all the shadows from the tall trees. And on two occasions during that afternoon they met with coyotes. She couldn't even imagine what it might be like at night.

She saw Bailey standing there waiting for her to leave and then finally heard her yell, "Go, just go!"

Sabre turned her lights on and moved forward. She saw a bicycle lying in the ditch just before she turned onto Mt. Acadia. *At least she isn't on foot.*

Chapter 26

"Thanks for coming by so early," Sabre said as JP entered into her condo at 7:15 on Saturday morning.

"No problem."

"Would you like some coffee?" Before he could answer she said, "You've probably been up for about three hours already so you must be on decaf by now, right?"

"Right."

JP followed Sabre to the kitchen. She poured a mug of black coffee and handed it to him. She picked up her own mug and said, "Follow me, I have something to show you."

They went into the living room. Sabre already had the disc in the DVD player and set on pause. She pointed toward a big comfortable chair. "Have a seat."

JP set his coffee mug on the coaster on a small table next to his chair. "What is this?"

"It's a video that Bailey gave me."

"From Bailey? You heard from her?"

"She called me late last night and asked me to meet her." His eyebrow raised. "How late?"

"Around midnight. She apparently received the message that Apollo sent through Shellie, and she decided I was the one she could trust." Sabre proceeded to tell JP all the details of her rendezvous the night before with her minor client.

JP stood up. Sabre could tell he was upset with her. "Why didn't you call me?"

"Because I promised her I wouldn't. I need her to trust me and she needs someone she can trust. It had to be done that way."

"Dang, Sabre. You're going to get yourself killed." He stepped away from her shaking his head, his back turned.

"I'm fine. She's a fourteen-year-old girl."

JP turned back toward her. She could see the mixture of anger and concern on his face. "Fourteen-year-olds carry guns and knives, you know! And you don't know who could've been with her." He shook his head again. "For a smart girl, you sure can be dumb. Sometimes I can hear your engine runnin' but I don't think anyone's drivin'."

Sabre covered her mouth to keep him from seeing her smile. "Okay, it was foolish. But I'm okay. All right?"

JP sat back down. He looked directly at the television, avoiding eye contact with her. "Show me the video."

Sabre hit "Play" on the remote. The film had an eerie kind of "Blair Witch Project" appearance. There was a quick camera shot of the front of a house. "Bailey said this was the 'Devil House' they showed on the news. She said Apollo taped that one as well."

"Rewind that and pause on it," JP said abruptly. He waited for a second. "That's definitely the same house."

"Now, look at this," Sabre said. She continued playing the DVD. The camera followed a fat man as he wobbled from his car toward the house. It was dark and the footage was obviously shot from behind the man.

"Do you ever see his face?"

"Not really," Sabre said. She paused the DVD on the man but his face was turned at about a two-hundred-degree angle showing his right ear and cheek. "This is about the best shot. There's another one in a few frames where he faces the camera more directly, but he's in such dark shadows you can't see him." Sabre went forward. "Here it is."

"Hmm, maybe a tech guy could do something with that one."

Sabre started the disc again.

"Wait," JP said. "Go back to the car."

Sabre rewound it and paused on the car. "Can you tell what it is?" Sabre asked.

"It's old, really old. The shape looks like it might be from the forties, either a Plymouth or a Dodge."

"It's so dark I can't even tell what color the car is. And all that's exposed is a small part of the front bumper and fender. How do you get all that?"

"No, look, you can see a lot more than that. There's part of the wheel well, the hood, and the headlight. You can even see a part of the grill. I can't tell you for certain what it is, but I've had a little experience with old cars. I have a friend who could tell us more. I'll show him the disc. He might even be able to tell us who the collector is." JP continued to stare at the paused frame. Then he stood up and walked up to the screen. "And look, there's some kind of bumper sticker."

"But all you can see is a curvy line. What good is that going to do?"

JP pointed at the decal outlining it with his finger. "It looks like a double line, but I think it's a line slightly inside the edge of the sticker. See how it comes to a point here to the left and then curves in and back out again."

"It could be anything . . . or nothing."

"The shape looks familiar but I can't figure out why," JP said.

Sabre hit "Play" again. They watched as the man walked stealthily to the back door, used a key to open the lock, and entered the "Devil House." A very dim light showed through the window, then faded, then came on again.

"What's with the light?" Sabre asked.

"It looks like he's using a flashlight instead of turning on the lights."

"Maybe the electricity isn't turned on."

"But it was on in the other film. I remember seeing a light bulb lit up."

Sabre looked at him with surprise. "You remember a light bulb?" She shook her head. "I guess that's why you're the detective."

"So, what else is on here?" JP asked. The edge started to leave his voice.

"Not too much. A lot of down time, like Apollo's waiting for something to happen, but then at the very end there's something especially interesting." Sabre ran through the rest of the film until she reached the last few frames. "Look who showed up."

"That's Scott. Scott Jamison."

"Yeah. Dead man, Scott. Bailey's mother's boyfriend."

They watched as Scott walked up to the house, circled around to the back door, and went inside without knocking. And then there was a blank screen.

"That's it?" JP asked.

"I'm afraid so. What do you make of it all?"

"So far we know that Scott and the fat man are connected to the 'Devil House.' We know that Apollo and Bailey are involved in this mess, or they have at the very least seen something they shouldn't have and Apollo felt compelled to film it." JP nodded his head. "This must be the 'special project' Apollo's friend, Josiah, was talking about. So, is this some kind of expression of art, or is it evidence?"

"Well, whatever it started out to be, Apollo must think it's important enough to bring it out in the open."

"But why wouldn't he try to send the disc to his own lawyer if he thinks it could help him?" JP asked.

Sabre's head shot up and she looked at JP. "Because he didn't want it 'out in the open.' He wanted to help Bailey." Sabre paused. "But why wouldn't he give us the third disc?

There must be another one because Apollo's message said to 'keep the third one hidden.'"

"Maybe they don't know who they can trust. Maybe this is a test."

"All the more reason why I'm glad I went alone last night."

JP shook his head. He took a deep breath and sighed. "Please don't do that again."

Sabre smiled a funny smile, scrunching her mouth to one side and wrinkling her nose. "Sorry, I can't make that promise. If she needs me, I'll have to go."

"Dang, woman. You're about as stubborn as a blue-nosed mule!"

Chapter 27

JP drove for the third time to the chicken farm near the Johnson family house where Cole's mother claimed she obtained the chicken feet. The first time he went unannounced. The second time he had an appointment, but the owner had an emergency and wasn't there when he arrived. So, JP still didn't have a definite answer about the alleged satanic ritual abuse evidence found in the Johnson home. The mother maintained that she bought the cheapest meat she could to feed her family and that the farmer often gave her the chicken feet for free. Eating chicken feet seemed pretty gross to JP. Although he had never tried it, when he was young he was well aware of families in Texas who did eat them. He felt fortunate to not have been one of them. He lived in Texas for a while with his grandfather on a small ranch and he always had plenty to eat.

The mother had offered no explanation for the goat blood.

JP turned off the pavement and onto a dirt road leading up to the chicken farm. He parked alongside a blue 1970 Toyota Hilux pickup. He couldn't remember the last time he had seen that make and model. It was in pretty bad shape, and it had a lot of dents and gray primer splotches along one side where the paint may have been stripped. Duct tape kept the passenger-side rearview mirror from falling off. The rear bumper appeared to be hanging on with the help of bailing wire. JP exited his car and walked around to the other side of the pickup, admiring its beauty even in its state of disrepair.

Just as JP reached the other side, a man came around the dilapidated building and walked toward JP. "What can I do for you?" he asked.

JP looked up. He took a couple of steps toward the man. "I'm JP Torn." He reached his hand out to shake. "Are you Elliot Hammouri?"

The man shook his hand. "Yes, I am."

"I was admiring the Hilux. Is this yours?"

"Yeah. I bought it recently off eBay for $500."

"One-point-five engine, right?"

"Yeah, they apparently didn't make the one-point-six in America until later. I know it doesn't look like much but it runs real good. The kid who sold it to me said his grandfather bought it when it was new. It doesn't have a lot of miles on it for as old as it is." Elliot walked up to the side of the pickup and ran his hand along the primer. "He said his grandpa saw some spots where the paint was thin, so he used white house paint to protect the metal. I removed most of the white paint. I'm hoping at some point I'll be able to restore it, but for now it's a work truck."

"You got yourself a good deal."

"That's what I hear. What can I do for you?"

"I'm here about Leanne Johnson. You may know that her children were removed from her custody. I'm the private detective for the attorney who's representing the children."

"I heard Cole was missing. Have they found him yet?"

"I'm afraid not, but what I'm trying to establish is something very specific and I think you can help."

"What's that?" Elliot asked. He took a step to the left. "Would you mind if we go into the office? Then I can hear the phone if it rings. With this economy I've had to cut back on office help."

"No problem." JP followed him up the steps to a small office on the end of an unpainted building. The building looked steady enough. It was warm inside and the relatively new paneling on the walls gave it a clean look. "Leanne Johnson claims she got chicken feet from you for food. Is that correct?" Elliot hesitated and JP continued. "It's important that we know the truth. The Department of Social Services thinks she's performing some kind of satanic rituals because of the chicken feet."

"She did get them from me. I gave them to her because I knew she and the kids were hungry. I don't know for sure what she does with them, but as far as I know she uses them for food. She didn't come here asking for them."

"What did she ask for?" JP asked.

"She asked for the cheapest meat I had. I mostly have the chickens for eggs. I sell a few chickens when they stop laying or I eat them myself. I don't eat the feet and I don't like the gizzards or liver, so I give it all to her whenever I butcher a chicken. I certainly didn't expect it to cause her problems."

"Did you ever sell her any goat or give her any goat blood?"

Elliot looked directly at JP. His forehead wrinkled. "I didn't give her any blood. I sold her some goat meat, but I told her it was beef. I didn't think she'd know the difference."

"She didn't, but DSS had the blood tested."

"I never meant to cause any harm. I sold it to her real cheap. The kids were hungry and I was afraid they wouldn't want it if they knew it was goat."

"It's not your fault. You were just trying to help someone in need." JP smiled at him. "Just one more thing. Has anyone from DSS been here to ask you about this?"

Elliot shook his head. "No one has talked to me."

JP pushed his hat up slightly with his index finger and nodded his head. "Please just tell them the truth if they come asking."

From the chicken farm, JP drove south on Interstate 15 to see his techie friend in Poway, where he had duplicates made of Apollo's DVD. He left one copy behind so his friend could try to enhance the portly man's face or anything else that might help identify him.

Then he drove straight up Highway 67 to Ramona. JP liked this small town. He took a deep breath, inhaling the smell of the livestock as he approached. It was the closest he would get to Texas living. Maybe one day he'd find a ranch for himself in this area. Before he reached the main part of town, which consisted of a few blocks, he turned left on a dirt road, past a row of about thirty mailboxes. He wound around for half a mile until he reached a house that was situated on his left in a clearing. A new metal garage, at least twice the size of the house, stood behind it. The yard contained a half dozen old cars in different states of disrepair.

JP drove around the house and pulled up in front of the garage. As he exited the car with the disc, he heard a loud banging noise. His friend stopped pounding when JP walked in. "Hi, Skip."

"Nice to see you, buddy," Skip said, as he pushed his goggles up to the top of his head with his left hand and reached out his right to shake hands.

JP looked around at the four-bay garage. One of the bays had a hoist hanging from the ceiling and three of the bays were filled with old cars—a 1956 Thunderbird, a 1952 Plymouth, and a 1938 Ford Club Cabriolet Convertible. "Whoa, that's a beauty. Is it yours?" JP asked, as he approached the Ford.

"I wish. But it's fun working on it, anyway. I can't wait to see it when it's completely restored. It belongs to a new collector, some trust fund baby."

"Do you know most of the collectors in the San Diego area?"

"I know most of the collectors in southern California, at least the ones that have been around a while." Skip took off his gloves and walked toward his desk at the end of the garage. "Show me what you have."

JP followed him to the machine, put in the disc, and fast forwarded to the frame with the old car. "I need to know what kind of car this is and anything else you can tell me about it."

"It's a Plymouth Special DeLuxe four-door sedan, likely a 1948. Very few changes took place on these cars from forty-six through the beginning of forty-nine because of the war. The changes came out around March of forty-nine. Ford and Chevy had already come out with their new styles, but Plymouth didn't bring theirs on the market until the spring. Anyway, this has the old grill and front lines so it was before 1949 for sure."

"Do you have any idea who owns one around here?"

"Most of the Plymouths that I'm aware of are from the early forties or the fifties, like this one over here." He pointed to the second bay. "There was a collector years ago who had every old Chrysler product ever made in the US. He lived in Fontana, and when he died I think some of the cars were placed in the Ro-Val Museum in Fontana."

"I've never heard of that museum."

"It's been closed for many years. I believe the cars were sold to Bill Harrah, the founder of Harrah's Casinos, who had them on display in his casinos. When he died they were going to sell them at auction, but the people of Las Vegas fought to keep them and they were ultimately donated by Harrah's estate. A new automobile museum was established for them in Las Vegas."

"You're just smarter than a circus dog," JP said, smiling.

"I couldn't tell you how many of the Chryslers ended up in Las Vegas or if any of them did for sure."

"Do you know the name of the man who had the collection in Fontana?"

Skip looked pensive. "It was Craven, or Cravitt, or Caret, something like that. I don't know, man. I'm digging deep here."

"Thanks, Skip. You've been a big help."

"I do know the collector was a doctor. A bigwig with Kaiser, I think."

Chapter 28

Early Saturday evening before dark found Sabre at the park searching once again for Cole. She had been out earlier in the day, as she had every day since he was missing. She carried a bag of groceries with her in case she met Mama T. Sometimes she'd stop at a fast food restaurant and pick up a bag of one-dollar burgers. Lately, she had been trying to bring healthier food with more fruits and vegetables. Today she brought a loaf of bread, a large jar of peanut butter, and some jelly.

Sabre walked along the park showing Cole's photo to everyone she met. Some people thought they may have seen him, but no one had any definite or helpful responses. About three-quarters of the way through the park, she spotted Mama T at a trash can working her usual "turn garbage into food" magic.

"Mama T," Sabre called as she approached her.

Mama T turned around quickly. She appeared more nervous than usual. "Uh," Mama T said.

"It's just me. Sabre. Are you okay?"

Mama T frowned and continued to methodically fish bags and cans out of the trash can.

Sabre held the photo of Cole up in front of her face as she had done so many times before. "Have you seen this boy, Cole, today?"

"Hmpf. Boy. Boy eats. Boy runs. Boy. Boy. Boy." Mama T pointed toward three children chasing each other nearby. "Boy runs."

Sabre looked carefully at the children, but Cole wasn't among them. She held the picture up again. "Mama T, have you seen this boy?"

Another "hmpf" was all Sabre received in return, as Mama T continued shuffling through wet papers, cans, and broken glass in search of her dinner.

Sabre held the bag of groceries out to her. "I brought you some bread and peanut butter." Mama T looked up and took the bag from her hand. "There's a jar of jelly in there, too, in case you want it with your peanut butter." Mama T caught Sabre's eye before she looked away and although she didn't smile, Sabre thought she saw a little sparkle in her eyes for the first time. She made a mental note to bring jelly again.

Sabre finished her trek through the park, still not finding anyone who could positively provide any information about Cole's whereabouts. It had been so long since there had been news of him. He had not returned to Hayden's school and no one had reported seeing him since then. That was four days without a word. Sabre felt helpless. She knew looking through the park and the neighborhood nearby was probably a waste of time, and talking to Mama T certainly was, but she didn't know what else to do. Her mind raced as she walked to the car. *What a pathetic way to spend Saturday night, not that I have a social life anyway.*

Sabre rang Bob's doorbell. He answered the door in a t-shirt, corduroy pants, and slippers. "You look comfy," Sabre said as she walked in. "Is Marilee here?"

"Hello to you, too. No, she's at the store."

Corey, Bob's son, darted into the room and hugged her. "Hi, Auntie Sabre."

Sabre hugged back, tousled his hair, and said, "Wow, you're getting so tall. You're going to pass me up soon." She turned to Bob. "Thanks for letting me stop in. I just came from the park looking for Cole and I wasn't quite ready to go home."

"Anytime. Would you like something to drink?"

"No, I'm good." Sabre removed her jacket and hung it on the back of a kitchen chair. "I'm not staying long. I just needed a reality check."

Bob put his hand on Sabre's shoulder. "I wish I could help in some way. I spoke with Cole's mother today. I can't even imagine what she's going through."

"Neither can I, but it helps seeing Corey." She turned to him. "Are you still playing your saxophone?"

"Yeah, I was just about to practice. Want to listen?" He tugged at her and then broke away, dashing up the stairs toward his room.

"You bet."

Bob rolled his eyes. "Are you sure?" he whispered.

Sabre laughed and they both followed Corey upstairs to his bedroom. Corey had already started playing when they entered his room. It was a new song and it needed a lot of practice, but Sabre and Bob listened patiently and clapped loudly when he stopped. Sabre glanced around at all the trinkets and fun things Corey had in his room. "I see you've made a few changes in here."

"Yeah, Dad and I painted and put up some posters and things."

"I see that. And you have the Justin Bieber poster I sent you."

Corey just smiled. Bob said, "Some of his friends made fun of him for liking Justin Bieber but Corey held his own. I was very proud of him."

Sabre's forehead wrinkled. "What's that?" Sabre asked, pointing to a partially covered black-and-white metal object on his dresser.

Bob reached over, picked it up, and held it so Sabre could see it. "It's an old US Highway Shield. Route 101. Corey found it when we cleaned out the garage and he wanted to keep it. It belonged to Marilee's father. I'm not sure if it had any particular significance to him, but it's nice for Corey to have something that belonged to him," Bob said. "Why, what's wrong?"

"Nothing, but look." Sabre picked up a piece of paper and covered all but the edge of the shield. "Remember, I told you there was a bumper sticker on the back of the car in that video I received from Bailey? That's the shape. It was a US Highway Route Shield."

"So what does it mean?"

"Heck if I know, but I'll bet JP can figure it out."

Sabre drove down the hill that led to Bob's house, calling JP as soon as she pulled out of the driveway. "It's a US Highway Route Shield," she told him.

"You're right. It all makes sense now. It's another connection to Scott Jamison."

"What?" Sabre asked.

"Scott had a Route 66 shield tattoo. I saw it when I jammed my knee into his back. I bet the one on the car was Route 66 as well."

"But we can't see enough of it to tell."

"I know, but it gives me another lead. It could be a car club or something. It might help lead us to the identity of the man in the film."

Chapter 29

The purple Jerry Garcia tie fit Sabre's mood this Monday morning as she dressed for her court hearings. It was bright and aggressive—a "fighter" tie. She needed to be strong in the Johnson hearing. The children were still spread all over the county, sibling and mother visits were nearly non-existent, and Cole was still missing. And all this was brought on by a case that she wasn't sure even warranted filing.

She wondered if she should take one last trip around the park and Cole's foster parents' neighborhood. She went twice each day on the weekends but saw no signs of Cole. She and Mama T were becoming buds . . . well, not exactly buds, but Sabre had spoken to her several times. Recently, when Sabre brought her food, she seemed thankful in her own way. She mostly grunted when Sabre gave her something, but sometimes she could see a slight change of expression on her face. It wasn't really a smile; it was more like a softening of her facial muscles.

The cuckoo on Sabre's clock in the dining room stuck its head out and tweeted seven times. She was out of time; she needed to go straight to court. She finished dressing, picked up her files, and drove to the courthouse.

Parking was easy, but in fifteen minutes the lot would be packed. She exited her car and walked toward the front door, passing no one along the way. A young, uniformed sheriff greeted her at the metal detector. He was a sub, but she had seen him before. Sabre picked up her files from the belt and walked directly to the lounge/workroom where the new petitions for the detentions were housed for the attorneys. She rummaged through the petitions looking for bizarre cases, even though she wasn't on the schedule. There were only two new cases. One was a tox baby, and the other was a child who had been purportedly hidden in a closet for over three years. Sabre's stomach felt queasy and her face turned red with anger. No matter how conditioned she was to cases like these, some of them stirred up deep emotions. She took a deep breath, put the petitions back in the file folder, and checked her mail slot for the reports for her morning hearings. The reports should've been there several days ago, but Gillian, the social worker on Johnson and Lecy, had not filed them last week. That had surprised Sabre because although Gillian wasn't her favorite social worker, she had to admit she was generally efficient and timely with her reports.

She pulled the stack of paperwork out of her mail slot. The Lecy report sat on top. It consisted of only a few pages with a recommendation to continue until the minor, Bailey, was picked up. That was no surprise. Neither were the recommendations on the Johnson case. The social worker wanted to keep the children in foster care. Sabre sat down on one of the metal folding chairs and looked through the rest of her reports.

Several attorneys came and went from the workroom, greeting her, gathering their reports, and then leaving. Sabre separated her reports, placed them in the appropriate folders, and opened the door just as Bob was about to enter the room.

"Hi, Sobs," he said.

"Good morning." Sabre stepped back and decided to chat with him. "We just received the reports on Johnson and Lecy."

"Let me guess. The social worker wants to go straight to permanent plans and remove the children forever."

"She's not that bad."

"That Johnson case should be a voluntary," Bob protested. He picked up his copy of the report and flipped through it.

"You may be right, but the court isn't going to even consider that until Cole is returned."

"I know," Bob said, as he glanced at the report. "Oh, look. It says she'll consider return if everyone is exorcised."

Sabre cuffed Bob playfully on the arm and chuckled. "It doesn't say that, you nitwit."

"The woman is nuts. Worse than that, she's evil."

"She's not evil. A little off the page, maybe, but not evil."

"When do you want to do these cases?"

"I'm ready whenever you are."

"My client's already here on the Johnson case, but Lecy's not here yet. Who knows if she'll even make it."

"So, do you want to wait for her?"

Bob shook his head. "I don't care one way or the other. We could wait all day for her, but there's nothing we can do anyway until Bailey is picked up. I'm here all morning with other stuff."

"I have a few cases in Department One, and I have one in Five. I'll go do those and then meet you back in Department Four."

Sabre walked out into the hallway, which was filled nearly to capacity. She wound her way through the crowd to the end of the hallway and went into Department One. She sat in the back of the courtroom, reading her reports until her cases were called. She pondered over the Johnson report and what to do with that case. It left her uneasy but she wasn't convinced that there was ritual abuse going on. She certainly didn't want to return those children to the home if there was, but her investigation hadn't led to anything except poverty and hunger, both of which could be fixed. The children didn't seem to know of anything strange in the home, but Sabre hadn't had a chance to speak to Cole about it before he disappeared. Hayden certainly didn't indicate anything but he wasn't the best reporter, either.

Sabre finished reading the report. She shuffled back through the pages again. Nowhere in the report did it indicate that the social worker had spoken to Hammouri, the chicken farmer. So either she hadn't interviewed him or she deliberately left it out of the report because it didn't support her recommendation. Both scenarios were unacceptable.

Sabre stepped into Department Four, closing the door quietly behind her. She sat down next to Bob in the front row directly behind the bailiff.

"Hi, snookums," he whispered. "This hearing is almost over. Watch Wagner's client. She keeps staring at Mike, the bailiff. She's practically drooling."

"Is that the one who keeps flashing her boobs at him?" she whispered back.

"Yeah, Mike's girlfriend." Bob spoke just loudly enough for Mike to hear him.

The bailiff turned around, leaned over the railing, and said to Bob, "Hush, or I'll throw you out of here."

Bob and Sabre both smiled. They knew he was joking. They teased Mike relentlessly and in turn he did the same. Sabre was certain Bob had been jabbing him all morning about his "girlfriend." Every time this client came to court she wore low cut dresses and she always made sure Mike saw her. He hated to be on the metal detector when she came to court because she would hang out near it trying to talk to him. She wasn't particularly unattractive, but her face looked weathered from the sun and when she smiled several gaps appeared in her teeth. Her hair was bleached and she was about thirty pounds overweight. Everything about her seemed extreme. Her skirt was too short, her heels too high, and her makeup too heavy.

Sabre and Bob watched her as the hearing continued. The woman had positioned herself so she was showing Mike plenty of leg. She seemed to be paying little attention to the judge, more interested in Mike than whether or not her children would be returned to her. Sabre glanced at Mike. He tried to look everywhere except at her. The client shifted in her seat, bobbing her head, and swinging her leg in an obvious attempt to catch Mike's attention. Even the judge saw it and smirked.

When the hearing ended the client wiggled her butt as she pranced out of the courtroom, looking back every few steps at Mike. He just shook his head. When the door closed behind her Mike said to Bob, "Don't even start, or I'll throw you in a cell with the other derelicts."

Bob laughed, "She's your girlfriend, not mine."

"Are you ready on your cases? I want you out of here," Mike said.

Bob went out in the hallway to see if his client on the Lecy case had arrived.

"Did she show?" Sabre asked.

"Naw. Let's just do it. Anyway, this hearing should've been vacated when they issued the Pickup and Detain Order on Bailey."

"They probably thought she'd be back by now."

The Lecy case was called and continued without further date until Bailey was picked up.

The Johnson case was called next. Bob brought his client, the mother, Leanne Johnson, into the courtroom. She appeared nervous or anxious. Sabre wasn't sure which. She felt sorry for the woman who had no idea where her oldest child was and who was unable to visit very often with the rest of her children. But Sabre felt even sorrier for her children. They missed their mother and their siblings terribly. They constantly asked for one another whenever Sabre visited them. Sabre saw the pain on this mother's face and thought how hard it must be not to see one's children. Sabre dealt with different cases every day and the hearings seemed to come up quickly to her, but to the parents and the children the waiting must seem like forever.

The mother came to court probably thinking something would actually happen for her today, even though Sabre knew Bob had explained the process to her. The parents always wanted the process not be prolonged. Instead, another hearing would be set and the parents and children would be required to wait for the wheels of justice to turn. She knew they didn't understand. Heck, sometimes she didn't either.

"In the matter of Cole, Hayden, Alexandria, Blake, and Wyatt Johnson ..." the court clerk called the case.

Bob stood up. "Your Honor, this will be a trial set on behalf of the mother."

County Counsel spoke up without standing. "Your Honor, since Cole is still missing we'd like to continue this matter for a couple more weeks."

Bob said, "The mother would like to have the jurisdictional trial set as soon as possible. Cole was not in his mother's care but rather in the care of the Department of Social Services when he disappeared. She has no idea where her son is or what has happened to him. The department has neglected to protect Cole and now they want to buy some time to make their case of neglect against the mother. So unless the department is willing to return the other four children to her care while they continue the case, she wants her trial date. These children have been out of the home too long already."

The judge turned to Sabre, "Counselor, what's your position on this?"

Sabre stood up. "My investigation is not exactly in sync with DSS so I think a trial needs to be set. Until I hear more evidence or a clarification of the evidence, I'm uncertain what my position will be at trial. Also, today I'd like to obtain a more specific order as to visitation for the mother and for the siblings. The familial ties are very close, but the foster home placements are quite a distance from one another. I'd like to see an order for at least a two-hour visit weekly for the mother and the same for the children. If twice a week is too much for the department, perhaps the social worker can take all of the children to a central place so they can visit their mother. The family can meet as a unit."

The social worker whispered something to her attorney. The County Counsel spoke up. "The social worker is doing her best to schedule the visits as it is. With so many children it's a scheduling nightmare, and the department usually only does one-hour visits."

Sabre remained standing. "It's a scheduling nightmare because the children are housed in three different foster homes, four if you count Cole's, and it's a four-hour bus ride for the mother because of all the stops and transfers. These children need to see their mother and their siblings. Wyatt cries himself to sleep at night and Allie asks to see her brothers every day. It would seem that one regularly scheduled visit for two hours a week would simplify scheduling, not create greater problems. And two hours in one visit is far less time than one hour in four visits. They can all be together as a family, which I believe they need."

"How many times have the children seen each other since the detention hearing?" the judge asked.

Sabre knew the answer but she waited for County Counsel to respond. He turned to his client, the social worker, spoke quietly, and then said, "There has only been one visit and that was between Allie, Blake, and Wyatt."

"And Hayden hasn't seen his siblings at all?"

"No, Your Honor, but the social worker is trying to coordinate the visits between the foster parents."

The judge didn't show any emotion. He looked down at his file and said, "Off the record and we'll pick a trial date." Once they agreed upon a date several weeks into the future, the judge said, "Back on the record." He read the trial date into the record and then said, "There'll be one two-hour visit with mother and all the children each week at a set time. DSS will coordinate the place and time."

The social worker said something to her attorney but he waved his hand slightly as if to dismiss whatever she was saying. Sabre assumed Gillian had objected to the order. County Counsel knew not to object. This judge always took a strong stand on sibling contact.

After the hearing, Bob and Sabre walked out together. "Are you finished with your calendar?" Bob asked.

"Yup, you?"

Bob nodded affirmatively. "Pho's?"

"Sure." Sabre turned her cell phone on as they exited the courthouse and listened to her three messages. Bob checked his as well and made a quick phone call. By the time they reached Bob's car, they were both off their phones.

Bob said, "JP is joining us for lunch."

"Good. Then I don't have to call him. He just left me a message saying he has some information about the old car on the video."

Chapter 30

"So, how's Louie?" Bob asked as he sat down at the table in the Pho Pasteur restaurant with Sabre and JP.

"Who's Louie?" Sabre asked before JP could answer.

"He's JP's gay, beagle puppy."

Sabre's face lit up with a smile. "You have a puppy?"

"He's not gay," JP said seriously.

"The dog's favorite toy is a pink flamingo," Bob teased.

"You're the one who gave it to him," JP protested.

"Yeah, but he wasn't supposed to become so attached to it."

"I don't think the dog cares much what color the toy is," Sabre said. The waiter walked up, interrupting their silly conversation, and took their orders. Sabre shook her head at Bob and turned to JP, changing the subject. "So what did you find out about the car on the video?"

"I just may know who it belongs to," JP responded.

"You were actually able to track that old Plymouth from a picture of just a fender and partial bumper?" Sabre asked.

"Actually, having part of the grill in the picture made a big difference," JP said.

"But still, you tracked it from very little information."

"I think I tracked it," JP said, correcting her. "I'm not one-hundred percent sure it's the same car. If we had a license number or serial number it would be very simple, but now I'm tracking what I think is a 1948 Plymouth from the Fontana area. I started by going backwards from the Las Vegas Museum."

"Huh? I'm confused," Sabre said.

"My friend, Skip, is an expert on antique cars. He's the one who verified the make and model of the car from the photo. He said they made the same body style from 1946 to 1948. Then the grill changed, so he knows it wasn't any later than that. He also told me that the only serious collector in the area was a doctor from Fontana, who had collected every Chrysler made in the thirties and forties, but that was many years ago."

"Anyone could have an old car. It wouldn't have to be a collector," Bob said.

"True, but most people who have a refurbished car have more than one, and generally they register them. Collectors are an unusual breed, especially collectors of antique cars. They like to show them off." He paused. "You're right. It could be a car that was bought new and handed down through the generations. If that's the case, it's going to be a lot harder to trace. This is the easiest place to start."

Sabre asked, "So why did you start in Las Vegas?"

"I'm sorry. I guess I was tryin' to feed the horse before I harvested the hay. Let me back up. In the fifties or sixties there was a small antique car museum in Fontana called Ro-Val. It had mostly cars from the twenties and thirties, but before they closed their doors, they had many cars from the forties as well, due partially to a generous donation from a wealthy doctor. The doctor in Fontana who had the collection of old Chryslers left all his cars to Ro-Val when he opened himself up a worm farm."

Sabre wrinkled her forehead. "A worm farm?"

"When he hit the dust. You know, passed on." He looked down at her, raising his eyebrows as if she should know what that meant. "Anyway, his cars went to the museum. Then

William Harrah, the big casino boss, bought all the cars when the museum closed its doors."

"When the museum opened itself a worm farm?" she teased.

JP shook his head slightly, but gave her a half smile and continued. "From there the cars went to the museum in Las Vegas. But when I checked on the Plymouths in Las Vegas, they had Harrah's 46 and the 47 but not the 48. There was a 1948 Plymouth in the museum but it was purchased from a guy in Indiana and the car had never been in the state of California. It was added to the collection about five years ago, so it was never a part of Harrah's collection."

"So the doctor had all the Chryslers in his collection, but the 1948 didn't make it all the way to Las Vegas," Sabre said. "So maybe Harrah kept it."

"That's what I thought." JP paused while the waiter set the food down in front of them. "But I was able to get a list of the cars in the Harrah Collection as well as a list of the cars Harrah bought from Ro-Val, and it didn't appear on either list."

"So, the doctor's estate either kept it or the doctor never had it." Sabre sat her chopsticks down on the side of her bowl.

"Oh, the doctor had it all right. The word was he had every single Chrysler ever made for that two-decade span. Not only that, with a little more digging and the help of a young filly from the Las Vegas museum, I was able to get the original list of cars that was provided to Harrah when he first started negotiating with Ro-Val."

"And it was on that list, but Harrah didn't buy it?"

JP nodded his head. "Yup. By the time they actually made the deal, the doctor's estate that had left the cars to Ro-Val bought two of them back, a 1931 Chrysler Imperial and a 1948 Plymouth."

"Do you have the name of the doctor?"

"Dr. Ronald Cavitt. He was a bigwig at Kaiser Hospital in Fontana. For some reason, which I haven't yet figured out, his estate bought those two cars back."

"So who got the cars?" Bob asked.

"I'm not sure yet, but I do know Cavitt had three sons—Roger, Robert, and Richard. I'm thinking the boys may have been given the cars."

"So why weren't three cars bought back then?"

"Roger was killed in Vietnam. So that left only two sons."

"Do you know anything about Robert and Richard?" Sabre asked.

"It appears Robert left Fontana after he graduated from Bucher High School. I haven't been able to track him down yet. The youngest son, Richard, followed in his father's footsteps and became a doctor. He went to UCSD Medical School right here in San Diego."

"So he could be the owner of the car," Sabre said. "He could still be living here."

"He could be, but that's as far as I've gone with my investigation, and as I said, I'm not entirely sure we're tracking the right car. I'm still investigating Richard. I don't have an address or much information on him yet. I hope to have it by this afternoon."

"Wow, you've been a busy boy."

"I aim to please, ma'am," JP replied in an exaggerated Texas drawl. "And now that I have a name, I can see what cars are registered to Dr. Richard Cavitt."

They all finished eating their rice noodle and pork dishes, the number 124.

Chapter 31

Chapter 31

When Sabre and Bob returned to court for their afternoon trials, JP drove to Poway to see his techie friend and pick up some enlarged photos of the portly man in the video. Some of them were pretty clear. Whatever he had done to enhance the photos definitely worked.

From Poway, JP drove back to his office to continue with his investigation of the Cavitt family. He made a few phone calls and did some digging on the computer. Although Richard seemed to be the most likely of the two boys to have the Plymouth, he searched equally as hard for Robert, or Ric and Rob, as he soon discovered they were called in high school.

JP's search for Ric Cavitt proved to be a fairly easy trail to follow, although he failed to find any recent photos to attempt a match to the photo from the disc. He called his friend, Kim, at the DMV and left a message on her cell asking which cars were registered to Dr. Richard Cavitt.

Delving into the doctor's educational background, he discovered Ric went straight from high school to college and then to med school. He received his BS in physiological science from UCLA. From there he went to graduate school at UCSD where he obtained his medical degree. He completed his residency at Scripps in the Department of Obstetrics and Gynecology.

Ric's work record was equally easy to research, partially online and the rest with help from two friends, one who worked for the U.S. Department of Justice and the other who freelanced ... and was extremely good at hacking into government and other necessary records. JP determined that after his residency, Dr. Ric Cavitt stayed on staff at Scripps for four additional years. He was named in a law suit during that time and although the terms of the settlement were not disclosed, they likely resulted in the doctor's resignation. Dr. Cavitt left Scripps in the early nineties and went to work at Alvarado Hospital Medical Center. After only two years there he moved on to a couple of local clinics, The Mountain Health Center in Campo and then the Clairemont Community Health Center. Approximately four years ago he appeared to be "retired." He was named in two more law suits after Scripps. One of them settled and the other appeared to be still pending.

JP obtained an address for Dr. Cavitt from his friend at the justice department and then drove to the San Diego County Public Records Department on Pacific Coast Highway. There, JP's research led him to the home that Dr. Ric Cavitt bought in the Clairemont area of San Diego in 1989. It was an older home but was located in a clean, well-kept residential neighborhood. He remained the owner of record.

It was nearly 4:00 p.m. as JP headed to the courthouse to research Cavitt's marriages. He drove to State Street, parked the car in one of the Ace Parking lots, and walked to the courthouse. He entered through the main door on Broadway, looking around to see if he recognized any of the sheriffs on duty, but he didn't see anyone he had once worked with. They all looked about twelve years old. Heck, he'd been gone from the force half their lifetimes. He passed through the metal detector, took the escalator to the second floor, and entered the first door to his right. The records department was a large room with a long counter about ten feet away from the door that stretched across the entire front of the room. The fifty feet or so behind the counter was filled with desks manned by clerks. Only three of the twenty stations at the front counter were open. Earlier in the day they all would've been buzzing with clerks serving the public. A row of computers lined the front wall stretching from the door to each end of the room. JP turned toward the wall just inside the door, found the nearest computer, and typed in the names he was looking for. After narrowing his search, JP took the elevator downstairs to the basement where the archived files were housed.

He handed the clerk a small form he had filled out upstairs for the file he was seeking. After waiting about ten minutes, the clerk returned with a manila file folder about two inches thick containing the records for Dr. Cavitt's first marriage and subsequent divorce. The marriage had taken place in the summer of 1986 during his residency. Two children were born of that marriage, a son born in January of 1987 and a daughter in 1990. The son was diagnosed with Down syndrome. Eleven years later the marriage dissolved in a messy divorce. Dr. Ric was awarded the house but was ordered to pay large monthly child support payments as well as alimony. The alimony had to be paid until his ex-wife died or remarried.

JP made copies of a couple of documents, wrote some notes in his notebook, and then returned to the second floor and requested the files he needed from the clerk. Dr. Ric had been married twice. His most recent divorce took place in 2003 from his then twenty-five-year-old wife and mother of his one-year-old daughter. The marriage had only lasted a little over two years. Although Dr. Ric again retained the house in the settlement, he added five years of alimony to his monthly payments and hefty child support payments each month until his daughter reached eighteen, or nineteen if she was still in high school.

JP simultaneously tracked Rob Cavitt's life, but his education and career took quite a different direction. However, both brothers appeared to be living locally at the present time. Rob was eleven months older than his brother Ric, but because of when their birthdays fell, they started school at the same time. JP couldn't find any DMV records, college, or work employment records for several years after Rob's graduation from high school. JP figured that he was probably moving from place to place, traveling abroad, or just bumming it at home. By 1980, while his brother Ric was graduating from UCLA, Rob had settled in Colorado in a little town called Florissant near Pike's Peak. He lived there for approximately one year and then returned to the Inland Empire in southern California. In his early twenties, he enrolled in Riverside City College. Before the school year ended, Rob dropped out and started working for a small trucking company, driving eighteen-wheelers cross country. Three trucking companies and eight speeding tickets later, he found himself without a driver's license or a job. For a couple of years there were again no employment or criminal records in existence for him. Then he reappeared in Colorado Springs, about an hour's drive from where he lived previously. There he picked up a DUI and a marijuana possession charge. His employment in Colorado consisted primarily of construction work.

In 1999 he moved to Ramona, a suburb of San Diego, and shortly thereafter he went to work for Home Depot, where he was apparently still employed. JP hadn't yet verified his most recent home address. His personal information was pretty sparse. There was nothing listed in the public records that showed ownership of a home. And according to the local records, Rob had no divorces or marriages—none that took place in San Diego County, at least. JP would have to search elsewhere to find out if Rob had been married or had children, which he decided may or may not be important to the issue at hand.

JP had one more thing to do before he made his evening jaunt around the park looking for Cole. He knew that was probably a waste of time, but he had nowhere else to look. The thought of that little boy out on the streets, lying somewhere dead or possibly being tortured by some sick pervert, turned his stomach. He brought his mind back to Cavitt as he pulled onto the bumpy pavement in the parking lot at the Clairemont Community Health Center, Dr. Ric's last place of employment. He picked up his hat from the front seat and after exiting the car, placed it on his head.

The old stucco building was a faded peach color. The wood trim was cracked and flaky and in desperate need of painting. The sidewalk leading up to the front door was lined with dead plants and it appeared the gardener had long since left the premises. Once inside, it was easy to see that the budget was used more leniently there than outside. JP glanced around the room, assessing it and drawing conclusions in his mind as he did whenever he performed an investigation. The walls were freshly painted within the last few months, JP determined. A young receptionist sat behind a simple, maple-colored desk that JP was sure came from Walmart or Target. The floors needed cleaning, not because they weren't kept up regularly but because it was the end of the day and there had been a fair amount of traffic.

Several people sat in the waiting room to his left. JP looked through the large window that led to the room. The chairs were padded as opposed to metal, but they were not so inviting that you'd want to fall asleep in them. Through the glass JP could see an Asian woman with two children, a gray-haired man in his eighties, and two pregnant women.

JP approached the receptionist and introduced himself. He spoke slowly and exaggerated his accent. "I'm looking for Dr. Richard Cavitt. He was my baby sister's doctor for her first child. Now Idella's gone and found herself in a family way again and she'd really like to have Dr. Cavitt for this baby as well."

"I'm sorry, sir, we don't have a Dr. Cavitt here," the receptionist said.

"Dang! I know this is where he was working when my sister saw him last. I don't know what to do now." He rubbed his chin and furrowed his brow. "Any chance you know where he went from here?"

"No, I'm sorry I don't."

"Did you know Dr. Cavitt?"

"No, but I've only been here for a few months. He hasn't been here since I came. The obstetrician on staff now is Dr. Kate Rutiger."

JP leaned in a little closer but not so he would be intrusive. "Does Dr. Rutiger have a secretary or a nurse that works with her? Perhaps they could help me."

"Mary Jo works in that department. She's been here a really long time. Let me check with her." The receptionist picked up the phone, spoke to someone, and then said to JP, "She'll be right out. Her shift ended and she's about to leave, but she said she can give you a minute."

JP stepped back out of the way as a patient from the waiting room came up to the desk. JP walked through an archway into the little room adjacent to the lobby and looked around. He noticed that no television hung on the wall as in most waiting rooms these days, but there were plenty of magazines and a small bookshelf filled with books. On top of the bookshelf was a sign that read, *Take it, Read it, Bring it Back Next Time*. He saw a woman enter the lobby through the door behind the receptionist's desk. She carried a purse and a shopping bag. JP walked back into the lobby just as the receptionist pointed toward him.

They approached each other. The woman spoke first. "I'm Mary Jo. I understand you're looking for Dr. Cavitt."

"Yes, my sister would like to find him." JP lowered his voice a little. "She's pregnant again, and would like him for her doctor."

"I don't know where he went from here. I've heard he's involved with a teen group home, but I don't even know which one." She was polite but her body language indicated she was ready to go home. "Dr. Rutiger here at the clinic is a wonderful doctor."

"My sister, Idella, really wants Dr. Ric, as she calls him. She has some problems and she doesn't do well with strangers." He lowered his voice again. "She doesn't have a full attic. It ain't her fault, mind ya. She's the sweetest thing you ever saw but she gets real confused about some stuff." JP watched Mary Jo's face as it softened, so he continued with his tale. "I'm not even sure I have the right doctor to tell you the truth." JP reached in his pocket and took out the photo his techie friend had made for him and handed it to Mary Jo. "She gave me this picture and said it was Dr. Ric. I know it's not a very good photo, but is that him?"

When Mary Jo didn't respond right away JP said, "I really want to do what's right by Idella. I came here from Texas to take care of her when I heard about her condition. She can't manage alone and she has nobody else. Our mother was taking care of her but just recently passed on." He cleared his throat. "I tried to get Idella to move back to Texas, but she wouldn't have it. I figure I'll stay until I can convince her to go back with me." JP stopped talking when he saw Mary Jo nod her head.

"That's him. That's Dr. Cavitt." She handed the photo back to JP and before she walked away said, "You really might want to consider a different doctor for her."

"Why?" JP asked as he followed her towards the door. "Is there something I should know about the doctor?"

Mary Jo waved her right hand in a gesture of dismissal and walked out.

Chapter 32

"You said if I needed anything to call you," Bailey said without any of the social amenities generally expected when someone calls your cell phone.

"Bailey?" Sabre asked, not entirely certain it was her.

"Yes. Hello. It's me."

"Are you okay?"

"I am, but I only have about ten minutes left on my phone. Can you add some minutes to my account?"

"Is it in your name?" Sabre asked.

"No. I got it from a friend."

"I'd need the information about the account." Bailey didn't respond. "Bailey?"

"I don't have it."

"Whose name is it in?"

"I can't tell you." Bailey's voice grew tougher. She sounded like the teenager she first met. "Can't you just get me another phone then?"

"Yes, I will. It'll take me about an hour to go to the phone store and find what you need. Where are you?"

"I'll meet you by the canyon, same as last time. You'll come alone, right?"

"Right."

It was approximately 8:40 p.m. Sabre had just enough time to drive to the store and purchase a pre-paid phone before it closed. At five minutes of nine she walked into the store, and twenty minutes later walked out with a new cell phone and one hundred pre-paid minutes. She arrived at Snead and Mt. Acadia, the entrance to the canyon, at 9:35 p.m. There were no signs of Bailey. Sabre turned her car around facing the street, just as she had done the last time. She felt a little nervous sitting there waiting but not as much as before. She found that interesting. It was no less dangerous, just more familiar.

The knock on the driver's window startled her as Bailey tapped on the glass. Sabre rolled it down.

"Do you have the phone?" Bailey asked.

"Yes. Come sit." Sabre nodded her head to the right toward the passenger seat.

"I've got to go."

"Please," Sabre said.

Bailey looked around and then walked around the car and opened the passenger door as Sabre unlocked it. She stepped inside and closed the door. "I don't have much time."

"What's your hurry?"

"I just gotta go."

"I need to know that you're all right."

"I'm good." Bailey didn't sit still. She kept looking around and squirming in her seat.

"Did someone follow you?"

Bailey shook her head in a negative response. "Do you have the phone?"

Sabre retrieved the phone from her front sweatshirt pocket and handed it to Bailey. "I put a sticky in there with the phone number. You only have one-hundred minutes. Please only use them to call me and to protect yourself. Be careful who you call. It's not as easy to trace a pre-paid phone, but it's not impossible. Be sure to save enough minutes to call me if you need more."

Bailey tucked the phone into the front pocket of the sweatshirt Sabre had given her the last time they met. Sabre wondered if she had anything else to wear.

"Bailey, I watched the video. Do you know who the people are in it?"

"Just Scott. I don't know who the fat guy is."

"Have you ever seen him before?"

"I . . . I gotta go," Bailey said as she reached for the door handle.

"Please wait."

Bailey stopped and turned back toward Sabre. "What?" she asked.

"Why did you give me the disc?"

"So you could help Apollo."

"But how can I help him? I don't know who the man is. Did he kill Scott?"

"I don't know, but I'm sure he's involved."

"How?"

"I don't know."

"Bailey, you're not making any sense. I need more information." Bailey shrugged her shoulders. "Where is the third disc? Maybe that'll help us find who killed Scott and get Apollo off the hook."

"I can't give you that. It's too dangerous. They're all liars."

"Who's a liar?"

"All of them. And they're mean and scary."

"Who are they?" Bailey didn't respond. "Bailey, I wish you'd turn yourself in. You'll be safe."

"It's not safe anywhere. I gotta go."

Before Sabre could say anything else, Bailey was out the door. It closed behind her. Sabre looked around but she seemed to have disappeared into the darkness.

Sabre drove home, made herself a cup of hot chocolate, and curled up on the sofa with the Lecy file. She read through every report again. Earlier in the day Bob had given her a copy of the detention report supporting the allegations against Apollo in the murder of Scott Jamison. She didn't ask him how he got it. She didn't really want to know, but since she had it she decided she may as well read it. It placed Apollo and Bailey at the scene at the time of the murder. Fingerprints of both kids had been found in the house, but that was to be expected since Bailey's mom still lived there and they had visited. They didn't seem to have any real motive, however. The report implied the murder may have been drug related, but they had no history or evidence of either Bailey or Apollo using drugs.

Sabre had glanced through the report earlier when Bob gave it to her, but this time she perused it carefully, reading every detail. Something caught her eye. She laid the report down, picked up her cell, and called JP.

"Are you okay?" JP asked when he answered the phone.

"I'm fine. Why?"

"Ah ... because it's nearly midnight."

"I'm so sorry. Go back to sleep. I'll call you in the morning."

"No. No. I wasn't sleeping." Sabre knew from his voice that she had woken him, but the damage was already done. "What can I do for you?" he asked.

"I met with Bailey again tonight. And before you reprimand me with some funny Texas saying, I'm home. I'm fine. And Bailey now has a new cell phone to replace the one she had. Her minutes had expired." Sabre gave him the phone number in case he needed it in the future. "I asked her about the video. She wouldn't tell me what they expected us to do with it, but I think she's still testing me. She said she didn't know who the fat guy was, but when I asked if she had seen him before, she changed the subject."

"So she knows more than she's telling you."

"For sure. I asked for the third disc, but she said it was 'too dangerous' to give it to me."

"Did she explain what she meant?"

"Nope." Sabre paused. "But here's something else you'll find interesting. I was reading some information on Scott Jamison, and guess what. He's from Fontana, just like our car collector."

Chapter 33

Fontana was at least fifteen degrees hotter than San Diego which put the temperature at about eighty-five degrees, a little too hot for JP's taste. He pulled into the parking lot at Bucher High School, where the Cavitt brothers had attended in the mid seventies. The school had opened in 1955 to house the thousands of post-war students whose parents came to work at Kaiser Steel, the largest steel production company west of the Mississippi. It was a blue-collar school with a nationally known football team. The remnants of "Cheetah Pride" lingered within its hallowed walls, and a huge trophy case displayed the evidence. It housed about a hundred trophies, but front and center stood the one from 1988 when the school football team ranked "best in the nation."

The school seemed to have lost a lot of its pride since then as evidenced by the graffiti on the walls, the attire of the students, and the guards at the gates. JP showed a guard his ID and explained he had an appointment with Mr. James Williams.

"Please check in at the office. It's straight through there and on your left."

"Thank you."

JP signed in at the office and then obtained directions to Mr. Williams' room. The teacher had scheduled the appointment for 10:00 a.m., his free period. When JP reached his closed door he wasn't sure what the protocol was for classrooms. Was he to knock or just walk in? He chose to knock, figuring it was the safest thing to do.

"Come on in," Mr. Williams called from inside.

JP walked into the warm room. It didn't feel as hot as it did outside, but neither was it air conditioned. A tall, physically fit man in his early sixties greeted him. His hair and tightly cut beard were gray and his face had received too much sun over the years. Other than that, he was in great shape. JP sucked in his stomach.

"Thanks for seeing me."

"It's my pleasure. I always love telling old tales about our school."

"And you apparently have first-hand knowledge. They tell me you've been here since Moses was a pup."

"Yup. It'll be forty years this spring. I started teaching here right out of college and never left. I've taught everything from P.E. to history at one time or another. History was my major and it's my class of preference, but I've filled in over the years wherever they needed me." He pointed to a chair at one of the tables. "Please have a seat." JP sat down and the teacher pulled out a chair and sat next to him.

"Did you ever coach?"

"I was the assistant football coach my first five years here. I played college ball and was real close to being drafted into the NFL, but I made some pretty foolish decisions and lost out on the opportunity. But Bucher High was just starting to make a name for itself on the football field and they were happy to put my expertise to use."

"Why did you stop coaching?"

"Teaching in the classroom was more rewarding for me, so that's where I decided to spend my energy. I continued to help out on the field when I was needed over the years, but I would never accept another position that took me out of the classroom." Mr. Williams smiled and said, "Enough about me. What can I do for you?"

"As I told you on the phone, I'm doing some research for an attorney on an old trust. That's about all the information I can give you, but I assure you it needs to be done."

"And you're interested in some students who attended here when?"

"They would've graduated around 1975 or '76."

Mr. Williams stood up and walked to a cupboard behind his desk. When he opened it, JP saw three rows of school annuals lined up on the shelves. "I have every annual this school published since I started teaching here." He brought down five of them ranging from 1973 through 1977. He sat them on the table in front of JP. "Who are you looking for? Can you tell me that much?"

"Yes, three brothers. Last name Cavitt."

Mr. Williams smiled. "I remember the Cavitt boys, especially Roger. He was one hell of a football player. My first year here he was a senior. Bucher High was just starting to make a name for itself on the football field." He walked over to the cabinet and took out another album, continuing to talk. "A lot of that was thanks to Roger Cavitt. That kid could throw a football better than anyone I've ever seen, at the high school level anyway." The annual read 1971 on the cover. He opened it up to the senior page and handed it to JP, pointing to a photo. "There he is. That's Roger."

"And you were his coach?"

"I just helped out. Coach Madrigal was the man. He inspired those young men to put forth everything they had. If Roger had been here a few years later, he would've been drafted for a major college football team instead of the military service."

"I understand he was killed in Vietnam."

Mr. Williams shook his head. "It was a pity. He came to me the day after he received his notice in the mail. He acted tough, but I could tell he was frightened. He told me a lot of things that day...stuff I don't think he ever told anyone else. He talked to me like a friend. Heck, I guess I was his friend. I was only a few years older than him."

"What kind of stuff?"

"He told me how mean his father was."

"He was abusive?"

"Yeah. He was some hoity-toity doctor who beat his kids. He'd belittle Roger all the time and even knock him around. Every once in a while he came to school with a black eye or bruising somewhere on his body. He always made excuses up until that day. That day his fear won out. He was really afraid he'd be sent to war, but I'll never forget what he told me. He said, 'Heck, I've been at war all my life with my father. At least now I'll have a gun to fight back.'"

"That's horrible. Did his father beat the other boys too?"

"Not until Roger went away. I think Roger protected them and took the brunt of everything his dad dished out. But when he was gone I started to see the signs on the other boys, especially Ric. I had the impression that Ric received more abuse because his father saw him as weak."

"Did you ever report him?" JP asked.

Mr. Williams sighed. "Several times, but nothing was ever done. Dr. Cavitt was an important man in the community and he contributed a lot to the athletic department at our school. I was warned by the principal to stay out of it."

"Did either of the younger boys play football?"

"Rob did. And he was quite good. In 1976 he played under Coach Madrigal as he took the Cheetahs to the CIF playoffs. Rob was good, but nothing like Roger. Ric didn't play at all. I think it was one more reason why his father was rougher on him than Rob. Ric played some tennis for a little while but that wasn't good enough for Dr. Cavitt. The old man was quite a football fan."

"Did the doctor go to the games?"

"Oh yeah. Football was sacred to him. I don't think he made it to any of the boys' graduations and I know he never went to a tennis match, but he never missed a football game."

JP picked up the 1976 school annual and opened it to the senior page. There were photos of Richard and Robert Cavitt, side by side. They didn't look much alike. Ric was already slightly overweight and wore glasses. Rob was handsome and muscular. The pictures throughout the annual depicted very different lives for these two brothers. Rob was athletic, prom king, and always surrounded by pretty girls. Ric was a member of CSF, captain of the debate team, and winner of the science fair several years running.

"Were the younger boys close?" JP asked.

"They were very tight in spite of their different personalities, at least until their senior year. They hung out together and supported each other whenever they weren't involved in an activity that conflicted with their own. They were just over a year apart and because of the way their birthdays fell, they ended up starting school at the same time. They went through school like twins. A lot of people thought they were."

"What happened in their senior year?" JP held the annual in two hands flipping it back and forth in front of his face in an effort to fan himself and then laid it on the table.

"Ric and Rob suddenly grew apart. A lot of people blamed it on the loss of their brother. Roger was killed that summer in Vietnam in one of the last battles of the war. He was also in the last group to be drafted. They had a draft lottery in 1972 for men born the year after him, but they were never drafted because the draft was abolished in 1973. So his was the last group to go." The teacher furrowed his brow.

JP noted Mr. Williams' expression. "But you don't think it was Roger's death that caused the rift between Ric and Rob. What do you think it was?"

"I don't really know, but something happened that September about a week after school started. When they began school everything was fine. They were both in my history class so I knew when they began acting differently toward each other."

"What do you mean, different?"

"They almost stopped talking to one another – not like they were really angry, but almost like they were afraid of something. I tried to get through to them, but neither of them would open up. It's hard to explain, but a few other things happened around the same time. Rob and his girlfriend, who he had been with for about a year, broke up."

"Do you think it was over a girl?"

"No." Mr. Williams stood up and walked toward his desk. "I'm thirsty. Would you like some water?"

"That would be great." JP could feel the sweat beading up on his forehead.

"I'm just saying lots of things changed for both of them. They had a couple of friends from Rialto they had hung out with all through high school until that September. Then it stopped. I never saw those boys again, and neither Ric nor Rob ever mentioned their names after that." The teacher took two bottles of water out of a small blue ice chest next to his desk. He handed one to JP.

"Thanks." JP took the water and unscrewed the top. He asked, "Are you sure it was in September?"

"I can almost tell you the exact date. If I had a 1976 calendar I could. School started the Tuesday after Labor Day weekend. On the following Monday they came to class and life was just different. I think something happened over the weekend. Rob's grades fell way below par. He only kept them up enough to play football. He didn't seem to care about anything else. Ric buried himself even further into his books."

JP took another drink of his water, downing almost half of the bottle. He didn't realize how thirsty he was until he started to drink. "Do you think the breakup between Rob and his girlfriend had something to do with what happened on the weekend?"

Mr. Williams nodded his head. "I do because I heard them arguing on Monday. She said she couldn't deal with what happened and for some reason she was worried about her little brother. It was so long ago, I don't recall exactly what was said, but she looked terrified."

"Do you remember her name?"

"Hmm...it was Maryanne or Marion something. I think her last name started with an M or an N, or a C. I can't remember. It was an Italian name." He picked up the 1975 annual. "She was in the class below Rob." He turned to the section with the senior class photos and glanced through it. It was only four or five pages long. "There she is. Maryanne Miconi." He handed the book to JP.

"Beautiful girl."

"And very sweet. Good student, too."

"Do you know the names of the boys from Rialto?"

"One was named Billy, or Barney, or something. He was a tall, skinny kid with more than his share of pimples. I think he graduated valedictorian in his class, so he must have been a pretty good student. The other boy was more athletic. He played football against us. It was always interesting when Bucher High played Monroe, that was the high school in Rialto, since the star quarterbacks were best friends and they wore the same number." He wrinkled his brow in thought and then sighed. "I can't for the life of me remember his name."

JP picked up the 1976 annual and turned to the photos of the football players. Rob wore jersey number six. The quarterback from Rialto must have as well. "Do you remember if the Cavitt brothers had any affiliation with Route 66?"

"You're good, JP. The two quarterbacks together were 'Route 66.' It was sort of a school joke. And they both lived on Foothill Boulevard, the old Route 66, which made it more interesting. I think at some point they called their little clique the Route 66 Club."

"They actually formed a club?"

"Not really. As far as I know it was only the four of them, the two Cavitt brothers and the boys from Rialto. They had Route 66 stickers on their notebooks. There was lots of memorabilia still around from the 'Route 66' television show back in the sixties. Of course, that all ended when the group disband in September that year. When they were about to play Monroe that fall, Rob became very angry at a pep rally when someone said something about 'Route 66,' referring to the two quarterbacks. He said, 'There is no Route 66, just one six kicking another six's ass.' There were a bunch of posters put up at school for that game with the Route 66 sign torn in half. One half was maroon and white and it had a foot on it kicking the green and white half. It was pretty clever, actually. Rob didn't really like that, either, and since he was the big man on campus, everyone pretty much dropped any reference to Route 66 after that."

"One other thing, do you remember a student by the name of Scott Jamison? He would have been here about ten years later."

Mr. Williams thought for a moment. "Uh, ah. I can't say that I do. You're free to look through the other annuals if you'd like." He nodded toward the cupboard. "I'll be at my desk correcting some papers. If you find him, show me. I might recognize his photo."

JP walked over to the cupboard and rifled through the books from 1983 through 1989. If he went to school there, it would have to be within that time frame. He found nothing under the name of Scott Jamison. The only Jamison he found was an African-American girl.

JP put the books back and walked over to the teacher's desk. He reached his hand out to the teacher. "You've been a big help, Mr. Williams."

"Jimmy," he said. "I'm Mr. Williams all day long in the class-room. The rest of the time I'm just Jimmy."

"Thank you, Jimmy."

Before JP reached the door he turned and said, "By the way, I understand Dr. Cavitt had quite a collection of antique Chryslers."

Mr. Williams nodded. "He did."

"Do you know if any of the boys ever drove any of them?"

"Just Roger. He drove a 1948 Plymouth for most of his senior year. It was a reward for playing football. Neither of the other boys drove any of the antiques, at least not that I'm aware of."

JP turned south out of the parking lot and backtracked to a Starbucks he had passed on his way to the high school. After finding it, he took his computer and went inside to have a cup of coffee and do some research online. He had a few things to follow up on before he left the area.

As soon as he had his coffee in hand, he found a corner table and sat down. He opened his computer, turned it on, and then checked his phone messages while he waited for it to boot up. Sabre had called but said it wasn't important and to just call when he had a chance. The only other call was from his friend, Kim, at the DMV. She called to let him know that Richard Cavitt never had a 1948 Plymouth registered to his name. He did have a 1931 Chrysler Imperial when he was twenty-one years old which he maintained for about four years. No other Chrysler products were ever registered in his name.

Chapter 34

Bob walked into Sabre's office late Tuesday afternoon. "I thought JP was going to be here to hash this out," Bob said.
B

"He's still in Fontana. Or at least he was a couple of hours ago. He's coming by when he gets back to town. If we finish before then, I'll call him and let him know."

"All right, let's get to it."

Sabre walked around to the other side of her desk and laid out the spreadsheet with all the alleged satanic ritual abuse cases. She lined up its pages so they could see all the columns and compare them. They both stood over them for several minutes trying to find a pattern.

"So, what do you see?" Sabre asked.

"Nothing glaring," Bob responded. "The age of the minors is all over the place, from newborns to teenagers. Geographically, there's nothing special. Now that we've added the cases from north and east counties and south bay, it's evident that they're everywhere in the county. They're a little more concentrated in Tierrasanta and downtown, but not enough to tell us anything. The social workers vary. Gillian is on more of the cases than anyone else, but then she happens to work primarily in Tierrasanta and downtown, so that's to be expected."

Sabre looked up. "But are more cases filed in those areas because she's the one investigating? Or is it because there are more cases that area?"

"Good point. Let's follow up on that." Bob studied the grid once again.

Sabre ran her finger down the column marked Attorneys. "There don't seem to be any attorneys receiving an excessive amount of these cases. You and I have as many or more than anyone else."

"That explains it then."

"What?" Sabre asked.

"It's you. You're involved in some kind of 'cult' thing. I've been suspicious for a long time. You don't sleep much, probably because you're out late at night doing your devil thing. When we have lunch and I order the number 124, sometimes you order the number six."

"That's one six. What does that mean?"

"I'm sure I've seen you order it three times in a row."

Sabre laughed and smacked him on the arm. "You're nuts. You know it?"

"It makes about as much sense as some of the reasons these cases were filed. The abuse indicators are all over the place and some of them not very convincing."

"So you're saying some of the cases aren't actually ritual cases?"

"That's exactly what I'm saying—overzealous social work. Like the Johnson case, for instance. I'm completely convinced there was nothing going on there."

"And you may be right. So let's make another column. We'll call it OZ for overzealous. We'll mark an X in that column where we think it might be exaggerated. Then we can take out the other cases and see what we have left."

"Good idea."

They searched through the grid and marked out only the cases that they could both agree were a stretch. Sabre marked through the ones that remained in yellow.

"Not much left," Bob said as he watched Sabre highlight the four cases they agreed on.

"Nope. And half of those cases weren't filed because of ritual abuse accusations. The Lecy case came in because Bailey was acting out and not attending school. One case is Wagner's with a thirteen-year-old girl who had strange graffiti all over her bedroom walls. And the other two belong to Collicott. One of them came in with ritual allegations, and the other was added because she had JP investigate the accusations about the cult thing at the group home for pregnant girls."

"So there are three cases with teenage girls. Do you think there's a group of teenage girls out there worshipping Satan?"

"Heck if I know. I'm at a complete loss. I'm just not seeing anything that helps." Sabre studied the chart again. "I'll give this to JP and see if he can see anything, but I think we're just wasting our time." She started to pick up the sheets, keeping them in order. Suddenly she swatted Bob on the shoulder with the spreadsheet and said, "That's it. They're teenage girls. I need to go."

"Huh?"

"I think I figured something out. I need to go see Bailey's friend, Shellie. I think she can help me." Sabre grabbed her briefcase, opened it up, and tossed the spreadsheet inside.

The sun was about to set by the time Sabre reached Shellie's house. She walked up to the front door and knocked. She saw the curtain move back and someone peek out. She waited a moment and then knocked again. After the third knock, Shellie opened the door and stepped out.

Sabre reached her hand out. "Hi. I'm Sabre Brown. I'm Bailey's attorney. Do you mind giving me a minute of your time?"

"I've already told your investigator everything I know."

Sabre pointed to the chairs on the porch. "Can we sit for a minute? I really need your help to protect Bailey. I think she's in a lot of trouble."

Shellie took a seat and Sabre followed her. "But I don't know anything. I don't know where she is," Shellie continued to object.

"I believe you don't know where she is, but I also know you've been in contact with her. Have you spoken to her recently?"

"No. The last couple of times I tried to call her I got a weird message. I think she's out of minutes."

"You two have been friends for a really long time, haven't you?"

Shellie nodded her head. "We met in fifth grade. I had just moved to a new school. At recess some of the kids teased me about being fat. I just stood there crying and that made them tease me more. I do that. I cry a lot. Bailey came to my rescue. She took my hand and led me away and encouraged me to ignore them. She said they teased her, too, but she wasn't as big as me."

"I'm so sorry. Kids can be so cruel." Sabre touched her hand to comfort her. Shellie didn't draw back. "And you and Bailey have been best friends ever since?"

"Pretty much."

"Even after she started seeing Apollo?"

"Yes, but we didn't see each other as much. She spent a lot of time with him."

"But you did know she was pregnant." It was a statement, not a question.

Shellie's eyes opened wide, and fear and confusion covered her face. She didn't respond, just nodded once affirmatively.

Sabre picked up the hand she was holding with her right hand and clasped her left hand over it. She looked her straight in the eyes. "Shellie, what happened to Bailey's baby?"

Shellie just sat there shaking her head as the tears rolled down her cheeks.

Chapter 35

The Monroe school library was quiet as JP sat thumbing through old annuals looking for the quarterback with jersey number six. He started with the year 1976 since that's when Rob and Ric graduated. The football photos took up seven pages. There were several shots of number six, but no name was attached. One page had individual photos of each varsity member wearing their jerseys and posing in football positions. Most of the players were bent over so the jersey numbers were not legible. Next to the photo was the player's name and position. Two quarterbacks were listed, Thomas Anthony Martin and Craig G. McGill. JP studied the photos and looked back at the pictures that showed number six in action shots. It wasn't enough to tell which one was the friend of the Cavitt brothers. JP turned to the senior photo page and looked for the quarterbacks. Both participated actively in sports, but Martin only played football the last two years, which left McGill as the more likely candidate.

Starting at the beginning of the annual, JP searched for any reference to valedictorian, but none was listed. He approached the information desk and questioned a woman behind the desk about why valedictorians weren't listed.

"Because they aren't determined yet when the annuals are released. The valedictorian and the salutatorian are chosen late in the school year, shortly before graduation."

"Of course. That makes sense." JP smiled. "Is there any record kept of the valedictorians? Say, from the seventies?"

"Everything used to be stored on microfiche and kept in bins. But I can see if it has been converted to the computer yet. Someone has been working on that for the past few years, but with budget cuts recently I think the process has slowed down if not stopped completely. But let me check." The librarian started typing on her computer. She looked up. "This may take a minute. I'll let you know if I find anything."

"Thanks. I'm looking particularly for the year 1976 and perhaps a couple of years before and after." JP walked to the table where he was previously sitting and thumbed through the senior photo pages. He didn't find anyone named Billy or Barney. He couldn't find anyone named Bernard, or anything similar for which Barney might be a nickname. He found one boy named William who could have been the Billy that the Bucher High teacher had referenced. There was no football affiliation next to his name where school activities were listed. The only thing stated there was his participation in Future Farmers of America for his four years at Monroe and his FFA presidency in his senior year. JP found the group photo of the FFA members as well as the photo of the club's officers. They stood side-by-side with the club president in front. He couldn't have been more than five-foot-five and not what JP would call thin. Mr. Williams had described him as tall and thin. This was definitely not the right Billy.

JP turned back to the first page of the senior photos searching for any more names that started with the letter B.

"Mr. Torn," the librarian called him. He walked over to her desk. "I'm sorry, but I can't find the valedictorians. Apparently they haven't been inputted yet. You could try the microfiche but I'm afraid you couldn't do that today because we're closing in about fifteen minutes. But you're certainly welcome to come back."

"Thank you."

JP returned to his desk and continued his search. He found five "Bobs" listed and one Robert, which seemed like an inordinate amount for such a small class. He looked for last names that might be twisted into Barney or Billy, again with little success. He continued his search through the class of 1975 and 1977 since he wasn't certain when the boy actually graduated. It was a long laborious hunt and in the end JP didn't feel like he had accomplished much. Before he left, JP copied all the photos of the entire 1976 graduating class, as well as anyone in the other classes that might come close to what he was looking for. Then he searched quickly through the annuals from the eighties looking for Scott Jamison. He struck out.

On his way back to San Diego, JP plugged in his new hands-free device that he had finally succumbed to and called Sabre. He gave her a quick rundown on the information he had gathered.

"I tried tracking Maryanne Miconi but so far I've had no luck with that, either. I expect she's married and has a different last name now, but I'll check it out when I get home. At the same time I'll try to find Thomas Anthony Martin and Craig G. McGill, the quarterbacks from Monroe High."

"Great."

"Any word on Cole?" JP asked, but he already knew the answer. If Sabre knew anything she would've blurted it out.

"Actually, I'm headed over to the park right now to take another look around."

"Sabre, it's getting dark. You can't go to that park alone after dark."

"I'll be fine. I'm just going to take a quick trip around."

JP raised his voice. "Sometimes you're about as dumb as a soup sandwich."

Sabre tried not to laugh, but she couldn't help herself. "Fine. I'll just circle around. I won't leave my car."

"Look, if you want to go when I get back to the city, I'll be glad to go with you."

"Thanks, but I'll be home in my cozy condo way before you reach the city limits."

The sun had set and the sky had darkened by the time Sabre reached the park. She drove slowly alongside the sidewalk looking for Cole. She didn't really expect to see him and she knew with every passing day the likelihood that he was still alive diminished. There had been no reports that he had returned to Hayden's school, and Hayden claimed he had hadn't seen or heard from him.

The sidewalk was empty except for a lone woman in her sixties walking towards her. She wore a pink waitress uniform and tennis shoes and carried a purse in one hand and a plastic bag in the other. Her steps were placed gingerly on the ground as if she had very sore feet. There were a few lights in the park but it was still difficult to see. She spotted three gentlemen at a distance inside the park near the gazebo, but there was no little boy. About twenty feet in front of her, to the right of the sidewalk, a shopping cart was partially hidden by a large magnolia tree. The woman in the waitress uniform was almost even with her car. Just then a man whooshed past her on a bicycle and snatched the woman's purse from her hand, knocking her into Sabre's car. The plastic bag flew up, splattering spaghetti in marinara sauce down the windshield. Sabre slammed on her brakes, and the woman fell to the ground. Just as the man on the bicycle reached the magnolia tree, the shopping cart flew forward. The bicyclist whipped to the right and smacked right into Mama T. She flew back with her legs in the air, and her head slammed against the tree. Before Sabre could get out of the car, the thief mounted his bicycle again and rode off into the dark.

She jumped out of her car and ran around the front of it as the waitress tried to stand up. "Are you okay?"

The woman straightened her skirt. "I'm fine, but he took my purse. It has all my tips." She sounded desperate.

Sabre reached out and placed her hand on the woman's arm. "Are you sure you're okay?"

"Yes."

Sabre dashed over to Mama T and the waitress followed her. Sabre checked Mama T's pulse. She could feel a beat but she was completely knocked out. "Watch her," Sabre said to the waitress, as she jumped up and scurried back to her car where she retrieved her cell phone and called 9-1-1. Then she went back to Mama T and the waitress. "You should call someone to come pick you up."

"I don't have a phone."

Sabre handed her cell phone to her. The woman dialed someone and explained what happened, then handed the phone back to Sabre. "My son will be here in about thirty minutes. He's coming from El Cajon."

"You should probably go into the hospital and be checked."

"No. I'll be fine. I'm really not hurt."

Sabre held Mama T's hand and talked to her, hoping she could keep her from slipping away. It frustrated her that she didn't really know what to do for her. She wished she were better trained for emergencies.

Sabre checked her phone for the time, wondering when the ambulance and the police would arrive. Several people had walked over and asked what happened. Most of them just hung around, waiting like vultures over a dead carcass. Sabre wondered why people did that. Why were people drawn to accidents and bad events? One woman came up close and then backed away when she saw, or rather smelled, Mama T. She wrinkled her nose and then covered her mouth as if she were going to vomit.

Sabre knew Mama T smelled bad. It wasn't the first time she had a close encounter with her, but today she hadn't noticed. She was too concerned about Mama T to worry about the stench.

Finally, Sabre heard the sirens. A large, red fire truck pulled up in front of her car. Four firemen exited the truck and approached them. One of them introduced himself and started asking questions about the incident. Sabre stepped back and let them work. Before she finished explaining what happened, she heard the sirens and saw the lights flashing from the paramedics. They were followed by two police cars with more sirens and more flashing red lights. Two of the men pulled the stretcher out of the ambulance and rolled it over as close as they could to Mama T. Sabre couldn't see what they were doing but she noticed someone had placed a cervical collar on her.

A policeman approached Sabre and asked her to explain what happened. Another one was talking to the waitress. The scene suddenly seemed very surreal with the lights, the sirens, and all the men in uniform buzzing around. She could feel her heart beating in her chest and realized it hadn't all really hit her until now. She had been operating on auto pilot. She took a deep breath and then answered the policeman's questions to the best of her ability.

"Can you tell me what happened?" he asked.

"I was driving slowly alongside the sidewalk and just as the waitress approached my car, the man on the bicycle came up from behind, grabbed her purse, and knocked her down. As he drove away, Mama T, that's the homeless woman, pushed her cart out onto the sidewalk toward him. It looked like she was trying to stop him, but he swerved and hit her instead, slamming her to the ground. She hit her head against the tree as she went down."

"You called the woman Mama T. Do you know her?"

"I've encountered her before here in the park on several occasions. I'm a child advocate and I have an eight-year-old child who is missing from this area. I've spoken to Mama T a couple of times while looking for the child."

"Did you see what the man on the bicycle looked like?" the officer asked.

"Unfortunately, no. I didn't see his face. He wore a black sweatshirt with a hood and black sweatpants. The hood was pulled up over his head. I didn't see him at all until he was by the side of my car and then I couldn't see his head through my window. I could only see his upper body. The car and the waitress blocked the rest of my view. I saw what he was wearing after he passed the car, and I saw the purse tucked under his arm."

Sabre watched as they loaded the stretcher into the ambulance. She reached into her pants pocket and took out her business card and handed it to the officer. "My office number and my cell are on there. If you don't mind, I'd like to go to the hospital and check on Mama T. I'm sure she has no one else."

"Sure."

Sabre looked over at the waitress who started to cry as she gave her story to the police officer. "That woman's son is on his way, but he may be a while. Will someone stay with her?" Sabre asked.

"You go ahead. We'll take care of her."

Sabre followed the ambulance to County Hospital. Her hands shook as she dialed JP.

Chapter 36

Chapter 36

"Hey, kid," JP said as he placed his hand on Sabre's shoulder.

Sabre stood up and wrapped her arms around him. They stood there in an embrace until Sabre finally let go. "You didn't have to come here," she said.

"Yes, I did." He smiled down at her. "How's Mama T?"

"I don't know much yet. The doctor should be out soon." Sabre took a seat and JP sat next to her. "I don't even know her name. I don't know who to call. I feel so helpless."

"You've already been a big help to her. You called the ambulance. If you hadn't been there she might still be lying in the park."

Sabre tipped her head to the side and gave him a half-smile. "So now you think it was a good idea that I was there? You told me not to go, remember?"

"You shouldn't have gone, but we'll have that discussion later. I've known mules that were less stubborn than you. But you were there and you helped her."

"Did I tell you she tried to stop the thief with her shopping cart? Mama T is quite the caretaker. She shares her food. She runs down thieves who attack strangers. I don't know why I'm so invested in this homeless person."

"Because you have a big heart, just like Mama T."

"I just wish I knew who she is. Why she's living on the streets. Who to call for her. If she has family. There may be someone looking for her who doesn't know she's even alive."

"Maybe the hospital will find out who she is."

"They told me they're sending a social worker in the morning, but I'm not sure what good that'll do. She's not coherent. So unless they run her prints . . . and that might not prove anything either."

A tall, grey-haired man entered the waiting room. "Is someone here for Jane Doe. . . er, Mama T?" he asked.

Sabre and JP stood up. Sabre raised her hand. "I am," she said.

The doctor walked over to them and sat down across from them. He started to speak. "Do you know this woman's name?"

"I don't really know her. I've spoken to her a few times in the park near where she lives. She . . . she lives under the bridge." Sabre felt almost like she was defying a confidence but the doctor had so little information.

"I figured she was homeless. But you call her Mama T. Why?"

"That's what they call her on the streets. She gathers food for some of the others and it's a play on Mother Teresa." The doctor had a concerned but not surprised look on his face. It was a look that said there wasn't much he hadn't seen. "Is she going to be okay?"

"The blow to the head caused some problems. She has a minor linear skull fracture, which isn't serious unless there's an additional injury to the brain. She has an intraparenchymal hemorrhage, a contusion. It's bleeding into the brain tissue. Like a bruise to the brain tissue, if you will."

"So what does that mean? What kind of treatment will she receive?"

"It's a minor bleed so it may not cause any further problems. The bleeding often stops without any treatment. For now, we just want to keep her here and watch to make sure it doesn't cause any brain swelling, which is rare. If it were a larger bleed we'd be looking at surgery, but this is minor."

Sabre sighed. "That's good then."

"That is good. But we also found a mass on her brain. We're running more tests to determine what it is. We have no medical history and we can't obtain any from the patient. Is there anything you can tell me about her behavior that you may have observed in your contact with her?"

"She has a strange speech pattern. She often repeats a single word or phrase. She really doesn't make sense most of the time. Yet, she seems to function like she knows what she's doing." Sabre shrugged her shoulders. "I don't know. It's hard to explain. Could the mass on her brain be causing that?"

"Maybe. We need to run more tests." The doctor forced a little smile. "She's awake, by the way."

"May I see her?"

"Sure, for a minute. It might be good for her to see a familiar face. We haven't been as busy tonight as usual so we already have her in a room. Come with me."

JP stayed behind as Sabre followed the doctor to Mama T's bed. She looked comfortable enough. Sabre wondered when the last time was that she had slept in a real bed. Her hands were strapped to the side of the bed, but they were clean and she was hooked up to an IV. The doctor stepped out.

"Hi, Mama T. How are you?"

Mama T looked at her with a blank stare for a few seconds and then recognition appeared in her eyes. "The boy. Help the boy."

"Yes, Mama T. I'll help the boy." Sabre gently touched her left hand. "You were very brave tonight, knocking your cart into that thief." Sabre smiled at her.

"Help the boy."

"Don't worry. I'll help the boy."

Sabre continued to talk to her for a few minutes. Mama T continued to repeat herself. That was the extent of their relationship. Their connection was Cole. They both wanted him protected. Yes, Mama T had a kind heart. Sabre wondered again if someone was missing their Mama ... Mama T.

Chapter 37

JP's search for Thomas Anthony Martin, the Rialto quarter-back, led him to an old bar in Bloomington called "The Ruins." Apparently, the bar had been in the family for fifty years or more, previously owned by his father Thomas Anthony Martin, Jr. The quarterback was technically Thomas Anthony Martin III, but he went by Tony. Other than his birth certificate, JP couldn't find any place where he used "the third."

JP looked up the phone number and called it but reached voice mail. He left a message for Tony to return the call when he came in.

The search for Craig G. McGill, the other Rialto quarter-back, took him to a nearby college where he had played football for a year. He had just started his second season when he met his death. McGill was driving drunk on the Ortega Highway on his way back from San Juan Capistrano when he crashed into the side of the mountain, flipped over, and landed part way down, stopped only by some very large pine trees. He and his date both died in the accident.

JP still didn't know which one was #6, the dead quarter-back or the bar owner.

He stood up from his desk; carefully stepped over Louie, his beagle puppy who lay asleep on the floor; and walked into his kitchen to get a cup of coffee. He stretched a few times before sitting back down to another round of phone calls. His next task was to find Maryanne Miconi. So far he hadn't been too successful. He had spoken to nearly every Miconi in the Inland Empire. After numerous phone calls he finally reached a man who worked in a tire shop, Stefano Miconi.

"Hello, Stefano?"

"Please. It's Steve. My grandfather was Stefano. Do you need some tires?"

"No, actually I'm trying to find someone. I'm on the alumni committee for Bucher High School and we're planning a class reunion for the graduating class of 1976. We're including the classes before and after, but it's thirty-five years for the class of 1976. I'm responsible for tracking down the addresses. We want to get the invitations out and if they can't come, maybe they could contribute a little background for the book we're putting out on the classes."

"So, who you looking for?"

"Maryanne Miconi. I thought she might be a relative. Do you know her?" The puppy started nipping at his hand.

"Yeah, that's my cousin, but I don't think she'll be coming to the reunion."

"Why's that?" JP asked.

"Because she's somewhere in South America in a convent."

"She's a nun?" JP didn't hide the shock in his voice.

"Yeah, my cousin the nun. It surprised us all. Head cheer-leader, social butterfly, even became a bit of a lush the last year or so of high school. Who'da thought? She joined the convent a few months after graduation. I've only seen her a few times since then."

"How long has it been since you saw her?" Louie kept tugging at him in an effort to get JP to play. JP gently pushed him away, but the pup returned immediately.

"She came home for Christmas once after she'd been gone about ten years. Five or six years ago she returned for her father's funeral."

"Were you two close when you were young?"

"No. She was quite a bit older than me. I hardly saw her, just family weddings and things."

"Thanks. You've been a big help."

"If you really want to get a hold of her you might want to crash her little brother's funeral. I expect she'll be home for that. They were pretty close."

JP hesitated. "I don't think that would be appropriate."

"Just sayin'. It might be a good distraction for her. And she might want to add something to your class book."

"Did her brother go to school in Fontana?" JP was trying any angle. Maybe there were others that knew something, or maybe Maryanne confided in someone. Then he remembered the teacher said Maryanne was concerned about her little brother when she broke up with Rob. He wondered if it was the same little brother.

"He went there as a kid, but he never made it to real high school. Spent the little time he did in continuation school. He was a real screw-up."

"When's the funeral?" JP asked, as he covered Louie's mouth to keep him from biting. " Maybe I can catch up with her before she leaves town."

"It's Friday at St. Joseph's in Fontana. That's if the coroner released the body."

"The coroner? How did he die?" JP was frustrated at Louie, but reached down and picked him up to keep him from growling or barking.

"The poor sap was beat to death. That kid just couldn't catch a break. But the truth be told Scottie brought most of it on himself."

Louie started licking JP's face. He moved his head quickly to the side and almost missed what Steve was saying. "Scottie? His name was Scottie Miconi?"

"Scottie Jamison. He was her brother by another father, but the party line from the family is that they were always very tight."

Chapter 38

Bob and Sabre had just completed their last hearing in Department Four, but before they left the courtroom Judge Hekman spoke to them. "Brown and Clark, Judge Shirkoff wants to see you in his chambers."

"Right now?" Bob asked.

"Right now."

"You can go this way," Judge Hekman said, as she moved her head in the direction of the back hallway.

They picked up their files and walked through the back door of the courtroom and into the hallway. They turned right and walked toward Department One. As they passed the sheriff's office, they both nodded at the sergeant.

"What do you suppose Judge Jerk-off wants with us?" Bob asked.

"I don't know, but when the presiding judge asks to see you in his chambers, you go to his chambers," Sabre said. "I feel like a kid being sent to the principal's office."

"Did that happen a lot?"

"Not often. Mostly I was in trouble for talking too much."

"Now there's a surprise."

"How about you?"

"I went a few times in high school. Once for smoking in the bathroom. Another time for drilling a hole between the girls and boys PE locker rooms."

Sabre shook her head. "Maybe Shirkoff found out you've been stealing information on the ritual cases," Sabre said in a whisper. They passed Attorney Jerry Leahy on his way to see a client in the holding tank and exchanged greetings.

"So why call you in, too?"

"Guilty by association?"

"Naw," Bob said. "He's not that smart."

When they reached the end of the hallway, they stuck their heads in Judge Shirkoff's chambers.

"Come on in," the judge said.

"Hello, Your Honor," Bob and Sabre both said at almost the same time.

"Have a seat," he said. "I'll get right to the point. As you know, there's been a rash of unusual cases filed here at Meadowlark. I also know that you two are on several of them and that you have your pulse on the happenings here at court."

"I don't know about that, Your Honor," Bob said.

"Don't be modest. You two know more about what's going on around here than anyone I know." He looked from Bob to Sabre and back again. "But here's the thing. I just want to hear your take on what's happening. I realize it's just your opinion and what you tell me stays here, but do you think there's a satanic movement afoot?" He looked directly at Bob.

"Personally, I don't think so. I think it's a series of misunderstandings, some overzealousness perhaps on the behalf of a few people."

Judge Shirkoff turned toward Sabre. "And you?"

Sabre chose her words carefully. "I agree with Bob. Something has obviously happened in this city, as evidenced by the so-called 'Devil House' they featured on the news. I know there were filings before that, but I think the news item sparked even more. My investigations on some of my cases are proving to have fewer demons than they first appeared to have."

"In your investigation have you discovered who might be behind the rituals?"

"No. I'm sorry, Your Honor."

"Are the attorneys panicking?"

Sabre said, "Not at all. There are a couple who seem more than a little concerned, but for the most part everyone is just trying to figure out what's going on."

Judge Shirkoff thanked them for their input and dismissed them. As soon as they left his chambers and were out of earshot of the judge, Sabre said, "What was that?"

Bob shook his head. "Beats me, but it was weird."

"I think he knows you stole the reports," Sabre teased. "And you better be nice to me or I'm going to squeal."

"I think he's under pressure from downtown. This is an election year, you know."

"Of course."

Sabre left Bob at the courthouse and drove to the hospital to see Mama T, silencing her phone before she entered. It was just past noon and she figured Mama T would probably be eating. At least she would have clean food while she stayed there. Sabre parked her car in the lot and walked inside. She went directly to the room Mama T occupied the previous evening. When she arrived, she discovered her bed empty. Sabre felt a knot in the pit of her stomach. She approached the nurse's stand, gave her name, and asked for Jane Doe in Room 312B.

"I'm afraid she's gone."

"What do you mean gone?"

"She left AMA."

"AMA?"

"Against Medical Advice. She left on her own. We tried to persuade her to at least sign a release, but she didn't seem to understand. She simply refused to stay and walked out."

"When?"

"A couple of hours ago. Shortly after breakfast. I tried talking to her, but she just wouldn't listen."

"Why wasn't I called?" Sabre asked, irritation evident in her voice.

The nurse looked at the records. "I'm sorry, ma'am but there's no one listed as a contact."

Sabre apologized for her behavior and hustled out the door, down the steps, and out to the parking lot. She was on the phone to JP before she reached her car.

"I'm going to drive back to the park and watch for her along the way. I'll call if I find her. If I don't find her, I'd like you to go with me back under the bridge where we first found her living, if you don't mind. But first I have an appointment with Hayden's foster mother at 1:30 and since she's close by, maybe we could meet in the park around two-ish."

"That'll work. And, Sabre, don't go to the bridge without me," he said sternly.

Sabre drove slowly, looking back and forth and in and out of alleys, watching for Mama T. She knew it was hopeless. There were so many different routes she could've taken and she may not even know the way. She could be anywhere. Sabre noticed she had missed a message on her cell. She turned the ringer back on and checked. It was from her mother.

"Sabre, sorry I missed your call earlier. Are you coming this weekend? Beverly's bridge partner is out of town and she wanted me to fill in, so please let me know. I'd much rather see you, of course, but if you're not coming then I may as well help her out. I have a Soroptimist meeting shortly. I'll talk to you later. I miss you, darling."

Sabre felt her muscles tighten. For a fleeting second she felt like a four-year-old. She needed her mother but she wasn't there for her. She dismissed the thoughts as quickly as they came.

Sabre called back and reached the voice mail. "Go ahead and play bridge with Beverly. Things at work are real crazy right now. I'll call later. Love you." Sabre hung up. She had too much to do anyway. She was even busier than her mother.

Sabre continued her search until she approached the park and it was time for her appointment. She made one last trip around the perimeter of the park before she drove the three blocks to Hayden's house.

Once inside, the foster mother offered Sabre something to drink and then sat down on the sofa with her. "The reason I called is because Hayden has been acting a little strange."

"In what way?"

"A couple of days ago, I saw him putting extra chips in his lunch bag. And I've noticed other food supplies are dropping quickly." The foster mother waved her right hand. "That didn't sound right. What I mean is that I wouldn't care if he took extra food for himself to eat, but I don't think he's eating it. This morning he asked for an extra sandwich, and when I put it in his backpack I noticed he also had three bananas in there."

"You know he didn't have enough food at home, right? Maybe he's just making sure he has plenty."

"That's what I thought at first, but this morning I asked him why he needed the extra sandwich and he said it was for Cole."

"For Cole? What else did he say?"

"I didn't question him any further. I thought it was best if you did. He'll be here any second now and you can ask him yourself."

"Thanks. How is he doing otherwise?"

"He's all boy, but very sweet. Even though he's constantly into everything and wrestles with the other kids, he's always so loving when he gets too rough. If he makes someone cry, it breaks his heart and he's quick with hugs and apologies."

"I heard he had a visit with his siblings and his mom yesterday. How did that go?"

"I've never seen a kid so excited to see someone. He ran to his mother and jumped on her lap. He wouldn't leave her side for a long time and he's not one to sit still very long. Then he finally started playing with his brothers and sisters."

"Did you stay there?"

"The visit took place at a park in El Cajon and I didn't want to drive home and come back, so I walked a ways away and sat on a bench reading my book."

"Did you observe Mom's reaction to the children?"

"What I saw certainly seemed appropriate. She hugged them all a lot but not in a smothering kind of way. I've seen parents hold on to their children when they wanted to leave. It wasn't like that. They were just as starved for her attention as she was theirs."

"Did Hayden talk about the visit afterwards?"

"Non-stop all the way home and most of the evening. He felt pretty down about having to leave them and devastated that Cole wasn't there."

The front door swung open and Hayden dashed into the house. He tossed his backpack on the floor. "Hayden," the foster mother said. Hayden looked up at her, picked up the backpack, and tossed it onto a chair. She just smiled. "Come over here, honey."

"Hi, Hayden," Sabre said.

Hayden walked over to the sofa. "Do you remember Ms. Brown, your attorney?"

Hayden nodded his head.

"She'd like to talk with you for a minute. Sit down here and I'll go fix you a snack."

Sabre questioned Hayden about school, his home visit, and anything else Hayden wanted to talk about. His comments about Cole not being at the park in El Cajon made a nice segue into the food issue.

"Your foster mother says you're taking food for Cole. Is that true?"

Hayden nodded his head. "Uh huh."

"Have you seen him?"

"Nope." Hayden squirmed.

Sabre put her hand on his shoulder to comfort him. "It's okay. We just need to know what you've been doing with the extra food."

"I just leave it for him."

"Where do you leave it?"

"At the fence. There's a hole I put it through."

"Did Cole tell you to do that?" Hayden shook his head from side to side. "So, why do you leave the food?" Sabre asked.

"Because that day when I saw him he said he was hungry, and we have plenty of food here."

Sabre wanted to reach out and hug this sweet little boy. Her heart ached for him. "Does he pick up the food you leave?"

"At first he didn't, but now it's always gone when I go back the next day."

Chapter 39

Being on a stakeout wasn't exactly the way Sabre had intended to spend the rest of her day, but JP wouldn't have it any other way. She could've returned to her office, but she still needed to check on Mama T and JP was adamant she not go under the bridge alone. Besides, she hoped the stakeout would culminate by finding Cole. So there she sat with JP in the park under a tree across the street from Hayden's school. The chain link fence at the end of the playground came to a corner near an intersection. Directly across the street was the outer edge of the park. Sometimes the cars blocked their view, but anywhere else they sat would've been too visible. Before they settled in, JP confirmed that the bag Hayden had left earlier was still there.

They had arrived a little after 2:00 p.m. and it was now almost 4:30. The students from the school had dispersed and there was little activity on that corner. The occasional pedestrian crossed the street toward the park. Sabre and JP leaned up against the tree like two lovers enjoying each other's company.

"Do you think he'll show?" Sabre asked.

"I don't know, but if it were me I wouldn't go there until after dark."

"It's going to be harder to see when the sun goes down. It's already starting to get dark."

JP pointed across the street. "After six we can park over there and sit in the car. There are no parking restrictions then."

"Good, because it's a little cold already."

JP took his jacket off and handed it to her. "Here, wear this."

She pushed the jacket back at him. "No, then you'll be cold."

"I'm fine. It's warmer than a preacher's knee out here."

"Yeah, right."

He looked at her and smirked. "I'm not wearing it. You may as well."

Sabre put the jacket on. She knew he wouldn't wear it now no matter how cold he felt. "And you call me stubborn. You're as stubborn as a blue-nose mouse."

JP laughed. "I think you mean mule."

"Mouse, mule, what the heck."

They sat in silence for a few minutes. JP broke it when he asked, "Bailey hasn't responded to any of your calls?"

"No, and now I'm afraid she won't. She probably knows by now that I'm aware of the pregnancy. I just wonder what happened to the baby."

"I hate to even think about the possibilities. By the way, I've been trying to track Dr. Cavitt down, but so far I've had no luck. I went to Clairemont Community Center, the last place he worked according to his tax records, and was told he was working at some group home. I've researched every group home where an obstetrician might be needed and no one has him listed on staff."

"So what now?"

"We have a home address for him, but I don't want to go there until we have to. It might tip him off." JP stood up slowly. "Look." He nodded his head and pointed with just his finger toward the school fence.

A man, wearing a knit cap pulled down over his ears and an overcoat that looked dirty even from across the street, walked straight to Hayden's bag.

"It's like he knew it was there," JP said.

The man leaned over and picked it up. Sabre stood up. "What now?"

"Let's just see where he goes."

The man opened the bag, took out the sandwich, and started eating it as he walked across the street toward Sabre, JP, and the park. From across the street the man looked to be over sixty, but as he approached Sabre realized he was probably closer to thirty. He had obviously been on the streets for a while. As soon as he reached the grass, he sat down and continued to eat his sandwich. He wasn't more than fifteen feet from their tree.

"Stay here," JP said, as he walked toward the man. Sabre followed closely behind. JP turned and scowled at her but she continued along with him.

"Excuse me, sir."

"What?" the man asked. His tone wasn't particularly friendly, but not hostile either.

"Do you mind my asking about your food there?" The man clutched the bag to his chest. "Look, I don't want your food. I just want to know if this is the first time you found the food there."

"No, it's there 'most every day. Not on the weekends, though."

"How long have you been getting it?"

"About a week. Maybe a little more." The man squinted his eyes at JP. "You a cop?"

"No, I'm not a cop."

"Cuz I ain't done nothin' wrong," the man said. "I figure it's just some fussy kid who don't like his lunch."

"That's probably it." JP reached in his pocket and took out a ten-dollar bill and handed it to him. "Here. Those lunches might not last forever. Take care." JP took Sabre by the arm and walked away.

They walked to their car and made a loop around the park looking for Mama T and her shopping cart. Sabre just realized Mama T had probably lost all her treasures in the cart that was left behind. She clicked her tongue in a gesture of frustration.

"What's the matter?" JP asked.

"I should've done something with Mama T's cart yesterday. She's probably lost it."

He looked at her. "And what could you have done with it? Put it in your car?"

"I know, but ..."

"But, there was nothing you could've done," JP finished the sentence for her. JP looked out as they pulled up to the curb on the side of the park that led to the bridge. "Why don't you go on home and let me do this alone? It's getting late."

Sabre stepped out of the car. "Then we better hurry. Come on."

JP removed two silver, three-D cell, LED flashlights from the trunk of his car and handed one of them to Sabre.

"It's not dark, yet," Sabre said.

"It will be. Besides, it makes a good club in case we need it." He raised the flashlight as if to clunk her on the head with it.

Sabre wrinkled her nose at him. "You're just trying to scare me."

"You should be scared more often. My grandpa used to say, 'Show fear a little respect, son. It'll keep you safe.'"

"Wise grandpa."

They walked across the field toward the bridge, maneuvering through the weeds and the garbage. Sabre was still dressed in court attire, but at least she had worn a pant suit and reasonably low-heeled shoes.

JP walked behind Sabre while keeping an eye on her. When she hit her foot on something and said, "Ouch," he switched spots and led the way, occasionally looking back at her.

Finally, he reached out his hand and said, "Here, take my hand. I need to know where you are."

Sabre slipped her hand into his and suddenly felt safer, but JP continued to grumble about how he should've come alone.

When they approached the "camp," Sabre recognized a few people from the last time. The young woman who had originally told them Mama T's name sat huddled against the wall. They approached her and asked for Mama T.

"She's not here."

"Have you seen her today?"

"No, not since yesterday, but she'll be back. She always comes back."

"I'm sure she will." Sabre didn't think it would serve any purpose to tell them about Mama T's trip to the hospital. Besides, she didn't know if Mama T would even want her to tell. A man reeking of alcohol and urine staggered toward her. She stepped out of the way just before he reached her, and he fell down against a pile of clothes. Sabre leaned over and asked him if he was all right. He moaned in reply, but didn't appear to be hurt. Something about him looked familiar, but she couldn't place him. She had probably seen him the last time they were here.

JP took the opportunity to show everyone Cole's photo again and ask a few questions. No one seemed to know anything. After a few minutes, they started the walk back to the car with no more answers than they came with. No information on Cole, and no Mama T.

Chapter 40

Bob knocked on Karen Lecy's door. At Sabre's request he had set an appointment with her, and to make certain she kept it he scheduled it at her house. Bob was as concerned about Bailey's baby as everyone else. If there was a baby out there who needed help, they all had to pull together. But no one had reported seeing a baby with Bailey or her mother. The social worker never reported anything nor had any neighbors. *Maybe she had miscarried.*

After much banging on the door, Karen finally answered it. "Huh?" she said when she opened the door. Her eyes were barely open, her hair was disheveled, her make-up was blurred, and she wore a short, see-through negligee. She was only twenty-nine-years old, but she looked fifty.

Bob looked at his watch. "It's 1:30 in the afternoon. Are you just waking up?"

"It was a rough night." She backed away from the door and said, "Come on in."

"Go put some clothes on; then I'll come in."

Bob waited on the porch. After about five minutes, he knocked on the open door and yelled to her.

"Comin'," she said.

Bob continued to wait, this time checking his watch to see how long she was taking. Five more minutes passed. "Karen, come on. I don't have all day."

"Yeah," she yelled back.

Bob lit a cigarette and paced in front of the house. The cigarette was nearly gone when Karen finally returned, wearing a man's long-sleeved shirt that she had apparently just slipped over the negligee. Her hair and face were still a mess, and from the look of her dilated eyes and numb lips, she'd spent the last few minutes ingesting something less than legal.

"What are you on?" Bob asked, never one to pussy-foot around his clients.

"Nothing."

Bob entered the house. He couldn't take a step without encountering some kind of trash, beer can, or piece of clothing. She directed him to the cluttered sofa, but he opted for a dining room chair. Before he sat down, he leaned the chair over and tapped it against the floor to remove any excess food that might be attached to the seat. Karen sat down across from him, but within seconds she stood up and moved around the room.

"Karen, something has come to our attention that needs to be dealt with right away."

"What?"

"We know that Bailey was pregnant. We need to know what happened to the child."

"I don't know what you're talking about. Who told you that? It's that bitchy social worker spreading lies, isn't it?" She opened the refrigerator, took out a beer, and popped it open.

"I haven't even spoken to the social worker. She may not even know," Bob said. "Karen, listen to me. We need to protect that baby. If you're hiding him or her, you'll be in a lot of trouble."

"It's not true. My baby was never pregnant. Why can't they just leave us alone? They want to pin something on her to cover their own asses, don't they. That's it. They put her in foster care and now they can't protect her, so they want to blame me or her for something. They're making up shit." She guzzled her beer.

"Think about that innocent little baby. He may need our help. Or is he with someone safe?"

Karen moved in closer to Bob's face. "There is no baby!" she screamed.

Bob tried several more times to reach her, but it was no use as long as she was high. He looked around the room before he left. "You really need to clean this pigsty up before the social worker comes back here. She'll have one more thing to rag on you about."

Bob smiled to himself as he walked to his car. *If Bailey had a child, Karen is a twenty-nine-year-old grandmother.* He shuddered. *That poor little baby.*

Sabre hadn't called the social worker yet about Bailey's pregnancy. She only told Bob because she thought he might be able to help, but she couldn't keep it from DSS much longer. She hadn't received this information in confidence, so there was no privilege attached. She just needed to gather a little more information. *Is* there a baby or not? And if there is, is he or she at risk? She called and left another message for Bailey, pleading with her to call back. Then she called the social worker.

"Hello, Gillian, this is Sabre Brown. I'm calling about Bailey Lecy."

"What can I do for you?"

"Do you know anything about Bailey being pregnant?"

"She's pregnant?"

"Not now, but apparently she was until about a month ago. Do you know anything about that?"

"No. That can't be. I've been investigating that family most of the year. I never saw her pregnant."

"I have good reason to believe she was."

"So, where's the baby?"

"I don't know. That's why I'm calling you."

"I think you're mistaken, but I'll certainly follow up and see what I can find out."

Bob walked into Sabre's office as she was finishing her call with the social worker. He started to walk back out and give her some privacy, but she waved her hand and motioned him to come in and sit down.

Bob sat down and picked up the antique mahogany hourglass that sat on Sabre's desk. He turned it over and watched the sand run down.

"Thank you. Please let me know if you discover anything." Sabre hung up the phone.

Bob examined the hourglass. "I like this. Where did you get it?"

"My mom came by the office today on her way to an appointment and dropped it off. It belonged to my brother, Ron. He collected all kinds of weird things."

Bob slid his glasses down to the edge of his nose and looked over them. "There's some very intricate woodwork on here. It looks Victorian."

"It is. And it keeps excellent time. It takes between fifty-nine and sixty minutes to empty." Sabre sighed. "Any luck with Bailey's mom?"

"No. She denies any possibility of Bailey ever being pregnant. Blames it all on DSS. She's such a charmer. Do you realize she could be a twenty-nine-year-old grandmother?"

"That's a lovely thought. You don't usually think about grandmas being druggies."

"What did Gillian say?" Bob asked.

"She's in denial, too. Says she hasn't seen any signs of a pregnancy and that she's been checking on them for the past year."

"Maybe Shellie was wrong?"

"I don't think so, but I'd like to hear what Bailey has to say. I wish she'd call me back."

After Bob left her office, Sabre finished some paperwork and then packed up her briefcase. She drove to the park and looked for both Cole and Mama T. She found neither one.

Chapter 41

A man pulled out of the parking spot directly in front of the bar as JP pulled up. JP maneuvered his car into the space, stepped out of his car, and donned his Stetson. A sign nearly as old as the building jutted out from the wall above the door. It had a palm tree on a beach and the words "The Ruins" in lights. At least a quarter of the bulbs were missing. Since it was daylight the sign wasn't lit, and JP wondered if it worked at all.

He stepped inside a very dark room. It took several seconds to adjust his eyes to where he could see anything. All he could make out at first were a couple of figures sitting at the bar. Although he saw no one smoking, the place smelled of stale cigarette smoke and fresh beer. Within a few seconds his eyes began to adjust to the lighting. Two customers sat at a table against the wall and six more were belly-up to the bar, all with what was presumably an alcoholic beverage in front of them at 9:33 in the morning. A slender fifty-something man tended bar.

"Good morning, Tex," he said, as JP sat down on a corner barstool. "What can I get you this fine morning?"

"Black coffee if you have it."

"Coming right up," he said.

From his barstool, JP could see that the room was long and narrow and was furnished with a few tables and chairs and four pool tables. Cheap tropical décor was scattered throughout the room. Several tiki masks hung above a ciga-rette machine on the wall behind him. In the corner stood a five-foot tiki god with a bobbing head and huge white teeth exposed by a freaky smile. A pineapple was carved into the top of his head. The head took up about two-thirds of the tiki and sat on a huge spring. The bottom half of the tiki was the shape of a man carved out of the trunk of a coco palm.

The bartender returned with the coffee and set it down on the bar. JP handed him a five-dollar bill. When the bartender went to the cash register, JP noticed some old football photos on the wall above it.

"Those yours?" JP asked, pointing to the photos.

The bartender nodded. "A hundred years ago." He picked up a glass half full of what looked like whiskey sitting next to the register and took a drink.

"Are you Thomas Anthony Martin, III, star quarterback from Monroe High School?"

"Do I know you?"

"No."

The bartender smiled. "That's my name, but friends and enemies alike all call me Tony. You can, too. And I wasn't a star, just second string, but I loved the game." He looked at JP and read him with all the knowledge of one who had observed people for many years. "So, if you don't know me, who are you looking for?" Tony asked.

"I'm a private investigator and I'm doing a little work on an old trust case. I'm looking for the Monroe High quarterback with jersey number six. Would that be you?"

"No. That'd be McGill, but I'm afraid he left us many years ago for the big stadium in the sky."

"Did you know him well?"

"Not really. I played football with him for two years. Damn good player. Much better than I was. But I never hung out with him in any other capacity." Tony took another drink.

"Did you know any of his close friends?"

"He hung out with the quarterback from Bucher mostly. I can't remember his name."

"Did you know a kid named Barney or maybe Billy that McGill hung out with?"

Tony shook his head. "Can't say as I did." Tony raised his glass toward JP in a toasting kind of gesture. "But then my brain isn't what it used to be."

St. Joseph's Catholic Church was empty except for a lone woman kneeling in the front row. JP walked about half way up the aisle and took a seat. He checked his watch. It was only five minutes before the funeral was scheduled to begin and no one was there. He didn't expect a big crowd for Scott's service, but he didn't expect to make up fifty percent of the attendance. He glanced around. Two stained glass windows looked out of place in an otherwise plain, almost austere, setting. The casket dominated the space in front of the altar.

JP wondered if the woman was Maryanne. She wasn't wearing a habit, but he knew the rules for nuns weren't as strict as they once were. She looked about the right age, but he couldn't tell for sure from where he sat. He would just have to wait until after the service.

A priest walked in from a side door and spoke briefly with the woman. JP couldn't hear the conversation. Then he began the funeral mass. "Eternal rest give to them, O Lord; and let perpetual light shine upon them."

JP had never been to a Catholic Mass before but he found it quite interesting when it first started. Then his mind began to wander. It had been some time since he had been in a church for any reason. He thought back. The last time was probably when his brother married some twenty years ago. He could remember going to church with his grandma when he was young. She'd always take him out for ice cream after the service, which encouraged him to go with her more often.

The funeral service was very impersonal. There was no eulogy, and at the conclusion the priest incensed the coffin and sprinkled it with holy water. He then walked over to the woman, touched her on the forehead, and said, "God bless you, my child." The woman stayed behind after the priest left and continued praying. JP waited for a while and then decided to go stand at the back of the church.

The woman remained on her knees for nearly fifteen minutes longer before she finally stood up and walked toward JP. When she reached him, she looked back at the altar and said, "It was once so beautiful in here. I remember coming here as a child. I thought St. Joseph's was the most beautiful church in the world. The candles were always glowing. There was lots of gold on a remarkable altar, and the way the sun would light up the stained glass windows all along both sides of the church just brought it to life." She paused. "Now it's just . . . another church."

JP opened the door for her and followed her out. He reached out his hand to shake hers. "I'm JP."

She reciprocated but her shake was very light; it barely squeezed his hand. "Sister Mary Agnes."

"Formerly Maryanne Miconi?"

She looked surprised. "Yes, do I know you?"

"No, but I hope you'll give me a few minutes of your time. I know it's not the best time to be doing this, but you may be able to save the life of a fourteen-year-old girl." JP realized he was being a little dramatic, but the truth was that Bailey could be in danger, especially if she knew who killed Scott. "I'm a private investigator. I work for an attorney who represents a young girl who may know how your brother died."

"What can I do for you?"

JP looked around. He felt very uncomfortable interrupting her grieving time. "Are you going to Scott's gravesite?"

"No. I'm finished here. I've done all I can except for my future prayers, which I will continue to say for him as I have for the past thirty years." She looked up at JP. "Come, we can go into the hall and have a cup of tea."

He followed her inside. There was a little table with two glass coffee pots sitting on the burners. One held coffee, the other hot water. "They had a class in here earlier, but there won't be another one for an hour or so," she said. She fixed herself a cup of tea while JP poured his own coffee. Then they sat down on metal chairs in front of a folding table.

JP began. "Sister, I really appreciate this. Again, I apologize for the timing." He realized how uneasy he felt questioning a nun.

"It's okay. I can use the distraction, but somehow I don't think I'm really going to like what I hear. It's about Scott, isn't it?"

"Yes, of sorts. It's about how and why he was murdered. I'd like you to tell me what you know about Ric Cavitt."

"Do you think Ric killed him?" She asked with little surprise in her voice.

"I don't know, but I do know they were involved in some rather unusual dealings in San Diego. And our client, the young girl I spoke of, knows more than she's telling. Now she's in hiding and I need to figure this out before it's too late. And we have reason to believe a baby may be in danger as well. Can you start by telling me what the relationship was between Scott and Ric Cavitt?"

"I hadn't seen Scott in many years. I know he was involved with drugs and some petty criminal activities, but I didn't know he had any contact with Ric."

JP thought she seemed either hesitant to explain or didn't know where to begin. He decided to lay it out for her. "This is what I know. I know that Dr. Ric Cavitt and your brother were involved with a place the news reporters are referring to as the 'Devil House.' It's a house that was filmed, and the video was provided to the media. It had a hospital bed with a circle around it in blood, albeit animal blood. A huge tree was painted on the wall along with the numbers 66. A couple of pig hearts were found on the premises. There are juvenile cases of ritual abuse popping up all over the city, and I can't help but think Ric and Scott were involved with those cases. Our client, Bailey, has a DVD of Scott and Dr. Ric at the 'Devil House.' She has another disc that I have reason to believe includes others or is more incriminating, but I don't know for sure what's on it. Bailey, the fourteen-year-old girl is involved because her mother was living with Scott and he was supplying the mother with drugs."

Maryanne shook her head. "I'm so sorry."

"What I don't know is just how Scott and Dr. Ric were connected or who else was involved, but I believe whatever they're involved in all leads back to Fontana. I realize Scott was a lot younger than Ric, but I can't shake the feeling that it had something to do with whatever happened to Ric, Rob, Craig, Barney, and you in high school."

"Why do you think that?"

"I know that something awful happened the first weekend of school. Something so awful it broke you and Rob up and sent you into a downhill spiral; it made you extremely worried about your little brother; it ruined your friendships; and it affected the relationship of two very close brothers."

Maryanne stood up, walked to the coffee pot, and poured more hot water into her cup. She returned to the table and sat down. "I'm not sure how it'll help, but I'll tell you what happened. I've never told anyone before except once in confession. They say confession is good for the soul, but when I confessed it didn't make me feel any better. I've lived with this sin all my life, but perhaps this information will help that young girl and give me a little peace."

Chapter 42

Maryanne took a deep breath and then started her story. "They called themselves the Route 66 gang. It wasn't really a gang, but they liked the way it sounded. There were four of them—Rob and Ric Cavitt, Craig McGill, and Barney Fife."

"Barney Fife?"

"Fife wasn't his real name. I'm not even sure Barney was. That's what they always called him because he was tall and thin and clumsy. He was smart as a whip, but didn't have much common sense. I'm quite sure he wouldn't have been part of the group if he hadn't been Craig's cousin. He was just so odd. The four of them did everything together."

"Who was the leader?"

"It's hard to say. Rob and Craig were star quarterbacks and used to having the attention and calling the shots, but sometimes Craig would go over the line. Barney was the brains, and Ric was there because Rob wouldn't have it any other way. Rob was the muscle. He wouldn't back down to anyone."

"Even his father?" JP asked.

"You know about that?"

"I know his father was abusive."

"Rob never wanted to leave Ric behind because he knew his father would mistreat him. The older Rob got, the more he was able to defend himself, but Ric couldn't so Rob had to do it for him." Maryanne looked pensive. "Anyway, when I first started dating Rob he spent a lot of time with me, but he soon went back to hanging more with the Route 66 gang and I'd see him on Friday nights. We hung out at school all week and I never missed his games, but he spent the rest of the weekend with his group. He'd try to make it sound like he needed time with his buddies, but I think it was about protecting Ric."

"Did you ever go anywhere with the gang?"

"A few times, but the other boys didn't have steady girl-friends so I didn't fit in very well. I don't think Ric or Barney ever had a girlfriend and Craig was a player; he was with a different girl every week. So, it was fine with me. I was involved in a lot of school activities and trying to maintain an 'A' average."

"So why were you with them on that particular weekend when 'whatever' happened?"

"It was the end of our first week of school. My parents were out of town for the weekend and they left Scottie with me. Rob had a scrimmage on Saturday afternoon so I took Scottie with me to watch it. He was eight years old at the time and loved to tag along with us. He thought Rob was 'rad.' He really looked up to him. In fact, Scottie thought all those boys were cool, and that night they treated him like their little mascot. Craig even gave him a Route 66 sticker."

"So the other boys were at the scrimmage?"

"Ric was. He sat with us. The plan was for Rob to come to my house after the game, but Craig and Barney showed up in the last quarter. Craig was angry because Rialto had lost their scrimmage. He was complaining about how his defense had let him down. He had been sacked several times and he wasn't happy about it. Anyway, I took Scottie and left and Rob was to come along shortly. We were going to have a movie night, eat popcorn, and watch Scottie."

"But?"

"But Rob apparently invited Craig, Barney, and Ric to my house because a half hour after I returned home all four of them showed up. They walked in ready to party. Craig was carrying a case of beer and Barney had a bottle of wine in each hand. I was upset at first but after a few glasses of wine I settled in. I had only drunk alcohol one time before that night, so it didn't take much to hit me pretty hard. Barney and I drank the wine; the others guzzled the beer. We mostly stood around and talked but we had the stereo blaring and the more we drank the louder it got."

"Where was Scott?"

"He was right there with us. The boys were treating him like he was real important. I think Craig even slipped him a few drinks of his beer." She shook her head. "I don't know what I was thinking. Then someone knocked on the door and I answered it. A neighbor had come over to complain about the music being too loud. So I turned the stereo down, but Craig kept turning it up so I shut it off. Craig suggested we take the party to a hilltop off of Highland. Apparently Rob had been there before and thought it was a good idea. I protested because I had Scottie and I couldn't leave him and it was nearly midnight. They said to bring him along and Scottie begged to go, so we all piled in the car and left."

"Whose car did you take?"

"Craig's."

"And he was driving?"

"Yes, even though he had had way too much to drink. Rob didn't want to drive his car and I don't think Barney even had a license—not that Craig would've let anyone else drive anyway."

"So you went to the hilltop?"

"No. Well, we went that direction, but Craig turned just before we reached Highland Ave. He drove through a residential neighborhood and pulled over by this little ridge that overlooked the street. He said, 'I have an idea.' Then he opened his trunk and took out a life-size dummy that his school used at the pep rallies to hang the other team in effigy. It was made of cream-colored cloth and was dressed in jeans, a t-shirt, and a baseball cap. The students changed the t-shirt to match the jerseys of whatever team they were playing and then hanged the dummy at the rallies. We had one at our school, too. When I think back on it now, even that was pretty creepy. I don't think the schools allow it anymore.

"Anyway, Craig told us to stay by the car and to just watch. He waited until there were no cars coming, and then he dashed out onto Highland Ave. and sat the dummy near the side of the road, just on the edge. Then he ran back to us. Before long a car came along and swerved to avoid hitting the dummy. After the car passed, Craig ran back and grabbed it in case he came back. He waited about five minutes and then he did it again."

"Did anyone else do it?"

"Barney did it once and I think Ric did it. Scottie begged to have a turn, but I wouldn't let him." Maryanne looked despondent and JP could tell she didn't want to go on.

JP stood up, "Can I bring you some more tea?"

"No, thank you. I'm good."

JP walked over to the coffee pot, filled his cup, and then sat back down across from Maryanne. "And then what happened?"

"Craig was becoming bored with that game and he encouraged us all to climb up on the ridge with him, which we did. Craig carried the dummy and told Barney to bring the rest of the beer. We were trying to be quiet because there were houses only a couple hundred feet away. The lights were out in most of them. By then we were all pretty wasted, so we kept falling down and then everyone would laugh. I'm surprised we didn't wake anyone.

"I thought we were going to the top of the ridge to sit and finish the beer. I actually thought this was the hilltop he was initially taking us to, but when we all reached the top Craig said, 'Now watch this.' There was a convertible driving east on Highland, and it was probably moving a little faster than it should have been. Music was blaring from the car. Just as the car approached the ridge, Craig threw the dummy. We could hear the thud as it landed on the front hood of the car. The driver swerved to the left and then back again. I heard brakes screeching and metal crashing. Then the car flipped over, and I saw what I thought was the dummy flying through the air. It wasn't until later that I realized it was the girl who had been driving the car. She landed on the street, and the car rolled over on top of her. And all of a sudden there was complete silence."

Maryanne stopped talking, took a deep breath, and slowly let it out. Then she began her narration again. "I started to scream, but Rob put his hand over my mouth and stopped me. As he was trying to calm me down, I saw Scottie start to run down the ridge. He was yelling, 'I'll get the dummy.' I ran after him, but he was too far ahead of me and I had had too much to drink. By the time I reached him, Scottie was standing near the car with his mouth agape looking at the young girl pinned under the car." Maryanne swallowed; tears were forming in her eyes. "Her torso was nearly severed where the metal had cut into her, and her insides were falling out. Her head looked like it was on sideways because her neck had obviously been broken, and there was blood everywhere."

JP reached over and patted her on the arm. "Are you okay?"

"Yes, I need to finish," she said. "I grabbed Scottie and tried to pull him away, but he just stood there. I don't know if he was in too much shock or if I was too drunk, but I couldn't make him move. The next thing I knew Rob picked him up and carried him to Craig's car. I followed behind. At first Rob was walking fast but he kept going faster and faster and soon he was in a full run. He kept yelling at me to hurry. I saw Ric over in the bushes looking for something when we ran past. By the time we reached the car Craig already had it running, Barney was seated in the front, and we climbed into the back. Craig flipped the car around and popped his trunk open. I looked back and saw Ric running toward the car with the dummy. He threw it in the trunk, jumped into the back with us, and Craig took off.

"I could see that lights in some of the houses had been turned on, and we weren't very far from the scene when we passed a fire truck coming towards us with its siren blaring. We turned and took a back way to Fontana, but we heard sirens for quite a while."

Maryanne took a deep breath and blew it out. "There, that's the first time I've told the whole story. Even in confession I just gave the highlights. God already knew anyway."

JP heard her take a few deep breaths and then she began to sip on her tea. "Do you think you can answer a few more questions?"

"Sure."

"None of you reported it?"

"No. Someone from one of the houses must have called in the crash because the ambulance and fire engines were there quickly. At least we assumed that's where they were going."

"And I assume none of you ever told anyone."

"I don't think so. I know I didn't. We drove back to my house and everyone came inside. We all sat down and Barney said, 'We need a plan.' It's the only time I ever saw him take charge. He started telling everyone what to do and everyone just followed along. He made Scottie and me members of the Route 66 gang, and we swore to never say anything about what had happened. We cleaned up the house and put all the empty bottles in Craig's trunk. He was to dispose of the dummy and the bottles on his way home. The gang agreed that we would forever be bound by the evening's events but we'd never operate as a gang again. We would for the most part go our separate ways."

"So you broke up with Rob?"

"He didn't want to, but I couldn't be around him without talking about it. I could hardly live with myself. Everything changed after that. I couldn't concentrate on my studies. I didn't want to be with any of my friends. I wouldn't get close enough to anyone for fear I would be compelled to confide in someone."

"What about Scott?"

"Everyone was worried that he might talk, so Craig went up to his room before he left and talked with him. When he came back down, Craig seemed confident that he wouldn't say anything. To tell you the truth, I think he threatened him."

"Did Scott ever say anything to you about it?"

"Nope, not a word. Nor did I to him. Looking back, I realize what a horrible disservice I did to my little brother. I wanted to talk to him sometimes but I didn't know what to say. And I had started consuming a lot of alcohol to drown out my memories. I would hear him crying himself to sleep at night, and that just made me drink more. It totally ruined Scottie. He was such a sweet little boy, but after that night he was never the same. He didn't smile much. Heck, he hardly even spoke for a year. My parents could see there was something wrong, but they thought it was just a phase. Then his behavior became much worse. He started smoking and stealing and skipping school. By the time he was eleven, Scottie had become a full-fledged delinquent. By the age of thirteen, he was a drug addict."

"Were you still at home?"

"No. I was in the convent by then. I moved as far away from Fontana as I could. But I'd receive letters from home. My mother always wrote that everything was fine. She never mentioned any of Scottie's problems, but my cousin, Yvonne, would tell me everything he was into and I would just pray for him."

"Was he ever into a cult or devil worship or anything like that?"

Maryanne shook her head. "Not that I'm aware of. He didn't really believe in much of anything. But who knows what he was into later."

"Did you ever hear what happened to Barney?"

"No. I know he always wanted to go back to San Diego where his mother was living, but I don't know if he did. His parents were divorced and I think he lived here with his dad, but I'm not even certain of that."

Silence ensued for several minutes. Finally JP said, "Did you ever think about reporting it all to the authorities?"

"Every day for the last thirty-five years, but I never knew what good it would do or how many lives it would destroy. I know it ruined a lot of lives anyway, but after some time had passed what was the point? We could've all been sent to prison, but I think we were punished enough. I think God's punishment for me has been the agony I've suffered just knowing what we did. He directed me to the convent, where I've been able to atone for my sins by helping others. I believe that's what I was meant to do. If telling you helps save that young girl then I'm glad I did, even if it means I have to pay my debt to society in prison."

JP thanked her for sharing her story. "By the way, do you know anything about a 1948 Plymouth that belonged to old man Cavitt?"

"The car Roger had in high school?"

"Yeah, that's the one."

"Rob always wanted that car, but his dad wouldn't let him have it even after Roger was killed in Vietnam. But apparently he took possession of it after his dad died. Yvonne wrote that she saw Rob driving it around town the summer after I left."

Chapter 43

Bob looked over Sabre's shoulder as she flipped through the computer screen pages of The Eagle, a local Inland Empire newspaper dated September 11, 1976. The front page carried the story with a large photo of a smashed 1976 Mercedes-Benz 450 SL.

Eighteen-year-old April Baker met an untimely death when she crashed her birthday present, a brand new Mercedes-Benz 450 SL convertible, on Highland Ave. at approximately 12:45 this morning. She had owned the car for less than six hours when it flipped over and pinned her to the ground, nearly severing her torso. Her parents presented her with the car at her birthday party at the El Rancho Verde Country Club in Rialto, Ca.

The cause of the accident is unknown, but there is no indication that another car was involved in the crash, nor was there any evidence of drugs or alcohol.

"She met an untimely death," Bob said. "I love the way reporters always say that. What exactly is a timely death? Is that when a death is scheduled? So if someone is murdered exactly when someone plans it, does that make it timely?"

Sabre smiled. "You're a nut."

Bob walked around to the other side of Sabre's desk. He picked up the hourglass and examined it.

Sabre looked at the article again. "My God, she was only eighteen years old," Sabre said. She printed the article and placed it in the Lecy file. "But what does it all mean? And does it tie in with the 'Devil House?'"

Just then JP walked through the doorway. He stopped and leaned against the wall. "I've been asking myself that same question ever since I left Fontana yesterday."

"So, did you come up with anything?" Sabre asked.

"Maybe. I'm thinking, what could a loser like Scott Jamison have in common with a doctor? A loser like Dr. Ric Cavitt?"

"You mean other than that they're both losers?" Bob asked. He turned the hourglass over and watched the sand start to trickle down.

"Yes, other than that?" JP said.

"They had a dreadful past in common," Sabre said.

"Yes, and that past gave Scott the ammunition to blackmail the doctor. I assume he wanted drugs, or money to buy drugs," JP said.

"And when he asked for too much, the doctor killed him?" Sabre said.

"Maybe," JP said.

"But does it have anything to do with the 'Devil House'? There was no evidence of drug activity there. What's with the animal blood? Or sacrifices? And let's assume Scott was blackmailing the doctor. Was it for drugs or money?"

"I don't think it was money because the doctor is pretty strapped himself. His credit cards are maxed out; he's paying child support; and he has no visible means of income, at least not that I've found. No, there's definitely something missing . . . something that we're not seeing."

"Maybe they needed each other for whatever they were doing," Sabre said.

"Or maybe they're just cult buddies who found each other," Bob piped in.

JP and Sabre looked at Bob. "Naw," they both said at the same time.

"I think the key is Bailey. She knows something else and she has another DVD. That might be the missing link," Sabre said.

"And if the doctor killed Scott, he may know about Bailey's disc and she could be in serious danger," JP said.

"That's it. Somehow I have to reach Bailey."

"And how are you going to do that?"

"I'm going to keep calling her until she calls me back. If I use up all her minutes she'll have to call for more."

"And this time you'll let me know when you're meeting her, so I can follow her and find out where she is, right?" JP tilted his head at Sabre and looked her straight in the eye.

"I'll think about it. We do need to get her off the streets."

JP handed Sabre a large white envelope. "Here's the report from my trip to Fontana. I've told you most of it on the phone, but here is everything in case I missed something in our conversation. Tomorrow I have an appointment to see Regina Collicott's teenage client at World of Hope. Regina called me this morning and said the girl was ready to talk. Maybe we'll find another connection to this cult thing."

After JP left, Sabre called Bailey again and left a message. "Bailey, I'm pleading with you to call me back. I am worried that your life is in danger, and I'm even more worried about Apollo."

Bob looked up at her. "You're worried about Apollo?"

"Not really, but I'm hoping it'll get her attention."

Chapter 44

Sabre bolted out of bed a little after one o'clock in the morning to answer her phone. It made her nervous. It was never good news when a call came in that late.

"Hello, Bailey?"

"I need to talk to you," Bailey said.

"Are you all right?"

"Yes, for now."

"Can I pick you up?" Sabre asked.

"No, I'll meet you."

"Same place?"

"No. There's a back entrance to the canyon just at the bottom of the hill on Boyd. Do you know where it is?"

"Yes, I'll be there in about ten minutes."

"First, promise me you'll be alone."

Sabre hesitated. "I'll be alone."

The more Sabre learned about the Route 66 gang, the more she realized she was at risk. She thought about calling JP, but she was afraid she'd lose any contact with Bailey. She drove down the hill on Boyd. She glanced at the gas gauge and saw she had a quarter of a tank. It made her uncomfortable when it dropped below the half mark, but there was plenty of gas to make it where she was going. She'd fill it first thing in the morning.

Just before the road curved, there was a small paved area off to the left where she could park. It sat between two housing tracts in front of an open field that led into the canyon. She pulled into the parking area and faced her car toward the road. She had just parked her car when Bailey knocked on her window. She had to have arrived before Sabre did.

Bailey stepped into the car. She was wearing a dark jacket, jeans, and a knit cap. She had apparently found access to some clothes. Sabre wondered if Shellie gave them to her.

"They came to see my mom," Bailey said as soon as she was inside the car.

"Who is *they*?"

"The worshippers. They were looking for me."

"Did your mom tell them where you were?"

"She didn't know."

"What do you think they want?"

"Probably to kill me like they did Scott."

"Bailey, did you see who killed Scott?"

"No, I didn't. But it had to be them, and if they know about the other disc then they're probably looking for it."

"What's on the other one?"

"Apollo said it has the worshippers on it. They're going to one of their meetings. I haven't watched it, but he said it shows the fat guy and some other people he didn't recognize."

"And they let Apollo film it?" Sabre was skeptical.

"No, they didn't know he was filming. They would've killed him and probably sacrificed him, if they'd known. I didn't know he was taping it, either, until later."

"So how did he do it?"

"He followed me a couple of times, so he knew where to go. I was with him when he filmed the 'Devil House' but not when he did the third video."

"Do you have the disc with you?"

Bailey shook her head from side to side. "No, I have it hidden. Apollo said not to give it to anyone until he said so."

"But Apollo can't tell you now. And he might need the disc to save himself from going to prison."

Bailey didn't respond. Sabre was sure she was trying to figure it all out. This poor little girl was trying to make decisions no adult should ever have to make. After about a minute of silence Sabre said, "Bailey, I know you were pregnant. Did you have the baby?"

Bailey looked up in complete surprise. Apparently, Shellie hadn't told her that Sabre knew. "How'd you know?"

"I figured it out from your behavior and a couple of things you said. Please tell me what happened. Maybe I can help."

Bailey started to cry. "They k . . . killed my baby. The worshippers killed my baby."

"Oh my God. I'm so sorry." Sabre reached her arm around Bailey's shoulder and pulled her close. For a second Bailey leaned on her accepting the comfort she offered. Then she slowly sat back up.

"How did you get involved with these people?"

"Scott took me there."

"To the 'Devil House?'"

"Yeah, but there was another one, too. It was out in the country somewhere. I was blindfolded when they took me there, but it was too quiet to be in the city. And Apollo followed me there and then he sneaked back and made the film."

"Maybe you could start at the beginning and tell me everything."

"Where's the beginning?"

"Last fall your grades started to drop and you began to miss school. Why don't you start there?"

"I guess it all started when my mom brought Scott home to live with us. He was creepy and I kept telling my mom that, but she said we needed him to help with the rent. I don't think he even paid rent. Maybe at first he did, but then he was just giving her more and more drugs. She'd get high and pass out, and then Scott would come into my room. I kept telling him no, but each time he'd stay a little longer and he'd keep touching me. I was so scared."

"Did you ever tell your mom?"

"I tried to tell her when she was sober, but she didn't believe me. She said it was all in my head."

"Then one night he came into my room and raped me. My mom came in and saw it. She pulled on his arm and he pushed her. She was so high she just stumbled and fell. Scott looked at me and said, 'See, you don't mess with me or I'll kill you and your mom.' Then he finished his business and fell asleep on top of me."

"What did you do?"

"I managed to crawl out from under him and out of the bed. I checked on my mom to make sure she was okay and helped her into her bed. And then I locked myself in the bathroom and showered until the hot water ran out."

"What did your mom say the next day?"

"Nothing. She probably didn't even remember it, or she just didn't care."

"And you never approached her about it again?"

"What was the point?"

Sabre felt sick to her stomach. She hated what this poor girl had experienced and she hated having to ask the questions but she had to continue. "Did it ever happen again?"

"A couple of times. Most of the time I would come home real late after Scott was asleep. When he passed out, he wouldn't wake up until noon. That's why I was missing so much school. I'd stay out late and then sleep in while he was asleep."

"When did you start going out with Apollo?"

"I met Apollo at the softball field around the corner." She stretched her arm out and pointed slightly to the left. "I would go there and watch the games. He did the cleanup after the games so he always stayed after everyone else left. I would hang out and wait for the time to pass. He was real friendly. Sometimes I would leave for a while and then come back after he left. One night I was sitting there in the bleachers and he came back. I had been crying and I guess he could see it on my face. My period was almost two weeks late and I'd been feeling sick a lot. I knew then that I was pregnant. When Apollo sat down next to me, we started talking. I didn't tell him what was wrong or anything. I just said I was having trouble at home. He seemed to understand."

"Then you started hanging out?"

"He came there every day and we'd talk awhile. Then we started doing other things together. I'd take him home sometimes in the evening because I knew Scott wouldn't be able to do anything if he was there. That only worked on the weekends because otherwise Apollo had to go home before Scott went to sleep. After a while I told Apollo everything. He wanted me to go to the police but I was too afraid. So Apollo came over one morning when Scott was asleep and put a deadbolt on my door so I could lock it from the inside."

"So then you were able to stay home at night?"

"Yeah, but I was still afraid he would break the door down. By then I had started showing and Scott and my mom both knew I was pregnant. Mom just acted like it was Apollo's baby, but I know she knew."

"So when did you start going to the meetings?"

"Mom took me to the first one."

"Your mother?" Sabre was surprised.

"It was Scott's idea. He set it all up. I heard them arguing about it. But my mom said she was going to help me through all this and it would ease my soul, or some shit like that."

"What happened at the meeting?"

"A woman wearing a mask greeted us. She made us put on masks, too. Then she took us into another room. They called it the inner sanctum. Three other people, all wearing masks, were standing around a pentagram under a tree painted on the wall. It's like they were worshipping the tree. There was one woman who looked real old. She could hardly walk."

"Did you see her face?"

"No, she wore a mask, too, but I saw her boney, wrinkled hands. She led the chants. They treated her like a queen or something. They started chanting and saying all kinds of weird crap, like how I had something evil in my belly and I needed to be cleansed. How Satan needed his child back. They made me feel like I had something bad inside me. I felt that way too because it was Scott's baby and he was a devil. It was real strange, but after a while I started chanting with them. About an hour later we went home."

"But you went back?"

"On the way home my mom promised that if I went to a few more meetings and 'did what needed to be done until after the baby was born'—those were her words—that things would be a lot better, Scott would go away, and we'd have money to live on."

"Did you know what she meant by that?" Sabre asked.

"No. I tried to get her to explain but she didn't make any sense. She just kept saying I needed to trust her. Like she ever gave me a reason before. But then one day at one of the meetings I found out what she meant. They wanted my baby. By then I was pretty well convinced that I had something evil inside me, but I still didn't realize that they were going to sacrifice it." She paused. "I don't even know if it was a boy or a girl."

Sabre grimaced. "Did you see the sacrifice?"

"Not exactly. When it was time to have the baby, they took me to the inner sanctum. They had me lie down on a metal table, put my feet in the stirrups, and they bound my hands and feet. There were candles all around and they told me the circle around the bed would keep me from having pain. But it didn't. The pain was so bad I could hardly stand it. There was one woman on each side of me. One was a really big woman and she kept getting in my face. I remember how bad her breath smelled and how she kept telling me to push. And then they all chanted, 'I believe in the power of the oak. I believe in the power of the oak.' I still wake up sometimes at night hearing that chant."

"Was anyone else there?"

"Just the fat man in the video. I'm sure it was him. I guess he was a doctor. Anyway, he's the one who delivered my baby. I remember what a relief it was when the baby was finally out and the worst of the pain was over. The big woman took the baby out of the room." Tears ran down Bailey's cheeks. "I heard the baby cry and then it stopped." She sniffled. "A few minutes later, the woman returned but she didn't have the baby with her. I didn't want to think about what they did to my baby so I just closed my eyes and imagined holding him next to me. I knew what I had done was real bad and I'd probably never be forgiven. I knew I'd never be able to forgive myself."

"You poor child. I am so sorry." Sabre didn't know what else to say. "And when it was all over, Scott didn't go away?"

"No. Mom didn't keep any of her promises. I think Scott paid her off in drugs. She got worse every day. But Apollo threatened to kill Scott if he ever touched me again, and with my lock on my door I wasn't as afraid. Apollo also fixed the window in my bedroom so I could sneak in or out, especially if I needed to get in without being seen."

"Did Scott ever go to the meetings?"

"Not all the time, but pretty often, and when he did go he always picked something up from the fat man or this other tall, skinny guy."

"And you never saw any of their faces?"

"No. They always had masks on."

"Did you ever see Scott give them money?"

"No, but one time the tall guy gave Scott some money. I couldn't see how much or anything."

Chapter 45

The first thing Sabre did when she woke up on Saturday morning was to call JP and tell him what she had learned from Bailey the previous night. He scolded her again and made another Texas slang remark about how stubborn she was and how they once again missed the opportunity to follow Bailey.

"I think she's living at home," Sabre said.

"At her home? Did she say that?"

"Not in so many words, but she left a lot of clues. First of all, she's very close to the canyon because she arrived before I did and this time she must've walked because there was no bike. Second, she told me someone *came* to her house looking for her—not that they *went* to her house. It sounded as if she was at home when they arrived. And third, Apollo fixed the window in her bedroom so she could sneak in and out if she needed to. Oh, and she had a change of clothes this time. The other two times I saw her, she was still wearing the same clothes she wore when she left the foster home."

"Hide in plain sight. It's possible."

"Bailey also told me where the third disc was, in case of an 'emergency' as she put it. I think she meant if she died or something and we needed to save Apollo, but she didn't actually say that."

"So where is it, in case of an 'emergency'?"

"It's in her room in a cardboard box under the bed. It's in the case her *Juno* DVD came in."

"Juno?"

"Yeah, it's a movie that was released a few years ago about a pregnant teenager. It was a big hit. Kind of apropos, don't you think?"

"But none of this excuses your behavior," JP said. "You have to stop meeting Bailey by yourself. These people are dangerous. They kill people. If they're crazy enough to kill an innocent baby, they sure aren't going to think twice about killing a lawyer."

"I hear you."

"By the way, I received a call from my friend at the DMV. She said that Robert Cavitt had a 1948 Plymouth registered in his name. And she gave me his address in Lakeside. I'll be going by there shortly to see what I can see, and then I have my appointment at World of Hope with Collicott's pregnant teenage client."

"Are you going to confront Rob?"

"No, not until we have something more. He may not even be involved. His brother, Dr. Ric, could've just borrowed his car the night Apollo filmed him."

Sabre dressed and went for a run on the bay. She ran the entire boardwalk from one end to the other, a distance of six miles; then she walked two more before she reached her car. The exercise cleared her head. When she returned home she took a shower, made herself a large cup of herbal tea, and sat down with the Lecy file. She parked a legal pad on the table next to her. The top sheet was divided into two columns labeled "Facts" and "Questions." The entries consisted of what she knew and what she needed to know. She read through every single report and bit of information she had, jotting down notes as she read.

When she finished the Lecy file she moved on to the Johnson file, creating the same columns on her yellow pad.

She read through the social workers' and JP's reports, taking diligent notes. She opened the envelope of photos JP had collected for her and dumped them out. She studied each one carefully until she came across one particular photo.

"Oh my God!" Sabre said aloud. She jumped up, grabbed her keys and phone, and ran for her car. She had forgotten to put gas in the car, but she still had just under a quarter tank. It was plenty for now.

As soon as she was out of her driveway she called JP and left a message to call immediately, and then she drove to the park. She looked around for Mama T but didn't see her. She wondered if Mama T would ever find her way back. Sabre crossed over the abandoned railroad tracks and across the field to the bridge. For the first time she was wearing decent walking shoes. Even so, it was difficult avoiding the glass. She felt a chill. The sun had disappeared behind the clouds.

Mama T was not there, as Sabre had hoped, but the other woman she had met earlier was there. Sabre reprimanded herself for not asking her name. She was treating her like everyone else did, like she was a non-person, and she suddenly felt ashamed. She approached the woman and extended her hand, "I'm Sabre, by the way. I'm afraid I didn't get your name."

She smiled. "I'm Megan Lily, Piccadilly, Princess of the Lily Pad People."

"That's a lovely name. May I just call you Megan?"

"No. Call me Piccadilly."

"Okay, Piccadilly it is. So, Piccadilly, has Mama T been back?"

"No, not yet, but she will. She always comes back."

Sabre remembered that was almost exactly what she had said the last time. "Has Mama T left before for any length of time?"

"No, but she'll come back. She always does."

Sabre looked around at the people lying on the ground or sitting against the wall. It was a regular little community with many of the same people. This was their home. The overpass provided shelter from the sun and the rain. Underneath was a flat area about the size of a Little League infield that abutted the concrete wall. The edge of that area formed an embankment with about a forty degree decline. Each resident seemed to have a personal space with his or her own pile of junk.

She spotted the man who almost fell on her the last time she was here. He was standing against a mound of clothes and junk on the edge of the embankment. He was drinking from a cheap wine bottle. She approached him.

"Hello, Dean."

"What do you want?" There was anger in his voice.

"I want your son, Cole. Where is he?"

"He ain't here," he said gruffly.

Sabre started to look around for any sign of him, but Dean staggered after her, following her wherever she went. "Get out of here," he yelled.

Sabre continued to look in any nook or cranny where he might be hidden, but there was so much trash it was hard to see anything, and she had to climb over boxes and around carts. "Where is he, Dean? This is no life for him."

Sabre started back toward the mound where Dean had been standing earlier. She heard Dean yell, "I said, get out of here, you stupid bitch." And then she felt the bottle hit the side of her head.

Chapter 46

JP drove to the Lakeside address his friend from the DMV had told him belonged to Rob Cavitt. The long driveway led to a huge, two-story house with a three-car-garage attached. The garage doors were all closed so he couldn't see if the Plymouth was there. The new home appeared to be rather expensive for a clerk at Home Depot.

Since there were no other homes within at least twenty acres, he dared not go too close. If anyone saw him, it would be obvious he was looking for something or someone at this address. So he turned around and headed back toward the road. Just after he turned out of the driveway, a yellow Volkswagen beetle approached him. As they passed one another, the driver, a brown-haired woman who JP estimated to be in her mid-forties, stared at him. He could see in his rearview mirror that she continued to watch him throughout her slow, calculated turn into the driveway.

JP arrived at World of Hope only to learn that Mena had run away. He spoke to the counselor in her unit.

"How long has she been gone?"

"The last time anyone saw her was about four o'clock. She checked into the day room to do her chores. We can't account for her whereabouts after that. When we sat down for dinner, we discovered she was missing."

"Do you know why she left?"

The counselor appeared quite upset. "I spoke to her about three-thirty and told her the doctor had pulled her pass for the weekend because she'd been having some pains."

"Was she in labor?"

"No. He examined her and said she wasn't. I looked at her records. It says she's not due for another month, but she's awfully big. That's probably why the doctor was concerned, but apparently not enough to send her to the hospital."

"So why was Mena angry?"

"She wanted to go somewhere this weekend and when she couldn't go she threw a fit. I guess she decided to go anyway."

"Did anyone see her leave?"

"I've asked everyone on staff, as well as the other girls. Either no one saw her or no one is fessing up."

"Do you mind if I ask around a little?"

"Go right ahead. I doubt if anyone will tell you anything. You earn a bad reputation around here if you 'narc' on someone." The counselor sounded frustrated.

JP walked around the campus. It consisted of nine small, cabin-like structures. Each cabin housed four students and had its own private bath. There was one large building with a reception area that doubled as a living room in the evening. A hallway led to three offices and an examining room for the pregnant girls. At the end of the hallway and to the left was the back of the house where the kitchen, dining area, and recreation room were located.

Since the recreation room was the last place Mena was seen, JP began his investigation there. He found several girls there. None of them could provide any significant information, but someone had seen Mena speaking to one of her roommates, a girl named Brenda who had just returned to her room. JP walked over to Mena's bungalow and knocked on the door. When Brenda answered the door he explained who he was. She stepped outside. She wasn't showing a lot. If JP had seen her in a different situation he wouldn't have thought she was pregnant. He guessed she was three or four months along.

"We're not allowed to have anyone in the room," she said.

"I understand," he said. "I won't take long. Did Mena tell you she was going to leave?"

"No."

"But you talked to her this afternoon?"

"Yeah, for a bit."

"I understand she was pretty upset."

"I guess. She just told me that Dr. Ric had pulled her pass."

"Did you say Dr. Ric?"

"Yes, he's the obstetrician on duty today."

"What's his last name?"

"I dunno. I've never had him for a doctor, but I haven't been here that long."

"Have you seen him? Do you know what he looks like?"

"Yeah. He's kinda . . . fat . . . and old." She quickly tried to cover what she said by adding, "But most of the girls like him okay."

"Thanks. You've been very helpful."

"There's one other thing you should know."

"What's that?" JP asked.

"Mena sneaks out sometimes after curfew with a couple of the other girls. I think she goes to the meetings."

"What kind of meetings?"

"I don't know exactly. They can't talk about them."

"Do you know where they go?"

"No, but it's not here on campus. They drive somewhere."

"And you've never been?"

"No. You don't get invited until you're at least six months along."

JP checked his messages and returned Sabre's call. She didn't answer. He called Collicott and left her a message in case she hadn't heard that her client was missing. Then he drove to Dr. Ric's house. He had to get there before another baby was sacrificed.

Chapter 47

Sabre opened her eyes. It was almost dark, and for a moment she wasn't sure where she was. The smell drove it home. She was under the bridge and Piccadilly was leaning over her.

"Are you okay?"

Sabre started to stand up. Piccadilly reached her hand out to help her. But Sabre stood too quickly and it made her head hurt even worse. She felt the large lump on the side of her head, and when she brought her fingers down there was blood on them. She felt the cut again. It was minor and had already stopped bleeding.

Suddenly, Piccadilly turned and ran toward the field. "Mama T," she yelled. Sabre could see a figure walking toward them pushing a cart.

Sabre went to meet her and walked with her back toward the bridge. "I'm glad you're okay, Mama T. I'm sorry I didn't bring any food this time. I left in a big hurry."

"Hmpff," Mama T responded.

"I told you she'd be back," Piccadilly said to Sabre. "She always comes back."

"I'm glad she's back." Sabre turned to Mama T as they walked underneath the cover. "I need to find Cole. I know he's been here or is still here." Sabre pointed to Dean, who was still leaning against the mound. "That's his father over there and he won't tell me where Cole is. Cole needs to go back to his mother." Sabre didn't know if she was wasting her breath trying to explain, but she had to try.

"Boy."

"Yes, the boy. Where is he?" Sabre said.

"Boy sick."

"He's sick? Cole is sick?"

Mama T reached in her basket and pulled out an old bottle of cough syrup. She handed it to Sabre. The side of the bottle was covered with dried syrup and dirt. She shook the bottle. It appeared to be empty. She supposed Mama T was trying to help but couldn't. "It's empty, Mama T. Where is Cole? If he's sick, he may need a doctor."

Mama T pushed her cart forward toward the mound where Dean was standing. "Boy," she said to him.

Dean stood up and took a step toward Mama T. "No! He's my son!"

Mama T pointed to the mound. Sabre looked at it but she couldn't see where Cole could be. She kept pointing. "Boy." Sabre climbed over some boxes and around an old dishwasher to the other side of the mound. Dean started to walk towards Sabre, but Mama T pulled back her cart and rushed forward, ramming it right into his gut. His bottle flew up in the air and Dean fell backward, rolling down the embankment and onto another pile of rubbish. Sabre looked down at Dean wondering if she should help, but he pulled himself up and staggered off.

She continued walking around the pile of trash that formed the mound until she spotted an opening in the side of it right where the ground started to slope downward. A shopping cart was lying on its side. Cardboard and clothes piled on top of the cart created a rain-free shelter in the form of a mound on the edge of the embankment. It looked like an igloo made of junk instead of ice. Old clothes placed inside the cart provided a bed for Cole. He lay there curled up inside the cart with an old sweatshirt spread over him for a blanket.

"Cole," Sabre touched his arm. He didn't move. "Cole," she said louder. No response. She felt his face. It felt hot. She pulled her phone out of her pocket and tried to dial 9-1-1, but there was no service under the bridge. She reached in to pull Cole out, but because of the slope and the loose trash she couldn't establish the leverage she needed and her foot slipped. She planted her feet on some cardboard and reached into the cart to release him, but she slipped again. She shook Cole in an attempt to wake him. He still didn't move. Sabre was scared. The sun was setting and the sky was cloudy, making it very difficult to see. She looked around for help. "Help me! Someone help me," she yelled. Several people looked at her but no one came to help. Mama T had pushed her cart back to her customary place at the other end of the concrete wall. Sabre spotted Piccadilly and yelled to her. Piccadilly walked over to the mound and looked over it.

"Piccadilly, I need your help." Piccadilly just stood there. Sabre tried again to pick up Cole, but she couldn't do it from where she stood. "Piccadilly, please." She motioned for her with her hand. "Come here and brace me. Cole needs our help."

Piccadilly walked around the mound and took two steps down the slope so she was even with Sabre. "What do I do?" she asked.

"Just stand behind me and hold onto my waist so I don't slip."

Piccadilly took her place behind Sabre and placed her hands on Sabre's waist. She didn't seem very strong. Sabre prayed it would be enough.

"Please don't let go," Sabre said.

Sabre placed her left hand against the top of the cart and her right arm under Cole's frail torso. She pulled with her right arm as she pushed with her left. Her right foot started to slip. Sabre could feel the pressure lighten. "Hold me steady, Piccadilly." Sabre felt another set of hands on her lower back. She glanced back to see a man she hadn't seen before. He was a lot stronger than Piccadilly and he was bracing her. Sabre pulled Cole's body out of the cart and held him in her arms. The man helped them up the embankment without saying a word.

"Thank you," Sabre said when she reached the top.

Picadilly smiled. The man walked away.

Cole lay there listless like dead weight against her body. Sabre walked quickly toward the opening, but Cole was too heavy. She'd never make it all the way across the field. She spotted Mama T's cart, but Sabre was afraid of what she might do if she tried to take it.

"Mama T, I need your cart."

Mama T shook her head, partly sideways and partly up and down. Sabre couldn't tell if it was an affirmative or negative nod. "Boy. Sick."

Sabre took a chance. She raised Cole up in a motion as if to lay him on the top of the clothes stacked in her cart. Sabre spoke slowly and deliberately in an attempt to make Mama T understand. "Can I please use your cart to take Cole to my car?"

Mama T didn't say anything. "Piccadilly will bring it back to you." Still nothing.

Sabre laid him down on top of the junk in the cart and pushed the cart forward. She felt a raindrop hit her face. "Come with me, Piccadilly." Sabre moved as fast as she could across the field with Piccadilly alongside her. The sun had just set and it was sprinkling. Sabre tried to stay on the path, but it was bumpy. She hit a rock, slick from the rain, and the cart started to tip. She leaned to balance the falling cart, but over compensated. Piccadilly grabbed the cart as Sabre let go and grabbed Cole, the three of them falling in a tangled pile.

Sabre moved Cole off of her and stood up. "Are you okay?" she asked. Piccadilly seemed to be fine. Sabre pulled the cart upright and picked up Cole. It wasn't far to her car and although it was raining harder, she knew she could carry him the rest of the way. "Thanks, Piccadilly. Please take the cart back to Mama T."

Chapter 48

Sabre sat down in the lobby at the hospital and took a deep breath. Her head was spinning as she thought about who she needed to call. She didn't have a cell number for the social worker, but Cole was under the jurisdiction of the juvenile court so the hospital would contact the Department of Social Services. Sabre called Bob.

"Hi, Sobs," he said.

"I found Cole."

"Is he okay?"

"He's alive but he's pretty sick. Can you reach his mom?"

"She doesn't have a phone and even if I could leave a message with a neighbor, I doubt if she could get a ride anywhere. Where is he now?"

"We're at Scripps Mercy in Chula Vista. It was the closest hospital."

"I'll go pick her up and bring her there."

"That would be so good."

"How did you find him?"

"He was with his father, but I'll explain it all when you get here. Right now I have to make a couple of phone calls."

Sabre checked her messages. JP had called three times and Bailey twice.

Sabre listened to JP's messages. The first message said, "Hey, kid, call me when you get this." The second one, "Hey, kid, I just left Rob Cavitt's house. I didn't really learn anything new." The last one concerned her. "Sabre, I went to World of Hope. Dr. Ric Cavitt is one of the obstetricians on call there, and a very pregnant girl is missing. In light of what Bailey told you, I'm worried. I'm going to try and track the doctor. Call me."

Then she checked her messages from Bailey. In both messages Bailey whispered into the phone. "They're here at my house. The social worker is with them." The second message said. "I'm sneaking out. Meet me by the canyon, the back side."

Sabre checked the time of the messages. It had been nearly an hour already. She called Bailey's cell. No answer. "Bailey, I just received your message. I'm going to the canyon right now. Call me." Then Sabre called JP. It rang four times, but he didn't pick up. "I found Cole. He's at Chula Vista Hospital. Bob's on his way there with Cole's mother. I'll explain when you call. Right now I'm going to the back opening to the canyon off Boyd to meet Bailey. Call me."

Sabre pulled into the paved parking area near the canyon and turned her car around. She thought she saw something move in the bush between her and Boyd Street, but it was raining so hard she could hardly see. She left her lights on for a minute and her windshield wipers were operating at full speed. Two figures emerged from the bushes—Bailey and a tall man in his mid-fifties. Bailey was holding an umbrella over their heads. The man was holding a gun to hers.

"Open the door," he yelled. Sabre unlocked the doors. The man yanked the rear door open on the driver's side. He told Bailey to close the umbrella and then he pushed her inside the car. He held a .22 caliber handgun in his left hand directed at Bailey and reached his right arm out to Sabre, palm open. "Give me your cell phone." Sabre dropped it in his hand. "Now drive," he ordered. "Take the 163 south to the 8 east. I'll tell you where to go from there."

Sabre heard Bailey crying and asked if she was okay.

"She's fine," the man said, "but she better stop her blubbering or she won't be."

Sabre ignored the man. "Bailey, did he hurt you?"

"No," she said.

"What do you want from us?" Sabre asked.

"I want the rest of the videos her little boyfriend filmed," the man said.

"I told him there weren't any more, but he doesn't believe me."

Sabre drove as slowly as she could, trying to formulate a plan. "Speed up," the man said.

"I can't see where I'm going. It's pouring." The roads were accumulating water. An eighteen wheeler sped past, throwing even more water on her car. For several seconds she was blinded by the waterfall that drenched her windshield. Sabre entered the 163 freeway going south and then exited on Interstate 8. She still had no plan.

Chapter 49

No one was home at Dr. Ric's house in Clairemont. JP had walked around the side of the house and even rung the doorbell, but no one answered. So, he drove to Lakeside to Rob Cavitt's house instead. The long driveway was completely dark. He parked and knocked on the door, but no one appeared to be home here, either. He walked back to his car, retrieved his flashlight, and then went around the house and tried the back door and windows. All were locked. He found another door with a small glass window that led into the garage. He shined the flashlight in the window and peered in. The 1948 Plymouth sat in the far bay; the other two bays were empty.

JP couldn't think of where else to look for Mena. He had ruled out her home and friends and feared she was with Dr. Ric somewhere giving birth for their latest sacrifice. Then he remembered Bailey's other DVD. This was definitely an "emergency." He called Sabre again, and when she didn't answer he left another message. Then he drove toward Bailey's house. It started to sprinkle. JP flipped the windshield wipers on. He had been hearing all week that there was a storm brewing, and now it had started.

JP dashed up to Bailey's house to keep from becoming soaked and knocked on the door. He could hear loud music coming from inside. Karen Lecy came to the door holding a drink in her left hand.

"Well, hello, cowboy," she said, stretching out the word "hello." She grabbed him by the shirt with her free hand and tugged, "Come on in out of the rain."

JP was caught slightly off balance but quickly steadied himself and stepped inside. "Are you Karen?"

"Yes. Are you my birthday present?"

"Not today," he said. JP swiftly sized up the room. It was a mess, but the way things were piled against the wall it appeared some attempt had been made to tidy up the place. A woman was lying on the sofa, and although she hadn't yet passed out, he guessed she would be soon. Several liquor bottles were scattered around the room. A half-empty bottle of Jack Daniels lay on the table with an ashtray full of butts. "So you're celebrating your birthday?"

"I'm thirty today . . . over the hill . . . shit, I'm too young to be over the hill."

Another woman walked out of what JP presumed was the bathroom, buttoning her jeans as she came towards them. She stopped and eyeballed JP from top to bottom. "Uh huh," she said. She turned to Karen. "Who's the hunk?"

"My birthday present."

"Sorry," JP said. "I'm looking for Bailey."

"Why is everyone looking for Bailey tonight?" Karen said.

"Who else was here?"

"That bitch, the social worker." Karen picked up a cigarette off the table and lit it.

"What did she want?" JP asked.

"I dunno. I just told her she wasn't here and she was ruining my birthday."

"Are you sure Bailey's not in her room?"

"No. She's not in her room."

"Do you mind if I check for myself?"

"Knock yourself out. It's just down the hall on your left." She stuck her cigarette in her mouth and reached up and ran her fingers across JP's cheek. "And when you're done there, I'll gladly meet you in my room."

JP forced a smile and removed her hand. He walked down the hallway, flipped on the light, and checked the room. The deadbolt was locked tight. When he walked back out Karen reached for his arm. "Let's dance," she said.

He spun around, pulling his arm away. "Not today. I'm in a hurry." He stepped backwards and out the door, tipped his hat and said, "Happy Birthday."

JP walked to his car and waited for about five minutes. The rain had let up a little. When he thought he could sneak by unnoticed, he walked around the back to Bailey's room. The screen was off the window. He pushed the window open as wide as he could, leaving plenty of open space. Putting both hands on the sill he started to boost himself up, but it was slick and his hands slipped. He took the end of his shirt and wiped the ledge off and repositioned himself. This time he went up and lay on the sill belly down. When he reached forward and down to determine if there were any obstacles, he felt the bed directly under him. JP rolled into the room, onto the bed, and closed the window behind him. Then he removed a small flashlight from his jacket pocket. He wasn't concerned about the noise because the music was so loud, and as long as the hallway light stayed on, they wouldn't see light coming from under the bedroom door.

JP turned on the flashlight and looked under the bed for the box of movies Bailey had told Sabre about. It was a big box. He rummaged through them as quietly as he could without taking too much time. He pushed aside *Napoleon Dynamite*, *Mean Girls*, *Bewitched*, *Mamma Mia*, and several Harry Potter movies before he found *Juno*.

JP shined the light around the room until it lit upon a DVD player. He removed the disc from the box, put it in the slot, and hit "Play." The camera panned the outside of an old home. It was not the "Devil House" or anything JP recognized.

The house was situated on a small rise and appeared to be somewhat isolated. The grass was in serious need of cutting and it obviously hadn't seen paint in several decades. To the left of the house stood a huge evergreen oak tree that towered above the two-story house and billowed out on each side of the trunk shading the entire left side of the yard. The camera focused on the tree for nearly a minute before it circled the house to the right and stopped on a door. The next shot was from inside the house. It looked like a hospital examining room but not as clean. There were instruments and supplies sitting on a counter. The corner of an examining table with stirrups showed in the next few frames. Then the camera zoomed out and showed the entire bed surrounded by a red-brown pentagram. On the wall to the side of the bed was a large drawing of a tree resembling the one outside. Candles glowed throughout the room. The film stopped abruptly and started again outside.

JP heard a noise. The light was gone from the hallway. As quickly as JP could push the buttons, the DVD player and his flashlight were turned off. He waited in the dark. Since he was quite certain no one but Bailey had a key for the door, he kept his eye on the window as he moved closer to the door to listen. With his ear pushed up against the door he heard the toilet flush across the hall, then the clink of high heels on the tiled floor. He continued to wait until he was sure there was no activity outside the room, and then he turned the DVD on again.

The film showed three men and a woman leaving the room through an outside door. JP recognized Dr. Ric but not the others, although he thought one could have been Rob, Ric's brother. The men all appeared approximately the same age, mid-fifties perhaps. The woman looked a little younger. He paused on the woman and decided it looked a lot like the woman driving the VW Beetle he had seen at Rob Cavitt's house, but he couldn't be certain. The rest of the film was mostly the ground flying by as the cameraman ran away.

JP removed the disc from the player, returned it to its box, and stuck it in his pocket. He pushed the rest of the DVDs back under the bed and climbed out the window. Once he was back in his car, he noticed he had another message on his phone. He realized the ringer had been off since his visit to the group home. The call was from Sabre. It said she was going to the back side of the canyon to meet Bailey. He hooked up his earpiece, drove off, and called her back.

"Sorry I missed your call, kid. I'm on my way to meet you right now. The canyon's just around the corner. Please call me back." He paused. "I may be repeating myself, but just so you know, Collicott's client, Mena has disappeared from the World of Hope. She's pregnant, about to give birth, and Dr. Ric is her obstetrician. I'm trying to find them before another baby is killed. They're not at Dr. Ric's house nor his brother's. So I went to Bailey's and picked up the disc she left behind. There are new players on it. I want you to see if you recognize anyone. Please call as soon as you get this." He hadn't hung up yet when he reached the parking area for the canyon entrance. "I'm here. Where are you? I'm getting worried. Call me."

"Damn it," JP said aloud. He sat there in the lot with his windshield wipers flapping and called Bob. "Have you talked to Sabre recently?"

"About an hour ago, at the hospital."

"She's in the hospital?"

"No, she's not in the hospital. She was at the hospital with Cole."

"That's right. She left a message saying she found Cole. That's great! Is he okay?"

"He's pretty sick. I just dropped his mother off there."

"So what happened?"

"I don't know. Sabre said she'd explain when I got there, but when I arrived she was gone. I tried her cell and her home, but there was no answer."

"It's odd that she wouldn't stay there with him until she knew he was okay. I've been trying to reach her, too, but she's not picking up."

"It had to be pretty important for her to leave Cole."

"She said she was going to meet Bailey. I'm at their meeting place but they aren't here. Say, are you busy?" JP asked.

"I was just driving home. Why?"

"I need your help. I want you to look at a DVD and see if you recognize anyone. Can I stop at your office?"

"Sure. I'll see you in a few."

JP put the disc in Bob's computer. When it started JP pointed out the house. "You've lived in San Diego all your life. Do you recognize this house?"

Bob shook his head. "No. Sorry." JP forwarded the film to show Bob the room. "It's like the 'Devil House' but with more equipment," Bob said.

"Yeah, but it's not the same room." JP paused the frame and pointed to an area on the screen. "See the little sitting room area. The other house didn't have that."

"I see. But it has the same satanic symbols, and the same tree."

"True." JP paused the film again. "Here they are. Look at these people. I know who the fat guy is. That's Dr. Ric. See if you recognize any of the others."

"Oh my God!"

"What is it?"

"That woman is the social worker on Bailey's case. That can't be. Maybe she was investigating something?"

"Does she look like she's investigating? I don't think so. That's the same woman I saw going to Rob Cavitt's house earlier today. What's her name? I'll call my friend and get an address."

"It's Gillian Lloyd. But that's not all. I know the tall, skinny guy, too. He's an attorney. He represents Bailey's mom in her criminal case and now he's Apollo's attorney."

JP was already calling his friend in the police department. "What's the attorney's name?"

"I can't remember. I always call him Ichabod Crane."

"Think. Is it Barney, by any chance?"

"No, it's Barry. That's it, Barry . . . Barry something." Bob jumped up. "Wait, my client gave me his card." He opened his desk drawer and shuffled through some business cards. "Barry Betts," Bob said, as he held up the card.

JP repeated the name to his friend on the phone. "I need a pen and paper," JP said.

Bob handed them to him. JP wrote Gillian Lloyd and Barry Betts on the paper, leaving space for the address as he waited. Another minute or two passed before JP wrote anything else. Then he scribbled the addresses on the paper. "Thanks, Ernie. I owe you one." He handed the paper to Bob. "Can you run Betts' directions for me?"

"Sure," Bob said as he typed in the address on MapQuest. "But how do you know it's not Gillian's we need?"

"Because that's Rob Cavitt's house. I was just there."

"She lives with him?"

"Looks that way."

"What the hell is going on here?" Bob stood up and grabbed the directions out of the printer. "Let's go."

"You with me?"

"You bet."

Chapter 50

The man with the gun directed Sabre onto the 805 south. The storm grew worse.

"Who are you?" Sabre asked.

"Just drive."

"You must be Rob Cavitt, the good doctor's brother." Sabre took a calculated guess. He didn't deny or affirm it. "So, Scott was blackmailing you, too?"

"Just how much do you think you know?"

"I know all about the Route 66 gang and your fiasco with the dummy. I don't know for certain which one of you killed Scott, but I'd guess it was you. You're the muscle of the group, right? You were always the muscle, the protector, and now you're still trying to protect your little brother."

"You don't know what you're talking about," he said.

Sabre continued in an attempt to engage him. "I know that you're the one who's going to be charged with murder when this all collapses. They sent you to kill Scott, didn't they?"

"That was an accident."

"You accidentally beat him to death?" She spoke louder to be heard above the rain that beat down on the car.

"Scott couldn't keep his mouth shut. It was a warning that got a little out of hand."

"A little? You like to minimize things, don't you? Is that how you justify killing innocent little children?"

Rob leaned forward. Sabre could feel his breath on the side of her face. "I don't kill babies."

"They make you do that, too, don't they? They're smarter than you and way more educated. They make you do the dirty work. And when it's time to pay the piper it'll all come back to you." Sabre watched him through the rearview mirror.

"You don't know what you're talking about. We each have our part." He waved his gun toward the overhead sign. "Take the 94 east."

Sabre followed the off ramp around and onto the 94 as she continued to goad him. The water splashed as she drove through a little dip in the road. "But Dr. Ric and 'Barney,'" Sabre emphasized the name for Rob's sake, "they're covering their bases, aren't they. They're setting you up to take the fall. How can you kill little innocent children?"

Rob raised his voice. "I don't kill babies."

"And what's with the cult thing? Do you justify your sadistic behavior by blaming it on the devil? You're sick."

"You don't know what you're talking about."

Sabre looked at her gas gauge. It was almost empty. She wondered if she should let it run out of gas in hopes someone would come along. Or should she suggest they stop at a gas station and see if she could get help. She opted for the latter.

"I know that we need to get some gas or we're going to be stranded."

Rob leaned forward and looked at the gauge. The needle was below the empty line and the gas light was on. "Damn it," he said.

Sabre kept driving east on the 94 her windshield wipers slapping back and forth. "There's a Shell station coming up. Do you want me to stop?"

"Okay. Stop. But no tricks."

Sabre took the next off ramp and turned right into the station. She pulled up next to the pump. A young woman was filling her tank on the other side of the pump while she waited inside the car. The other pumps were unoccupied.

"Here's what you're going to do. You get out, run your credit card, start pumping the gas, and then get back in the car until it finishes. Do not talk to anyone."

"I don't have a credit card with me. I only have cash."

"Don't lie to me. You're not going inside."

"I'm not lying. I left the house in a hurry. I don't even have my driver's license. Look, she pulled some cash out of her back pocket."

"Where's your purse?"

"I don't carry a purse."

"Every woman carries a purse."

"Not me."

"Me neither," Bailey said. It surprised Sabre when she spoke up. She had hardly said a word since they left.

"I'll gladly use your credit card," Sabre said. "We can get gas and leave a paper trail."

Rob took a minute to respond. "I have a better idea. Give me the keys." Sabre took them out of the ignition and handed them to him. "Now get out of the car slowly. One wrong move and Bailey is dead." Sabre stepped out of the car. He opened his door. "You too." Rob pulled Bailey's arm as he backed out of the car, keeping the gun in her back as he walked around to Sabre. They stood there for a few minutes in the cold air facing the woman in the car next to them. Although they were under the cover, the wind was whipping cold air through them. Sabre shivered.

When the woman exited her car and took a step toward the pump, he moved the gun from Bailey to the woman. He popped her on the back of the head with the gun. Bailey screamed but with the noise from the wind and the rain, the scream didn't carry very far.

"Shut up and get in. Both of you." He motioned for them to get into the woman's car, while pulling the gas hose out of the tank and flinging it to the side. Sabre buckled up and looked back at Bailey, giving her a quick nod. "Move it," Rob yelled. Sabre heard the click of Bailey's seatbelt. Sabre yanked her door shut, looked forward, and saw no cars coming on the street. She pushed the accelerator to the floor and sped forward, making a quick turn to the right around the side of the convenience store. A glance in the rearview mirror told her Rob had lost his balance. He slid to the left against the door. "Slow down," he yelled. Rob grabbed onto Sabre's seat with his right hand and flung his left arm with gun in hand around her neck.

In the downpour, the car was losing traction. Sabre pulled the steering wheel with both hands as quickly as she could toward the right. They slid onto the street and into a spin, throwing water into the air like a fountain. She no longer had control of the car. She let go of the wheel and grabbed onto Rob's gun with both hands. He pulled his hand and hit her in the face with the butt of the gun, but she still held on tightly. She turned her head to the left and used all the leverage she could muster to push the gun away. The car made a complete 360-degree turn. She felt like she was inside a washing machine the way the water was spinning past her. She caught glimpses of wet buildings and trees. Then there was a crash of metal and a deafening sound in Sabre's ear as the gun discharged and flew forward against the windshield.

Sabre turned around. Someone had turned off the sound, except for the church bells ringing in her ears. "Bailey!" Sabre felt her mouth open and the word formed on her lips, but she couldn't hear her own scream. She saw the shocked look on Bailey's face and the blood running down the side of her mouth. Bailey's eyes were opened wide and her mouth was agape as she stared at Sabre. She thought she saw Bailey's lips move but couldn't hear what she said. The world was completely silent. The ringing came from within. She looked down. Blood covered Bailey's chest and Rob lay slumped across her lap.

Chapter 51

"It's raining so hard, the animals are starting to pair up," JP said.

"Can you see where you're driving?" Bob asked.

"Not too well. It's a good thing you know your way around here. We'd never be able to read these street signs."

"Speaking of which, you need to take the next exit and stay to your right."

JP drove down the off ramp and made the turn. "I hope we're going to the right place."

"Don't you think we should call the police?" Bob asked.

"And tell them what? That we think we know one of four people who might have killed Scott, and those same four people are using satanic rituals to kill babies? No, officer, we don't have anyone who has actually seen any babies killed, nor do we have a witness to Scott's murder, but we're pretty sure because there's a pregnant teenager missing from a group home."

"We know more than that. We know there was a social worker and an officer of the court seen leaving a house where rituals are practiced," Bob said.

"Yes, a private home and we don't know if there's any evidence in there now. Everything could have been removed since the film was shot. And furthermore, the only one who can authenticate the film is sitting in juvenile hall charged with Scott's murder."

"Okay, maybe we need a little more. But what do you expect to find?"

"I don't know, but maybe it would be better if I do this alone. You really shouldn't get mixed up in this."

"Are you kidding me? I haven't had this much fun since our joy ride with Sabre."

"Don't remind me."

"Next right." JP turned. "It should be straight ahead."

JP drove forward until he saw lights from a house surrounded by bushes. He drove as close to the driveway as he dared and then stopped the car on the country road. From there he could see the enormous oak tree.

"Are you going out in that rain?"

"No, we're going out in that rain." JP looked out the window. "It is a bit of a gully-washer isn't it? Hey, make sure the ringer is off on your phone." Then he stepped out of the car, walked around to the trunk, and removed two flashlights. He handed one to Bob. "Here, don't turn it on unless you have to and use it as a club if you need to."

JP walked toward the house with Bob following closely behind him. They were completely soaked before they had gone twenty feet. "Stay near the bushes," JP said.

"Look," Bob said, pointing to a window on the second floor where an old woman sat in a chair. "It looks like something from the Bates Motel."

"Just make sure she doesn't see you." JP pulled Bob back a little closer to the bushes. "There are only two cars in the driveway and there's no garage. The Beetle belongs to the social worker. She and Rob probably rode together. The other car must belong to Barney or Barry, whatever his name is. So maybe the doctor isn't here."

"Barry goes to court in a taxi, so maybe he doesn't have a car."

"Maryanne told me that he didn't drive in high school. Perhaps he never learned." They continued along the bushes until they were even with the house. The door they had seen in the video stood about fifteen feet from them just beyond the oak tree. "That's probably the room they're in if Mena is having her baby. You stay right there under that tree near the door, but back where they can't see you if they come out. I'm going to see if I can get inside."

"Are you crazy?"

"Crazier than a dog at a hubcap factory."

JP creeped around the back of the house and tried the back door. It was locked. He reached inside his jacket and removed a piece of plastic. He leaned against the door and slid the plastic in the crack between the door and the frame. Then he tilted the card so it nearly touched the doorknob, pushed it a little further in and then back in the opposite direction. The lock released. He slowly and carefully opened the door and stepped inside.

Bob watched as a cargo van turned onto the property, flipped a U-turn, and backed up close to the door near him. Bob stepped back further into the shadows and dropped down behind a bush. A man stepped out and dashed the ten feet or so to the door, opened it, and went inside. Bob could see a woman sitting in the front seat.

The floor creaked as JP stealthily moved through the house. Only two of the rooms downstairs had lights on—the room from the film and what appeared to be the living room. JP hid in a bedroom and peeked through a crack in the door. He was close enough to see across the hall, through the large archway, and into the living room. He watched as a man handed Barry a box. Barry opened it and took out a pack of what looked like one-hundred-dollar bills. JP tried to keep up as he counted the packs. If he was right, the bills totaled about two-hundred-thousand dollars. Gillian entered the room carrying a bundle swaddled in a pink blanket. She pulled the blanket back, showed the man the baby's face, and then handed the newborn to him.

As they walked toward the front door with the baby, JP slipped out of the room, down the hallway, and out the back door. He walked next to the siding until he reached Bob. Then he dropped down behind him and whispered. "Can you see the license number on that van?"

"I already got it."

"Good job, partner."

"What's going on in there?"

"They're not killing babies. They're *selling* babies."

"Selling them?" Bob said a little too loudly.

"Shh ... yes, selling."

Bob whispered again. "That's good. I mean, it's better ... at least the babies are still alive."

So now what?"

"I don't want to risk the baby getting hurt. And Mena must be in the house as well. It's time to call the police."

Barry held an umbrella over the man and the baby as they walked to the van. The car door opened as they approached, and JP and Bob could see what appeared to be an incubator in the back of the van. After the woman stepped out of the passenger seat and into the back seat, the man handed her the baby and the doors closed. Barry returned to the house through the side door. The van drove away headed west on the country road.

As soon as the van pulled away, JP called his friend at the sheriff's department and reported the events. Then they circled around to the other side of the bushes and headed back to the car, moving as quickly as they could. They waited in the car in case anyone else tried to leave.

Within five minutes there were more cops surrounding the place than a Dunkin' Donuts on a Saturday morning. JP's friend, Kevin, from the sheriff's department, came over to talk to him. JP briefly told him everything he knew. Then they sat there and watched as everyone in the house was taken out in handcuffs and placed in police cars, starting with Barry, then Dr. Ric Cavitt, two women JP didn't recognize, the social worker, and finally, the old woman in the window. An ambulance arrived shortly thereafter, loaded Mena in the back, and drove off with siren blaring.

Kevin went to JP's car to let him know that they had picked up the couple in the van and the baby was being transported to the same hospital as Mena.

"What's the story on the old woman?" JP asked.

"Apparently she thinks she receives special powers from the tree--that somehow Satan communicates with her through the mighty oak. I guess she's a tree witch or something. She's been having meetings like this for over forty years. She's a total crackpot."

JP shook his head. "As my granddaddy would say, 'I've been to two goat ropin's and a county fair and I ain't never seen nothin' like this.'"

Chapter 52

Sabre's mind was still in a fog as she looked around at the blood surrounding her. Her ears were ringing and the pain was excruciating. She tried to unbuckle her seat belt with her right hand, but pain shot through her arm when she applied pressure. She reached over with her left hand and undid the belt. After opening the car door and stepping out into the pouring rain, she found the drops to be soothing on her face. But after a minute or two, she just felt cold and wet. The deluge did, however, rouse her from her daze as she watched the pink rainwater run down her shirt. She felt a draft on her leg where her pants were torn and bloody.

She saw people running towards her in the rain. "Call 9-1-1," she yelled. She didn't hear a response. Her ears still ringing, she dashed around to the other side of the car to reach Bailey. The front passenger side enveloped a telephone pole. The pole took up half of the front seat. Sabre grabbed the handle on the back door with her right hand. Pain shot through. She switched to her left, but the door still wouldn't open. A man tapped her on the shoulder and directed her around to the other side.

"I need to help Bailey," she screamed. "The man in there is a killer!"

The man said something but she couldn't make it out. Sabre could hear the garbled sound of voices around her as the ringing subsided slightly. The sirens sounded so far away but the flashing lights were close. Two police cars pulled up alongside her. Four officers exited the cars. Three of them advanced toward the car and one toward the convenience store. A female officer took Sabre's arm and moved her aside.

"He was holding us hostage," Sabre said to her. "He made me drive here. He stole a car." Sabre looked around. Her eyes landed on the gas pumps. "Where is she? The woman? He hit her with his gun and stole her car."

"You need to sit down," she said. The officer appeared to be shouting but Sabre could barely hear the words.

"I'm sorry. I'm having trouble hearing. There's a loud ringing in my ears." More flashing lights and quiet sirens ensued—a fire truck, an ambulance, more police cars. The place lit up like a carnival. "I'm okay. Please see how Bailey is."

The officer attempted to direct Sabre to an ambulance. Sabre raised her hands and waved her off. "I'll go when they get Bailey out of the car." She walked to where she could see what was happening, but stood back so she wouldn't interfere. Another ambulance arrived. The ringing wasn't as intense and the voices and noises around her became louder. Sabre stood in the rain and watched the carnival unfold. They removed Rob from the car, placed him on a stretcher, and wheeled him into an ambulance.

The second ambulance backed up closer to the crashed car. A fireman reached inside and picked up Bailey. He carried her to the ambulance and placed her inside on a stretcher. Sabre followed him in and sat next to Bailey, squeezing her hand.

"I'm so sorry."

Bob and JP rushed into the examining room and found Sabre sitting on the edge of her bed awaiting release. Her right arm was wrapped and in a sling. Her forearm and leg were bandaged, and the side of her face was bruised.

"How are you, kid?" JP asked.

Sabre smiled. "I'm all right. Thanks for coming."

JP remained standing while Bob took a seat on the bed next to her and put his arm around her, gingerly squeezing her shoulder. "You had us pretty worried when that cop called."

"Sorry, I would've called myself, but I was a little preoccupied."

"So, what's the diagnosis? Any broken bones?" Bob asked.

"No. My injuries are minor—a sprained wrist, bruises, and a few cuts. That's it. Oh, and that dreadful ringing in my ears. At least it has toned down a lot. At first I couldn't hear anything except a pounding gong. Now the intensity is more like a doorbell. The doctor said the ringing could last a few days but should gradually fade, and we're hoping for no permanent damage."

"The officer said you were with a young woman and a man. Was it Bailey?" JP said.

"Yes, and Rob Cavitt."

"Damn it," JP scowled. "How's Bailey?"

"Not bad. Her leg is broken, but there don't appear to be any internal injuries and there is no serious head trauma. They're still checking her and they're going to keep her overnight."

"And Cavitt?" JP asked.

"He's dead. I guess he should've been wearing his seatbelt." Sabre tried to smile but she was still angry and it reflected in her face.

"To hell with him," JP said.

"Yeah, forget about him," Bob added.

Sabre sighed. "You two arrived here in a hurry. Where were you?"

"We were taking care of a little business," Bob said. "First, tell us what happened."

Sabre explained the events of the evening, and JP and Bob told her about their adventure in turn. "So, what did the two other women look like who were arrested?"

"One was tall and thin; the other was shorter and wider," JP said. "By wider I mean she was solid and muscular."

"It sounds like the two women Bailey described who were there when she gave birth. I wonder how many other people are involved."

"I still don't quite get what's going on," Bob said. "What was with all the satanic ritual stuff? And just who all is involved with this baby snatching ring?"

"Beats me," Sabre said.

JP stood up. "I'm going to go check on Mena and her baby."

"They're here?"

"This was the closest hospital," JP said.

"Hey, you may want to call Collicott. She'll be relieved to know her client is safe."

JP sent one nod of the head in Sabre's direction. "I already did."

Bob stayed with Sabre until she was released. They walked over to the bed where Bailey was being guarded by a sheriff. The female police officer who Sabre had encountered earlier at the scene of the accident came in to talk to Bailey.

Sabre addressed the officer. "She's represented by counsel, and I've advised her to tell you everything you want to know about the events of this evening. Since there is still a warrant for her arrest for the murder of Scott Jamison, she will not be discussing anything else until I've had a chance to speak with the DA."

"Okay, counselor," the officer said. "I just need to know about the accident."

Bob brought Sabre a chair and set it next to Bailey's bed. Sabre sat down. "I'll stay until you've finished your questioning."

After the officer left, Sabre leaned down and kissed Bailey lightly on the forehead. "They told me you'll be going to your own room soon. For now you have a guard with you, but after they take you to a room they'll probably handcuff you to the bed. There's still a warrant for your arrest and you are considered a flight risk, so that's the way it has to be." Sabre put her hand lightly on Bailey's shoulder. "But don't worry. It won't be for long."

"I'll be okay," Bailey said.

"I'll be by to see you in the morning." Sabre desperately wanted to tell Bailey that her baby might be alive, too, but first she needed to find out for certain. She was dealing with sick, crazy people; one even claimed to be a witch. Who knows what happened to Bailey's baby or any other babies they encountered. There were likely more.

Chapter 53

It had been two days since the accident and the ringing and most of the pain was gone from Sabre's ears. She sat in the back of Scary Larry's courtroom with Roberto Arroyo awaiting Apollo's and Bailey's hearing.

"He's a good kid, you know."

"So is Bailey, in spite of her role models."

The judge walked into the courtroom and took the bench. The bailiff brought Apollo in through the back. His parents were brought in and seated in the back of the room. The case was called.

"Roberto Arroyo present with the defendant, Apollo Servantes," Arroyo said as he stood up.

Sabre stood up. "Sabre Brown appearing on behalf of Bailey Lecy who's not present in court, Your Honor. She's still in the hospital, but expected to be released this afternoon."

The assistant district attorney announced himself. "Your Honor, on behalf of the state ..."

"Save it. I've read the file," the judge said. "I just have a couple of questions." He addressed Apollo's parents. "Are you willing to take your son home today?"

"Yes, Your Honor," the father said.

"And will you see that he gets back in school immediately?"

"Yes, Your Honor."

"All right then." The judge looked at Sabre. "Ms. Brown, you represent Bailey in the dependency system. Is there a plan in place for her to live with someone other than her mother upon her release?"

"Yes, Your Honor. Mr. and Mrs. Venable were her foster parents before she ran away, and they're happy to have her back."

"All right then. My colleague can take care of Bailey next door. Both cases are dismissed without prejudice. Mr. Arroyo, make sure the parents know where to go to pick up their son." Arroyo nodded.

Sabre smiled and whispered to Arroyo. "Scary Larry is so weird."

Sabre went directly to Department Four for the special she had put on calendar on Bailey's case. Bob was waiting for her when she arrived.

"How's Cole doing?" he asked.

"He was a pretty sick little boy, between the flu and the pneumonia, but he's doing much better now. Has his mother been able to visit him?"

"She's been at his bedside around the clock. The social worker who replaced Gillian has been great about helping her with transportation. He even got her a meal pass so she can eat in the hospital cafeteria while she's there. And as soon as they receive the go-ahead from the doctor, he's going to take Hayden and Allie to see him."

"That'll be good for all of them," Sabre said.

The clerk called the Lecy case. Sabre had the Pick Up and Detain Order removed and a new detention order put in place for foster care for Bailey.

Bob announced his presence on behalf of his client, Karen Lecy, who did not appear. "My client may very well be at the hospital visiting her daughter, Your Honor."

Sabre rolled her eyes at Bob.

"She may very well be, Counselor," the judge responded sarcastically. "Are you keeping the trial date?"

"Yes, Your Honor," Bob said. Bob and Sabre knew the trial was a useless endeavor in light of the new information regarding Karen's involvement with the Route 66 gang. The case would likely settle before the trial. Bob would attempt to get his client to see the light but he wouldn't pressure her. It was her choice and she was entitled to go to trial if she so chose.

"JP, will you please keep track on the white board. My hand hurts and if Bob does it we won't be able to read it."

"My handwriting isn't that bad," Bob said.

"Yes it is," Sabre and JP responded in unison. They all laughed.

"Okay, what we're really trying to do here is figure out what happened to Bailey's baby," Sabre said. "Was he sacrificed or was he sold?"

"And since the defendants have all lawyered-up we're going to have to figure it out ourselves," JP said. "According to my sources, none of the suspects are talking except for the old lady."

"Barry Betts' mother?"

"Yeah, she's singing like a bird, but unfortunately she's way out of tune."

"What's she saying?" Sabre asked.

"She's really into the satanic rituals and has been having them in her home since Barry was a child, which could explain why his father was awarded custody of him in their divorce. She truly believes that she is connected to Satan through the large oak tree in her yard and that she can make things happen, but she doesn't seem to know about the babies."

"Maybe she's just not telling," Sabre said.

"No, she's spilling her guts about everything that ever happened in her life. And apparently there's not much corn in her silo. She's way out there. She carries a photo of the tree with her everywhere she goes. She says it's a picture of her 'mother.' Her first words in the morning are to the tree. No matter what the weather was like she would kneel in front of it and pray to the mighty oak. She called it her 'hour of worship with my mother.' Since she hasn't been able to get around as well the last while she would have to pray from her window when no one was there to take her to her tree. She really believes in the power of the oak. I think if they were sacrificing babies she would know about it . . . probably even be a part of it if she thought the tree needed it to flourish."

"You gotta love the old coot," Bob said.

Sabre cuffed Bob lightly on the shoulder. "Try to stay on track. You can admire the crazy lady later."

Bob smiled. "Okay, let's assume they weren't killing any of them but instead selling them all on the black market. We know Barry has been dealing with these strange rituals since he was a kid."

"So for some reason he figured it would make a good cover," Sabre chimed in. "And he had access to everything he needed and probably used real believers like his mother when he needed to."

"So, it's all about the money?" JP asked.

"It usually is," Bob said.

"Rob pretty much confirmed that Scott was blackmailing them about the Route 66 incident, and he said 'they all had their part,'" Sabre said.

Bob added, "So, Rob was the muscle. Ric delivered the babies. Barry was the brains. And Gillian found the babies for them."

"She probably created the ritual cases to draw attention away from what they were really doing. She'd plant evidence, or just twist things to make them look like abuse cases," Sabre said.

"Like on the Johnson case with the chicken feet and goat blood. And the picture of the unicorn," Bob said. "That's why she's on so many of the cases."

"She tried her best to not file on Bailey. She had been going into that home for nearly a year and had plenty of reasons to file, but she kept it out of the system. It was only because Bailey missed so much school that Gillian was forced to file. With the new law now that makes it a misdemeanor for the parents who don't make their kids go to school, she couldn't sweep it under the rug any longer," Sabre said.

"So if they check Gillian's caseload to see what she didn't file on they'd probably find more victims," Bob said.

"There's one other thing that Rob said when I suggested Gillian was involved. He said, 'There's better positioned people than her.'"

JP spoke. "It sounds like there's someone else involved that we don't know about. And how do babies disappear without people noticing?"

"I know," Sabre said. "They do it so it all looks legal. So it doesn't draw attention to them. They have a social worker that brings them the mothers. And in doing so, she looks like she's not filing because she's trying to keep families together. Then they have a doctor who performs the deliveries. He makes the paperwork say whatever he needs to. And then there's the attorney who specializes in adoptions who finalizes the package. They all look like they're providing a service for humanity. As Rob said, 'They all do their part.' So who else do they need to help them? A banker for the money maybe?"

"Maybe he was talking about Betts. He's an attorney, in his mind that could be a better position than the social worker," Bob said.

"He probably did count him, but he said 'people' in better positions. So even if he counted Betts, there's still someone else," Sabre said.

JP made a timeline on the board and they filled it in with everything they knew. Bob's phone rang and he stood up. "Excuse me." Bob answered his cell. When he hung up he said, "You can add another fact to the board. Karen Lecy was just arrested for numerous counts of PC 273a."

"Child endangerment," Sabre said. "Well she should be."

"They got her on both Bailey and her grandchild," Bob added.

"Good. It makes me feel better but I don't think it helps our puzzle. It does, however, take care of your trial set. It'll be moot if she's in jail."

The three of them went back and forth for several more hours challenging each other's brains, but failed to come up with who might be the one who was "positioned best."

Chapter 54

"Hello, Cole," Sabre said when she walked into his hospital room. "You're looking better today."

"I am better."

"Where's your mom?"

"She went to the cafeteria. She'll be back."

"Good. Do you feel like answering a few questions?"

He nodded.

"I need to know what happened when you left the foster home. Could you tell me about that?"

"When I woke up that morning no one was up yet and I wanted to see my mom and my brothers and sisters, so I snuck out. I was going to go to my brother Hayden's house 'cuz I knew he lived close, but I couldn't find it."

"So, what did you do?"

"I was walking through the park and that's when I saw my dad. Well, he saw me and he called my name. I was going to run but then he said, 'Cole, it's your dad.' It didn't look too much like him but it was his voice, so I looked closer. He took me home to the bridge and I stayed there with him."

"Did you ever go out?"

"I went out a couple of times to find food. Mama T always gave me the best food but I went to the store a couple of times and stole some things." He looked down. "I'm sorry," he added and then continued. "I went to see Hayden at school one day, but then a teacher came and I had to run. I wanted to go back home but then I started getting sick."

"Is that why you stayed under the bridge?"

"At first I stayed to help my dad. He really needed me. But then I got sick, and I really wanted my mom."

Sabre pictured that poor little boy stuck inside a shopping cart in a pile of rubbish, sick, afraid, and missing his mother and she felt her eyes get misty.

Cole's mother walked into the room. "Hello, Leanne," Sabre said. "Could I talk with you a minute?"

"Sure."

Sabre directed her out of the room and Leanne led her down the hall to a waiting room. "Have you spoken with the doctor today?"

"Yes, he was in early this morning. He said Cole has really improved the last twenty-four hours."

"That's good. Did he tell you how much longer Cole will have to stay here?"

"He doesn't know yet but it'll be a few more days for sure, maybe longer."

"And the social worker, have you spoken to him?"

"Yes. He's been very good to us. He arranged for Hayden to visit tomorrow, and Allie the next day. I think one at a time is best. And he lifted the supervision requirement."

"Leanne, the social worker recommended a 360. It's a voluntary agreement, of sorts. Your attorney can explain the particulars to you. The social worker will see that your aid is reinstated and your heat is turned back on, and then the children will be returned to you."

"All of them?" A pained look appeared on her face, like she wanted to smile but feared it wasn't warranted.

"All of them."

Leanne burst into tears. "I'm sorry," she said. She jumped up and hugged Sabre. "Thank you. Thank you so much."

"You don't need to thank me. Those kids need you. You're a good mother and with a little guidance you can do this. Once Cole is well and you are settled in, you can look for work again. Maybe DSS can even get you some kind of training."

"Can I tell Cole?"

"Just tell him we're all working on a plan to get your family back together, but the main thing for him is to get well. You don't want to say too much, but he does need to have hope. And this is all contingent on the court's approval. But as long as you do what you're asked to do, the judge will approve it."

They walked back to Cole's room. Leanne couldn't stop smiling.

"There's one other thing. Cole's father was arrested for child endangerment."

Leanne shook her head. "Maybe it'll sober him up."

Sabre waited outside Department One for her trial to begin or to settle. Bob walked up to join her. "Hi, Sobs. My trial was just continued. What's happening on yours?"

"It looks like it may settle. I hope it does. Judge Shirkoff is grumpier than usual today."

Bob sat down on the bench next to Sabre and leaned back against the wall. "That guy needs to get laid. Maybe you could do that for us ... you know, for the greater good."

"Eww ..."

"For a million dollars?"

"No."

"Two million?"

"Not for any amount."

"Ten million?" Bob kept at it.

"Stop. You're creeping me out."

"Usually with a judge, one side or the other likes him. But with Judge Jerk-off nobody does."

"Because he's so abrasive and he doesn't know the law. He's always making the wrong calls," Sabre said. "And it wouldn't kill him to laugh or even smile once in a while."

"I saw him laugh once."

"When? Did you record it?"

"A week or so ago. I went into his courtroom and he was talking to Gillian. They were both laughing."

Sabre looked at Bob and wrinkled her brow. "She was in his department a lot. Every time she came to court it seemed like I'd see her in there." Sabre's eyes opened wide.

"Yeah, I saw her in there a lot, too." Bob smirked, "Are you thinking what I'm thinking?"

"Oh, my God! That's why he called us into his chambers. He was fishing. Trying to see what we knew."

"He's certainly positioned well. That's all the Route 66 gang would need. The adoptions would go off without a hitch."

"Should I sneak into his chambers and see if I can find some evidence?"

"No, don't be crazy," Sabre said.

"Our hunches won't be enough. We need to find some connection between the judge and one of the other suspects."

"Are we just seeing what we want to see because we can't stand the guy?" Sabre said.

"Maybe, but there's some reason why he had that bizarre conversation with us that day. And Gillian *was* in his department an awful lot. It won't hurt to check it out."

"I'll get JP right on it."

Chapter 55

The next day JP walked into Sabre's office. "I've got it," he said. He walked around behind Sabre and tossed a small packet of papers onto her desk. "After we knew who we were searching for, it was so simple. Look at this."

Sabre thumbed through it. Her smile grew with each page. "Yes!" She jumped up and hugged JP. "I love you, cowboy! You're the best!" She looked at the papers again.

"Who'da thought?" JP said.

"Things aren't always what they seem, are they?"

"No, ma'am. You can put your boots in the oven, but that don't make 'em biscuits."

Sabre picked up her phone and dialed. "I'm calling Bob. He's going to love this." When he answered, Sabre said, "We found the goods on Judge Shirkoff. You'll never guess who his mother is. Old Lady Betts!"

"Are you serious?"

"She gave birth to him before she married Barry's father so they're half brothers, hence the different last names."

"And he was raised by the crazy woman?"

"For the first thirteen years of his life. Then he went to live with his father."

"That's great, but it still may not be enough for an arrest or even a search warrant."

"JP's on top of it. He talked to the investigator on the case and they've already questioned Mother Betts. She told them enough to nab him. She didn't realize she was giving anything away, of course. She was a wild card for them, but I expect no one ever thought we'd make the connection between Shirkoff and Betts. Besides, what are they going to do? Kill their own mother?"

JP caught her eye. "Tell him to meet us at the courthouse. They're picking him up as soon as he's off the bench. We can watch it go down."

"Yes!" Bob said before Sabre repeated it. "I'll be right there."

Sabre, Bob, and JP sat in the chairs nearest the metal detector at San Diego Superior Court Juvenile Division. The lobby was still full from the morning calendar. At 11:05 a.m., Mike, the bailiff in Department Four, approached them.

He leaned over and spoke softly. "Department One just started their last case. It shouldn't take too long. You may want to go outside. Judge Shirkoff is meeting with a traffic commissioner across the street for lunch. The plan is to take him as soon as he goes out the door."

"Thanks, Mike. We would've been very disappointed if we'd missed this."

"By the way, they're searching his house as we speak."

The three of them walked outside and stood against the building. Several other people were milling around near the door. Most of them were out there to smoke while they waited for their cases to be called. Three detectives were strategically placed near the entrance. JP pointed them out. Bob lit a cigarette. They watched in anticipation every time the door opened. They waited.

Seven minutes passed. The door opened. The judge walked out letting the door fling back, paying no attention to the young woman with the baby behind him. Mike was close behind. He stepped forward, grabbed the door, and said, "Your Honor." The judge turned around.

"That jerk, he didn't even hold the door for that woman with the baby," Bob said.

One of the detectives stepped up and slapped the handcuffs on him. "You're under arrest for kidnapping and conspiracy to commit murder." Mike smiled. Several camera phones snapped, including Sabre's. Before they had a chance to escort him away, eight more sheriffs emptied out of the building. A few of them walked behind the detectives to the car. Others dispersed the crowd that had gathered. Bob, Sabre, and JP waited until the detectives drove off with him in the backseat. Bob waved as they passed.

Chapter 56

A week had passed since the judge was arrested. His arrest had made national news, and every day some new piece of the "Devil House" puzzle was uncovered. Sabre listened as the news reporter gave her account of the events.

"Another teenage mother has come forward this morning in the 'Devil House' case. Our sources tell us she was forced to participate in tree-worship meetings for the last three months of her pregnancy and to continually chant, 'I believe in the power of the oak.' The satanic hysteria that has hit this city has shaken each and every one of us. Judge Shirkoff, a man whose job it was to protect our children, has been allegedly terrorizing families for nearly two years."

Sabre muted the sound and answered her doorbell. "Thanks for going with me this morning."

"No problem, Sobs," Bob said, as he walked into her living room and saw the news story running on television. "I see you were watching the latest on the 'Devil House' case, as the media is calling it. And juvenile court is rid of Judge Jerk-Off."

"Yeah, they have most of their facts straight. This is the first time the chant was released to the public. JP said the cops have been chasing a lot of bogus reports." Sabre walked toward the kitchen. "Would you like some coffee? I'm afraid it's decaf."

"That's okay." Sabre poured Bob a cup of coffee and then picked up her half-empty cup. They stood in the kitchen at the counter.

"I hear DSS has been scrambling to right the wrongs they've created. All but one of the juvenile court cases that had been filed proved to be either Gillian's handiwork or that of a couple of social workers who were diligent but overzealous. Several of the cases were dismissed. The rest were re-filed with new allegations. The one case that is still pending wasn't one of Gillian's cases, but it had evidence of devil-worship throughout the household. Did you hear about that case?"

"Yeah. The mother had two young children, ages two and four, and a long history of mental illness. It was that case that gave Gillian the idea to plant and twist evidence to create a diversion."

"Have they tracked all the missing children?"

"Not all of them. Since the judge was arrested the rest of the suspects have been talking like mad, each trying to get the best plea bargain. The DA thinks they have the information on all the marketed babies, but the buyers have a lot of money, so some of them have been hard to catch." Sabre took a drink of coffee. "And on top of it all, some of those children have been with these families for two years. Now, they'll be ripped out of those homes."

"Have the children been treated okay in those homes?"

"It appears that most of them have, but the only screening ever done on the adoptive families by the Route 66 gang was to their bank accounts. Who knows what the children have had to endure."

"So, was Shirkoff the leader?" Bob asked.

"They're all pointing the finger at him, but it seems his brother Barry Betts came up with the idea. Apparently, Barry and Ric had remained friends. Ric persuaded Rob and Gillian to help. It was a natural move for Rob. He had been protecting his brother all his life and when he needed him, all Ric had to do was ask."

"Only this time it got him killed," Bob said. "But why would Shirkoff do it?"

"Apparently, it was all about the money. They were taking in some really big bucks. In two years, they raked in over five million dollars."

"And it would've continued except for Apollo's film project."

"Yup." Sabre nodded her head. "And, they hadn't counted on Scott showing up and blackmailing the doctor about the Route 66 situation. Dr. Ric was keeping him satisfied with a few drugs here and there and that would've been it, but when Scott got Bailey pregnant it opened up an irresistible opportunity for another baby sale. More greed."

"So, Scott wasn't really involved in the black marketing?"

"No, he only knew what Dr. Ric told him. He directed him to get Bailey to the meetings and paid him off in drugs. Scott in turn bought Bailey's mom off."

"Yeah, my client's the mother of the year."

"Well, at least they have Bailey's baby back unharmed. Are you ready to go see her?"

Bob poured the rest of his coffee in the sink and set the mug down. "Let's go."

Sabre and Bob arrived at the foster home where Bailey's baby was temporarily detained until some decisions could be made. Shortly thereafter, Mrs. Venable, Bailey's foster mother, drove up with Bailey. Bob and Mrs. Venable waited at the car while Sabre and Bailey walked together up to the house.

"Are you sure you're ready for this?" Sabre asked.

"Yes. I'm sure. I've given it a lot of thought and I can't raise this child. I'm not even fifteen years old yet. That's how old my mother was when I was born, and look what she did to me. I can't do that to my child."

"I'm not trying to convince you to keep your baby. Giving her up is a very brave and unselfish decision. But it is your decision. Just know that you're not your mother."

"I know. And I know the Venables are willing to take us both, but it wouldn't be fair to anyone, especially my baby girl."

Sabre put her arm around Bailey's shoulder and gave her a quick hug. The foster mother greeted them and then retrieved the baby and showed her to Bailey. She had big round blue eyes, a head full of platinum colored hair, and a tiny dimple in her left cheek. Bailey's eyes opened wide. Sabre could see the pride in her face when she looked at the tiny little pink face.

"She's so beautiful," Bailey said.

"Would you like to hold her?"

Bailey nodded. The foster mother placed the baby in her arms. Bailey stood there mesmerized, first smiling, then the tears slowly rolled down her face. Bailey gently rocked the little one back and forth.

After several minutes Bailey whispered to the baby, "Wherever you are, whatever you do, I'll never forget you."

She handed her back to the foster mother and walked out.

Sabre said her goodbyes, walked to her car, and drove to see her mother.

From the Author

Dear Reader,

Thank you for reading my book. I hope you enjoyed reading it as much as I did writing it. Would you like a FREE copy of a novella about JP when he was young? If so, scan the QR code below and it will take you where you want to go. Or, if you prefer, please go to www.teresaburrell.com and sign up for my mailing list. You'll automatically receive a code to retrieve the story.

SCAN ME

Teresa